The Gulf

ALSO BY CHARLIE MCDADE

Almost Dark

HARCOURT BRACE JOVANOVICH, PUBLISHERS

San Diego   New York   London

The Gulf

Charlie McDade

HBJ

Library of Congress Cataloging-in-Publication Data

McDade, Charlie.
The Gulf.

I. Title.
PS3563.C3534G8   1986   813'.54   85-21964
ISBN 0-15-136446-X

Designed by Michael Farmer

Printed in the United States of America

First edition

A B C D E

For RBM and MBM
with love

The Gulf

1

VIEWED from above, the Gulf of Mexico looks like a gaping mouth, either malevolently grinning or venting an agonized, silent scream. Through high, thin clouds, the turbulence of the currents can be ignored; the Mayan ruins, broken teeth in a rotting jaw, seem impotent and distant. The unblinking sun, as old as time, looks on, an indifferent eyewitness.

Isaac Roth was on his own.

He wasn't prepared for the intensity of Witman's summer heat. During a restless night, after he had risen repeatedly, he finally despaired of getting any sleep at all. It was June, and between the incessant buzz of insects and the heat, which had come down so suddenly the afternoon before, he was beginning to understand what he had let himself in for, and how completely his life had changed.

He put on jeans and a light cotton shirt with short sleeves, went to the kitchen and made himself some coffee. Resigned to wakefulness, he sat there at the table, the small light over the stove a beacon to the flying bugs battering against the screen. It was nearly five o'clock, still dark. The kitchen seemed no cooler than the bedroom, but it was too early for the porch. Hardly summer, but the mosquitoes were already so fierce he had to stay indoors until sunrise.

Knowing he could never nurse a single cup of coffee for that long, he gulped the first as soon as it had cooled enough to swallow, then poured another. He tried reading the paper, but the county weekly was long on advertisements and short on everything else. Putting the paper down, he got up to turn on the radio. Three weeks, and he still couldn't get used to the music. The twang of the singers was as strange to him as their names. No worse than the noise on New York radio, but it would be a while before this sound stopped reminding him how far he had come.

Back at the table, he wiped a smudge of newspaper ink from his fingers with a paper napkin. That stain, at least, was universal. The ink irritated him, accentuating the paleness of his skin. He glanced at the slenderness of his arms, his uncallused hands. He wondered whether he might not, after all, be too fragile for this new life. He had always taken good care of himself, but now he was merely healthy in a town where robustness, even bulk, seemed essential. Even his pale gray hair, beginning to thin a bit, seemed too delicate for Witman.

New York couldn't have seemed farther away than it did now. Little more than a month away from it and the city was as fuzzy in his memory as his reasons for coming to Texas. He had had a long, quietly successful career as a general practitioner, a dwindling breed in this era of medical specialists. The dispensability of that form of practice and the increasingly brusque turmoil of the city had led him and Rose, more than once, to consider pulling up their roots, what few there were, and going elsewhere. But they had never done more than talk. When Rose died, though, stricken by leukemia that no one, neither he nor the specialists, could cure or stop, the need for change became obsessive.

Moving was one thing, but Witman was another. He had never heard of the place until he passed through it on the way to Mexico from New Orleans. He was taking a ritual vacation at the insistence of friends after Rose died. *You need a change. Get away for a while; it'll do you good.* Witman was a way station, a casual stopover, nothing more. The night he had spent there—of all things, delivering a baby to a woman whose name he did not even know— had somehow connected him to the town. *You a doctor? Oh, God, I need help!* It wasn't that simple, but it sufficed to explain to him how so remote a place could have appealed. Certainly it was not the desperately dry, sandy streets and the barren hills that sloped away from the Gulf. But it was different from anything he had known before, and that may have been the key. Or one of them.

The stunted vegetation of the place seemed more desert oriented than subtropical, despite the humidity he was coming to loathe, almost as if the trees realized that Witman was inhospitable in ways other than climate and thought better of rising to their full height. John Halsey, who had been there for thirty years, told him that even he had never gotten used to the contrary climate, which couldn't decide whether it should be dry or wet, settling only on hot. Halsey was his first friend in Witman, and for a time seemed its only saving grace. When Halsey started calling him Doc, he took it as a mark of friendship. By now it was how he thought of himself.

But he hadn't known any of that the night he delivered the baby. Instead of wondering at a duality that was no less subtle, for all of its blatancy, than that of New York, he seemed to have formed an attachment, however superficial, to the sandy streets and the sandier people. Most of the latter were the same dark beige as the soil that regularly collected against the curbs and had blown through the cracks around the door of his motel room that night, gathering in small ridges at the edge of the carpet and against the baseboard. Those deposits had been cause for wonder that first morning. Now they were no more than another nuisance he would have to tolerate.

The following morning, he had been on his way, and didn't think about Witman in the next few months. He went on to Mexico, stopping briefly at Padre Island, which baffled him with its blend of contraries. Windblown dunes and luxury hotels marked the island's cultural, as well as geographical, extremes. He told himself that he really needed to find some dormant Mexican volcano, beneath whose slopes he could sit and drink himself blind from noon to sundown, which he began to do as soon as he found one.

He sat on the hotel veranda every day, with his head slowly sinking to a gritty table top, keeping pace with the setting sun, only to wake up in the middle of the evening. Groggy, he would stumble off to his room, pointedly ignored by all but the most gossipy of the hotel's clientele, to sleep it off. *Well, at least he's a quiet drunk . . . and stays by himself.* Then he'd begin the cycle all over again whenever he managed to wake up.

The Mexican binge failed, as he knew it would. It was nothing more than an emotional formula dimly remembered from some novel, which had drawn him by melodrama disguised as romanticism. He abandoned the pointless performance after two weeks of increasingly disgusting awakenings and surrendered to the far less romantic knowledge that Rose was dead and he had to get on with his life. Heading back to New York, he accepted what now seemed the only viable alternative: resuming his practice.

But instead of an anesthetic grind, he found self-doubt. He couldn't honestly say that he regretted being a doctor, but he was no longer satisfied with his life as it had been. Its primary justification was the money he made, and that began to make him uneasy. Without Rose to interpose between reality and bank account, he felt guilty about his income, which now seemed built on the frailties of others. He had been less aware of such things when Rose was alive, because she was less introspective and less inclined to guilt. Not that she had been heartless or more callous than he was, but she had been insulated from the pain and suffering.

When Rose died, the money had continued to come in. Jennifer Greene, his nurse, and Kimberly Kostos, his technician, kept his professional accounts in order, depositing checks and paying bills. But his personal finances slid into wild disarray. Jenny and Kim had tried to organize his affairs, but, despite his promises, he seemed to wander off in a fog as soon as each discussion ended. His practice seemed remote to him, and that was not lost on his patients. It was not too long before his appointments calendar showed gaps and his hospital schedule was no longer crowded. He thought he might give more time to the free clinic, where he probably was needed. Where *was* he needed? Where did he need to be? And that was when Witman had drifted back into his consciousness, almost as silently as the sand he remembered drifting under his motel door. The need for change was now every bit as real as those small, dun-colored drifts.

When he first recalled Witman, he wasn't even sure

where it was. *Padre Island's too long a drive, but you can stop over in some town for a night.* He spent a half hour looking at a map of Texas, and finally found Witman, just when he was beginning to doubt he had ever been there at all. For a few days he thought about a sober vacation, but slowly the idea was replaced by that of relocation, so subtly that it seemed a natural thing for him to do. Only when he started talking about it was he fully aware that he had decided to leave New York permanently.

Even then, eager to get away, it never occurred to him that Witman was as alien to him as he would prove to be to it. He was only too willing to dismiss that possibility when it was mentioned by friends in the weeks before his departure. *Isaac, be realistic. You never even spent a full day in the place. It's a hell of a risk.* He pushed on with his plan, if so inchoate an urge could be said to be a plan, and made arrangements to spend a few days in the same motel where he had spent his only previous night in the town.

He went about the business of closing down his New York practice with a peculiar sense of satisfaction, dismembering it with a detachment and efficiency he hoped he could translate into assembling a new one in Witman. He referred his patients, some of whom he had been treating for twenty years, to other physicians, rather than go through the awkward formality of selling the practice. He discouraged all but a few leave-taking drinks and dinners. He found excellent posts for Jenny and Kim, and gave them liberal severance pay. His only dread was the last visit to the cemetery, but after an hour's quiet reflection at her grave, he realized that, wherever Rose might be, she wasn't there.

Once he had arrived in Witman, however, it had almost immediately begun to seem less promising a cure for his malaise than he had hoped. The exultation he had felt on leaving New York quickly evaporated. Unwilling to concede, even to himself, that he might have made a mistake, he hadn't written to anyone and, after a burst of phone calls to his closest friends during the first week, made no further contact. It was as if he was hoping the deliberate alienation from his origins would mitigate that of his current surroundings, as if he felt he had to betray the past in order to be accepted by the future.

Kate Riley wandered around the house in a daze. Unable to sleep, she had passed most of the night staring at the ceiling. Now and then she would get up for a moment to pull aside the lace curtains that hung limply in the breathless dark. Her mother was sleeping in the next room, and Kate walked on tiptoe to avoid waking her, preferring restless solitude to the nervous solicitude her mother would offer. The following day, David Hodges, the man for whom she had been waiting for more than four years, was coming home. He'd asked her to wait, and she had. He'd been gone twice as long as she expected, and he'd written less and less frequently as time wore on. What now kept her awake was not knowing exactly what that meant.

Kate was nervous, too, about the plans she had made for the afternoon. She had planned a celebration at the bus terminal to welcome David home, believing it would re-establish his ties to the town. In the last few weeks, there were times when the preparations seemed the only thing keeping her going. She was too distracted to eat, more often than not, and frequently seemed less a human being than a battery drawing near the end of its charge.

At three-thirty, her mother tapped on the door, softly, so as not to wake her if she were sleeping. Kate ignored it and heard her mother move back to her room and pause a moment before closing her door. To Kate, the shadows on the ceiling read like script in Linear B. She was convinced they meant something, if only she could understand the language. The past four years had been lonelier than she had imagined they could be. At first, David had written regularly. For nearly two years there wasn't a week she hadn't received at least a note, scribbled God knew where. David talked about everything but the war, and the letters were remarkably tranquil when she considered the circumstances of their writing.

Then, suddenly, came the letter to Maggie, the only one David wrote to her mother during his tours of duty. The following two years of uncertainty had not diminished her yearning for his return, but they had frightened her. It hadn't been easy to imagine a convincing explanation for the sporadic nature of his subsequent correspondence. Each attempt only heightened her fear that something was terribly wrong. In the second month after the letter to Maggie, she started sifting through his letters, looking for something, anything, that would explain what had happened. But she found nothing that hadn't been there all along. Nor was there anything missing that *had* been there before.

At five o'clock, she went to bathe and wash her hair. While the water ran, she dropped her robe and examined herself in the full-length mirror on the bathroom door. Inch by inch she explored her reflection, looking for some sign of deterioration, some discrepancy between the way she looked and the way she imagined David remembered her. She was four years older, but at twenty-five, there was little change in her face or figure. She scrutinized her face, looking for wrinkles, any apparent signs of aging, but there were none. Determined to find some fault, she cupped her breasts and gently lifted them, convinced they had begun to sag. Their nipples, dark pink against the pale skin, were prominent, but not fully erect, as if uncertain whether they should cooperate with her determined self-criticism or her anticipation of David's return. Her hair, a lustrous black that fell nearly to the tops of her thighs, seemed for a moment shot through with gray, which, on examination, proved to be nothing more than streaks of condensing steam bright against the dark background as her reflection slowly faded under the clouds rising from the bath.

She grabbed a towel and rubbed the mirror with broad, rough strokes. Before the steam could mask her image a second time, she turned to stare over her shoulder, as if to catch herself defenseless. Her long, muscular legs were taut, the skin the reddish brown it assumed every summer. Her buttocks were round and firm, sweeping away from the trim waist in assertive curves.

Turning to the mirror again, she leaned forward to peer at her own features as if they belonged to a stranger. The lips were full and, even without lipstick, a soft red. The nose was somewhat angular, but not unattractive beneath its sprinkling of freckles burnished by the sun. The face that peered back at her was accentuated by the stark cascade of black hair framing it. Uncertain and tense despite the pleasing impression given by her naked body, she turned away from the mirror and walked to the windowsill for a bottle of shampoo before slipping into the hot water.

Once in the tub, she worked a generous lather into her hair before leaning back to close her eyes. Images of David, like stills in a photomontage, slipped past. Now and then she would hold one that particularly pleased her. It had been so long, and seemed longer still, but she could see him as clearly as if he had left only the week before. He must have changed, she knew, but could not imagine how, since none of his letters had enclosed photographs. He was probably leaner, and more muscular, than when she had last seen him, his face perhaps more rugged than it had been. That her recalled image of him would not be that of the man who would get off the bus that afternoon was foregone. But the question that haunted her was whether he would still be the man she remembered, no matter what he looked like. Had he been horribly disfigured? Had he lost a limb? It wouldn't matter. She wouldn't *let* it matter. She owed him that much, at least.

He had been handsome, though in a quiet way. Despite his heroics on the football field, he had not been considered a catch by anyone but her and one or two of her more discerning classmates. While many of the boys in school had openly shown their attraction to her, there had never been any doubt in her mind that David was the one she wanted. To her sweet surprise, there had been no doubt in his mind that he wanted her. While he was away, there had been no lack of would-be replacements, but she had never wavered in her belief that he would return and that, when he did, they would pick up exactly where they had left off.

She had missed him in dozens of ways, not the least physically, although she tried, not always successfully, not to dwell on the emptiness she felt. Now, just hours away from the reunion, the physical need she had striven to suppress yawned in her like a chasm that only David could fill. Looking at her wet body shimmering under the surface of the water, she tried to imagine what it would be like to hold him again, to feel the muscles of his back ripple under her gently raking nails, but there was no way the imagining could answer the need. As she began to soap her skin it seemed as if the caressing hands were not her own, and she became aroused. Rubbing her thighs, she struggled against the urge to put aside the soap and bury her fingers in the tangle of dark curls between them. She had waited so patiently, given in so seldom, a few more hours were a small price to preserve the full force of her desire, saving it for the man who inspired it.

Pulling the plug on the tub, she got to her feet, closed the curtain, and turned on the shower to rinse away the lather in her hair and the soft film of soap that clung to her skin. Stepping out of the tub, she toweled herself briskly, as if to erase the years that lay between the present and the last time she had stood before David as vulnerable as she now felt. Before putting on her robe, she went to the mirror, now clear again, and looked at her body one more time. There was nothing to cause her concern, no flaw in her skin, no absence of curve. Her breasts, she decided, didn't sag after all. She wasn't perfect, but she felt beautiful, and that would have to be enough.

Her hair in the complicated folds of an oversized towel, she went to the kitchen to make some tea. When the water was hot, she poured it over the tea bag, then watched it slowly turn from pale gold to dark amber, the color diffusing in gentle swirls. She removed the bag, squeezing it once between tag and spoon, then tossed it into the trash under the sink. At the table, she casually stirred two spoonfuls of sugar into the tea, until little but a thin glaze was visible on the bottom of the cup. David liked tea, she realized, much more than she did. She could count on the fingers of one hand the number of cups she had had since David left.

She noticed the sky was beginning to grow gray. As she sat there sipping her tea, almost mesmerized by the simplicity of her activity, her mother's door opened, and Kate heard footsteps coming toward the kitchen. She turned to the doorway as her mother looked in.

"Is everything all right?" her mother asked.

Kate looked at the older woman, in whose features she thought she could detect her own future. She had seen photographs of her mother as a woman her own age, and the likeness was overwhelming. Still striking, Maggie Riley wore her years well.

"I hope so, Mother. We'll know in a few hours, won't we?"

At seven, in the silence after shutting off the coffee, Doc noticed that the bugs had packed it in for the night. He walked out on the back porch, where the sun was dazzling, having already burned the haze off the Gulf. He looked at his garden, thought briefly of spending a couple of hours pulling weeds, then dismissed the notion with a wave of his hand, as if to explain his decision to someone else.

A drive in the country, though less charming than such a thought would have seemed in New York City, was the only idea that appealed to him. He had been in Witman for two weeks before it dawned on him that every trip was a drive in the country, and whatever charm such leisurely meanderings had held in theory was permanently dissipated by hot, dusty reality. It was a small discovery, the kind that should have been obvious to him even before he relocated. But he hadn't been thinking about such things, and when he finally realized it, it was more disturbing than so simple a thing should have been. As he settled into Witman, he was still discovering the obvious. The town wasn't yet home, and he was starting to doubt that it ever would be. He might call it home, someday, perhaps even without hesitation, but whether he would ever feel that way was something else.

Once in the car, he hadn't the faintest idea where he wanted to go. There was no longer pleasure in aimless wandering, but, still a stranger, there was at least the accumulation of familiarity to recommend it. He was out on the flats, and tired of the assertive sameness of the terrain. For some reason, he was feeling uneasier than usual this morning. He was aware of his anxiety, but not of its cause; then he remembered the coffeepot on the stove and the flame under it. Or had he turned it off? He made a hurried K-turn on one of the endless stretches of asphalt that radiated out from Witman toward other towns in the county and headed back.

It was usually possible to see the town for several miles before actually entering the city limits. Witman was largely of a single height, most of the buildings no higher than two stories. Even the hotel was only three, just two of which catered to transients, its street level given over to a barbershop and a bar. But this morning Witman was only hazily apparent at first, and the buildings wiggled in the early heat. As he speeded up, attempting to outrun the flames he imagined licking at the walls of his kitchen, he saw a small, faded sign off to the left that announced Witman by name, a rather perverse placement, as if the sign had been erected by an Englishman. Still, there was a consistency, an aptness, to the location of the sign, as if it were intended to announce not only the town itself, but the peculiarity he felt there.

Finally, the buildings stopped shimmering. He had gotten close enough to recognize particular specimens of the local architecture. The hotel, despite its unimposing stature by urban standards, asserted itself solidly at the center of town, still two miles away. He slowed down as he approached, allowing the car to coast with his foot off the accelerator, but not soon enough. He spotted, just off the shoulder ahead, the familiar dome of a county sheriff's patrol car, a broad, Stetsoned figure leaning against the driver's side. The deputy's arms were folded across his chest, and his hat was tilted over mirrored sunglasses. His lips puckered, as if whistling, he pointed casually to a spot in front of the patrol car.

Doc pulled over, feeling a rising flush of embarrassment and indignation. As he stopped the car, the deputy approached him with a slight frown, almost indistinguishable from a squint, and one hand draped over his side arm, the butt barely visible beneath a fist the color of old leather. Reaching the back door of Doc's car, the deputy leaned forward, informed him that he had been doing thirty-seven in a thirty-five zone, and asked him to hand over his driver's license.

As he did so, Doc responded angrily. "I didn't see any sign. How am I supposed to know what the speed limit is?"

"If you ain't sure, you go slow's how." He paused to look at the license, then continued, "Isaac Roth, it says here. That you? You live around here?"

"Yes, it is. And I do."

"This here ain't no good, then. It's a New York license."

"Well, I haven't been here that long. I still have time to change over, as long as that license is valid."

"Valid? This here *ain't* valid, mister. I just told you that. This here's a New York license. See here, this says 'New York State' right here in the corner."

"You mean I can't use that license?"

"Nope!"

"Why's that?"

"Cause this is Texas. If I was you, I'd hurry up and get a valid license."

"I plan to, but until I do, I'll use my New York license."

"Good luck! But I'll tell you what . . . I'd find out when I was on duty, if I was you, less you got a lotta money to pay tickets with. Then again, you're Jewish, ain't you? Guess you got more money'n I got tickets. Well, we'll probly see, anyway, won't we? I mean, you keep on driving around here without a valid license."

"Is that a threat?"

"Buddy, I don't have to threaten nobody. I'm a deputy sheriff . . . the law. That counts for something around here. This *ain't* New York!"

"So you told me."

"Well, I just do my job. There's always somebody stepping outta line. Sometimes real hard cases . . . and sometimes just Jewboys from New York. Don't matter to me, though. I can handle the pressure. Ask around, on one of your *walks*, you don't believe it."

"I'll do that. Maybe I'll stop by and ask the sheriff."

"He ain't gonna tell you no different."

"Maybe not, but I'll find out." Doc was irritated by the man, but his temper had cooled. The last thing he needed was to have the police against him. When he continued, he was conciliatory. "On the other hand, I'm going to live here, so there's no point in us not getting along, is there?"

"Not long as you mind your manners, there ain't. What you gonna do, here, anyhow?"

"I'm a doctor."

"That figures."

The deputy handed Doc his license, along with a speeding ticket, before walking back to his patrol car. He got in and started it, watching as Doc pulled away. The patrol car followed Doc halfway into town, then peeled into a U-turn with a squeal of its tires. Doc sighed as the car gradually disappeared from his rear-view mirror. "Be it ever so humble," he said.

2

IT hadn't been his first rude encounter since arriving in Witman, but it was the roughest yet. After locking his car, Doc headed toward Halsey's for aid and comfort, and some advice on getting along with the town's more obstreperous elements. By the time he reached the store he was fuming.

A few customers were already there, so he waited in the back until Halsey was free. He sat down at the battered table that held a checkerboard, a clear plastic box of red and black checkers, and the gold-hasped oak chest housing Lucas Darby's chess set, a reminder that Luke would likely be around later, looking for him. They were the only ones in town who bothered with the game. Doc drummed his fingers impatiently, tapping his foot in stiff accompaniment. When Halsey finally stepped in, Doc was wound tight. The storekeeper recognized his agitation.

"Doc, anything wrong?"

"Damn right, there's something wrong!" Doc snapped. "This damned town has a funny idea of who ought to be a lawman!"

"Hold on a minute. What happened?"

"I got a ticket. For speeding! And the guy who gave it to me is no public-relations asset for Witman."

"Six two, built like a linebacker?"

Doc stared at the merchant a moment before answering. "How did you guess?"

"I know everybody who carries a badge in these parts. There's only one man who could provoke that response. Congratulations, you just met Pat Riley."

"That so? Well, Pat Riley makes me mad as hell."

"I can understand that. Pretty near everybody is, the first time they meet Pat. He has the habit of introducing himself in a way that's hard to forget."

"Why?"

"Doc, that's a long story, and I don't know all of it, so you'd best discuss it with Luke. I got to get Tom set up at the register. Don't go away."

Halsey pushed through the swinging door into the store. Alone again, Doc looked around the room. Its spareness, homey on earlier occasions, now seemed barren. In the three weeks he'd been in Texas, the majority of his happy moments had been spent in this room, where he had felt most comfortable. Now, seeing it through the eyes of a man who had been insulted, whose pride had been assaulted, he disparaged his surroundings as if that would somehow make him even.

Idly, he flipped open Luke's chest to heft one of the heavy marble pieces while he looked around. Coming full circle, his gaze returned to the table and the checkerboard. It dawned on him that almost anything could be something

17

else. The simple board of sixty-four squares could support either the simplicity of checkers or the elegance of chess with equal ease. It wasn't the board; it was what one did with it.

Instead of shaping the future, he had been reacting to the present. The morning made that all too clear. Not that he should have argued; there was no point getting into a fight he could only lose. But he could have handled things differently. He'd allowed himself, almost instantly, to become as unreasonable as he assumed the deputy was going to be. Now, his frazzled nerves reminded him there might have been another way, one that would have left him feeling more in control of his own life than he currently did.

When Halsey bounced back through the door, Doc didn't hear him, until he said, "Come on, Doc, it ain't *that* bad, is it?"

"I'm sorry, John, I didn't realize you'd come back."

"Hell, Doc, you look like somebody just run over your dog. Sitting there feeling like a victim. You got to take *charge* of things, you're gonna live around here. Folks is just like other critters, you know; they can smell fear. You walk around waiting for somebody to get a whiff, and, by God, they do."

"You mean the deputy I met this morning?"

"Exactly."

"And there are more like him?"

"Well, he's got family, if that's what you're asking. Fact is, one of 'em's out in the store right now."

"You're kidding." Doc shuddered in mock horror.

"Nope, I ain't. Come on, I'll introduce you."

"Let me see, first. Point him out." Doc walked over to peer through the scratched Plexiglas window, and Halsey joined him, pointing over his shoulder.

18

"Right there, in the work shirt."

"*Her?*"

"Her." Halsey nodded. "Yessiree. Her."

"It can't be," Doc said, shaking his head.

The woman in question was tall and slender. Her face, in profile, was nearly obscured by long black hair. Watching a moment, Doc noticed that she didn't smile so much as erupt into a grin, showing small, even teeth, as she chatted with another customer. She appeared to wear no make-up, except possibly a light lipstick.

"Well? She look familiar?"

"Nope." Doc laughed. "She can't be related to the man I met this morning. Not in this world."

"Well, sir, it's Kate Riley, all the same. Pat's sister."

She was standing near the door. Doc was taken with her large, dark eyes. Something about her reminded him of Pat Riley, but as she walked down an aisle, her gait was supple and graceful and bore no trace of the deputy's lumbering stride.

"Are you *sure*, John? If I remember my biology, there's no way she and Pat Riley can be brother and sister."

"Katie's made a few in these parts remember biology they never even knew, Doc." Halsey was grinning like a schoolboy. "Come on out and let me introduce you."

"Wait a minute." Doc hesitated. "Why?"

"I can give you a dozen reasons, but a man shouldn't need an excuse to meet a beautiful woman. Even a backward fellow like you. Besides, the next time you have a run-in with Pat, you can tell him you're a friend of the family. Come on, now."

Before Doc could refuse, Halsey pushed through the door. Kate had moved to another aisle, wheeling a grocery cart. Doc lagged behind, embarrassed by Halsey's exuberance. They caught up with the young woman as she made the turn at the end of the aisle.

"Kate, hey, Kate. I got somebody wants to meet you. Katie, this here is Doc Roth. Doc, meet Kate Riley."

"Doctor Roth, how nice to meet you."

"Nice to meet you, too, Miss Riley."

"You've already made a bit of a mark around here, Doctor Roth." Kate smiled warmly.

"Oh, how so?"

"You treated the brother of one of my friends, Julio Guzman."

"I'm afraid I . . . "

"The man with two broken fingers, about two weeks ago?"

"Oh, yes. My first patient. How is he? He was supposed to come back and see me in a week. I've been meaning to look in on him."

"He's doing fine. It would be difficult to look in on him, though. He's out in the Gulf."

"But that's ridiculous. I told him not to do . . . "

"Doc," Halsey cut in, "one thing you gotta learn. People around here don't have time to wait for things to get better. Long as they can do something, they do it."

"But the man has two broken fingers!"

"Mr. Halsey is right, I'm afraid, Doctor Roth. As it is, Julio got much better care than he normally would have. It must take some getting used to for you, but medical care is a bit of a luxury for a lot of people."

"You'll get used to it, Doc, if you don't let anybody run you off." Halsey laughed.

Kate, in surprise, looked at each man in turn, before asking, "What's wrong?"

Halsey opened his mouth, but Doc interrupted before

he could speak. "Nothing, Miss Riley. A slight misunder-standing."

Taking the hint, Halsey asked, "You all ready for the parade, Katie?"

"As ready as I'll ever be."

"What parade is that?"

"Katie, here, put together a shindig for David Hodges this afternoon. Sort of a welcome home from the folks in town."

"I hadn't heard," Doc said. "What's the occasion?"

"Katie's boyfriend is coming home this afternoon. Ka-tie's sort of grand marshal. It was her idea. Then, I guess that's no surprise to anybody, them being sweethearts and all." Halsey laughed again.

Kate smiled, trying to hide her embarrassment, but Doc noticed a blush under her suntan. At the mention of David Hodges, she seemed vaguely distracted.

"Actually, I have a few last-minute things to buy. If you'll excuse me?"

"Sure thing, Katie," Halsey said.

"Will you come this afternoon, Doctor Roth? It would be nice to have you there. You could see another side of Witman."

"I'd be delighted, Miss Riley," Doc said.

After Kate left them, Halsey led Doc into the back room. He assumed, rightly, that Doc wanted to know more about Kate. She taught history in the county high school, and had been well thought of until her candid consideration of the Vietnam War in class aroused some local contro-versy.

"For some folks around here, Doc, you were suspect if you even suggested the war might be unpopular. There were a few, of course, who sided with Katie, but it was

21

rough on her. It didn't stop her, though. She's a tough cookie. Every bit as tough as Pat, in her own way. And her mother, Maggie, is no softie, either."

"I'd like to know more about *all* the Rileys, John."

"I bet you would. Let me give old Tommy a hand for a minute. I'll be right back."

While he was alone, Doc speculated on Kate. She seemed to be in the town, but not of it, as if she had somehow come to be what she was in spite of the place, rather than because of it. There was no mistaking the freshness, even innocence, of a country girl that radiated from Kate's open smile. Neither was there any way to miss the slight hint of wariness, the guarded look that crept into her eyes from time to time.

Almost as abruptly as he had left, Halsey was back, this time holding the door open for Kate. "Katie wants to tell us all the good things we got in store this afternoon, so's we'll be sure to show up," Halsey said, rolling his eyes behind Kate's back. "Well, go on, Katie, twist our arms."

Kate ignored the teasing and started ticking off items on the tips of lacquerless fingers. "Well, there will be a speech by Mayor Willard. I didn't see how I could get away without that, so I asked him to keep it short."

"If Frank Willard manages to give a short speech, it'll be the first time in modern memory," Halsey observed.

"Now, Mr. Halsey! He promised me."

"If I were you, I'd consider the promise itself a small victory and hope for the best. What else you got on tap?"

"The high-school band, playing some patriotic songs, Sousa and the Marine hymn, of course."

"And . . . " Halsey prompted.

"Then there's the parade, with David in an open convertible, over to the high-school gym."

"Anybody else in the car, by any chance?" Halsey asked.

Although she blushed, Kate ignored the question. "Finally, there will be a buffet lunch in the gym for anyone who wants to attend."

"That sounds right nice, Katie," Halsey said, "especially the food part there at the end. Even if I get there after His Honor's speech, I can still eat, can't I?"

"Mr. Halsey, aren't you ever serious about anything?" Kate asked, laughing.

"Course I am. You just watch me at that buffet table, if you think I ain't. And I seriously believe you're mighty anxious for David to get home, Katie. What do you think, Doc? She look anxious to you? I don't think she ever looked prettier in her life, neither."

Kate turned away from the two men. "I have to see about my packages, Mr. Halsey," she said.

"Good idea, Katie. Lets us all go on out and make sure Tommy didn't foul anything up."

Before she could protest, he swept open the door for Kate to lead the way. As they moved toward the front of the store, threading their way among shelves and around barrels, Halsey chattered to Doc.

"You'll like David Hodges, Doc. There's something about you that puts me to mind of him."

"How so?"

"Don't quite know, really. He spent some time in Austin, to study some sort of science or other, before he enlisted. Maybe that's it. Enlisted, he did, not like Petey."

"Who is Petey?"

"His brother . . . Now there's a boy I never could figure. Always getting in scrapes when he was a kid. Then, an honest-to-God war comes along, and what does he do? Ups and goes to Canada. Didn't want to fight, he said. Didn't believe in war."

They had reached the front of the store, where Tom

was ringing up the last of Kate's order. The two men stood aside, Halsey whispering while Kate helped Tom pack the groceries. Halsey seemed to think Kate wouldn't hear him, but Doc wasn't so sure.

"The Hodges boys don't sound as if they're exactly typical Witman kids," Doc said.

"Now that's the truth, Doc. Neither one of 'em's typical. David's all right, though. A good boy, like Katie's other brother, Donald. In fact, they was in the Marines together, David and Donald. Like brothers, they was. Donald won't be coming home, though."

Doc glanced at Kate, who had moved to the front of the counter. It was obvious she had overheard. Her body quivered, although she had not uttered a sound. Halsey was about to continue, but Doc interrupted him. "John, excuse me a moment, will you? Can I give you a hand with anything, Miss Riley?"

She shook her head and pushed through the door. Her shiny penny loafers clicking on the sidewalk outside, the stiff denim of her jeans rasping, Kate ran as the door closed behind her.

"Damn shame about Donald Riley," Halsey said. "Killed a couple of years ago. David was there with him. He wrote to Katie. I guess that's the only thing that let her get through it. They were as close as any brother and sister you ever saw."

"It was a terrible war," Doc said, somewhat lamely, not knowing what else to say. He waved good-bye and walked out into the hot sun.

The tar on the street looked as if it would catch and hold anyone trying to walk across it. He sat down in an old wooden chair and leaned back against the front of the store, tilting his hat forward over his face to cut down the glare. He had taken to wearing a Western hat and found it more practical than he had imagined, though less easy to get used to. He was forever bumping the brim into something or poking himself between the shoulder blades if he looked up too suddenly with the hat at the wrong angle. Halsey kept telling him to be more careful, since there'd be no one around to treat him if he hurt himself with it.

Doc saw Kate across the street, in front of the bakery, talking to an older woman whose brilliant white hair was drawn back into a tight bun. He watched as they spoke earnestly for a few moments. When the older woman left, Kate came back in his direction, her face more composed than he last had seen it. She deliberately sat down next to him and apologized for her abrupt departure. He assured her that it was understandable.

"Mr. Halsey told you about Donald."

"Yes, he did. I'm sorry."

"Thank you. I'm almost used to it now. Besides, David's coming home. That damn war . . . " She clenched one hand into a fist.

They lapsed into silence. Doc wondered what it must have been like for her, losing her brother when the person to whom she would have turned for consolation was inaccessible to her.

"I understand that David is . . . was . . . your brother's best friend."

"Yes, he was. In fact, all four of us were very close. Before the war, that is," she added.

"Four?"

"Yes, David and Peter—that's David's brother—and Donald and me."

"What now?"

"I don't know. I don't really know what to think. It all seems so very far away, and so . . . pointless."

"Did you always feel that way?"

"No, I suppose not. But now, after what happened to Donald . . . I mean, it's all over, and nobody seems to know why we were there in the first place. Hawks, doves. It's so damn . . . crazy! My brother's dead, and I don't even know why. What was it all for?" She paused to stare at Doc before resuming warily. "Why are you asking me all this?"

"I guess I'm just trying to understand why you're going to all this trouble today."

"It's not political, if that's what you mean. Maybe if David gets to see everybody at once, he'll know he's home, and safe. After all he's been through, I think we owe him something."

"Yes, of course we do. And we owe all the others, too."

"You mean those like Donald, those who won't be coming home . . . "

"Yes, but *all* of them. Those who went . . . and those who didn't."

"Why do we owe *them* anything?"

"Because they made us think. It's the first time most of us had to think anything about a war except how to win it. It might take us a while to get into another one, because they made us think about war in a way we never had. At least, I hope so."

"Still, they could have gone," Kate said.

"Maybe you resent them because they survived and Donald didn't."

"Maybe I . . . No! I don't think that's true. I wouldn't want anyone to die needlessly. So I wouldn't be alone in my loss. Still . . . "

"What?"

"They might have saved Donald, don't you see? It's not that I wanted them to die themselves. I wanted them to go so that Donald might have *lived*. Oh, God! I don't know the answers. Donald's dead, and this afternoon David will be home. As soon as he gets here, I'm going to try to forget all about that war."

She rose abruptly. There was no sound but the soft hiss of the sandy wind swirling down the deserted street. Behind her, the sky was bright blue and cloudless. Except for her hair drifting lazily behind her, she stood so still she could have been no more than a pastel drawing hastily filled in with broad, quick strokes of the chalk.

"I'm sorry, Miss Riley," Doc said. "I didn't mean to upset you, or to argue with you. I was only asking you the kind of questions I ask myself all the time, thinking out loud. I meant no harm."

She smiled and sighed. "I know that, Doctor Roth. It's just that I don't have the answers, and I so desperately need them, to know why all this happened to people I love. I try . . . but I don't understand." There was a long pause before she spoke again. "When David wrote to my mother about Donald, I couldn't believe it. I got angry. I couldn't deal with it. Now, I'm beginning to accept it. The anger has started to seep away. It's still there, but nothing like at first. I need to find some way to get rid of what's left, and get on with the rest of my life. David will help me. We were planning to be married when he enlisted. That much, at least, hasn't changed."

She turned once more to the sky, her eyes scanning the unclouded blue above them. In a voice hardly above a whisper, she said, "At least I hope it hasn't."

3

EVEN on the largest map of Texas, Witman is only a tiny dot, halfway between Port Arthur and Brownsville. Matagorda Island protects it from all but the worst weather. Every so often, a hurricane sweeps in off the Gulf of Mexico, and then Witman, like the rest of the coast, hangs on as best it can. If, when the winds have died, it's still there, everyone breathes a sigh of relief. Those who prayed might even walk a little taller for a few days, taking credit for the town's survival. Port Lavaca is the nearest thing to an urban center, and its six thousand residents are nearly thirty miles away by car. By boat, it's a little closer, but not much.

That Witman is small is no problem to most of its residents. That it depends on shrimp more than anyplace ought to depend on any one thing is another matter. The town spends its energy eking out a living from San Antonio Bay and the Gulf. By sundown, it's difficult to imagine anyone with enough left to get into trouble. In the inland towns, though, they tell a different story, about how shrimpers have nothing *but* energy, most of it spent making trouble. The inland opinion, shared by those Witman residents fortunate enough to make their living from the sea at some remove, is that all that time out on the boats builds tension to a high level. *When them shrimpers make port, first thing they do is let off steam . . . or, the second thing. First they stoke it up with a little booze.* The shrimpers, of course, disagree.

Witman's people are suspicious to a fault. Not exactly xenophobic, they're never sure it's worth the trouble to accept a stranger. Most newcomers don't stay long; more than a few leave no farther ahead of the sheriff than when they arrive. Being a stranger in such a place is grounds for suspicion. Being different can be altogether unforgivable.

Even the contours of the town suggest that it is more comfortable with the sea than with the land and its people. At the shoreline, viewed from the Bay, it's little more than a ramshackle collection of metal sheds and weathered wooden buildings, all of a height and seemingly built from the same sheet of rusty tin and one colossal piece of driftwood. The shingles and battered sheathing are bleached bone gray by sunlight and salt water. The docks show the same merciless attention of the elements. There is a touching vulnerability in their haphazard sprawl into the water.

Beyond the sheds and fish houses are newer, better tended structures, the prosperity of their owners inversely proportional to their dependence on the sea. In succession, there are bars, rooming houses, shops, then homes. The merchants and more prosperous shrimpers, the captains and owners, live on the outermost edge, if they live in town at all. *I see enough water. Some grass and a few weeds'll be just fine, thank you.*

Many prefer living in one of the two housing developments separated from the town by tree-lined avenues and the small parks built to buffer the town against the encroaching dune grass and prairie brush. Approaching from inland, one is hard put to guess the town's principal industry. Witman wants to pretend there is no such thing as the sea, let alone a living to be made from it. It reserves its candor for those who make that living and who, in the process, support the town. The shrimpers themselves ignore Witman's ungratefulness, knowing they'd be no different if they had the chance.

If there is one place in the entire town that embodies all of Witman's contradictions, and comfortably contains them, it's Halsey's General Store. It stands at the intersection of Route 94, the main access to Witman from the west, and Allen Street, the first commercial street after the docks. Close enough to the waterfront that shrimpers frequently shop there, it's still far enough removed that no one holds it against the genial merchant. It doesn't hurt Halsey's business that his is the only place in town you can be sure of finding what you need. There are a number of other stores, mostly specialty shops, but Halsey makes a practice of having some of everything they have, and a lot they don't. He has more hardware than Witman Hardware, and more food than Meacham's Grocery. About the only area of commerce he is willing to forgo is clothing. He explains the omission by pointing to his own attire. *Would anybody in his right mind buy clothes from a man who dresses like I do?*

The centerpiece of Halsey's is the portly merchant himself. His small stature makes him seem rounder than he is. Unlike most Witman residents, he spends most of his time indoors, a fact testified to by his pale complexion. With his pale hair and congenial smile, it suggests some nocturnal animal with a sense of humor. More easygoing than most, he manages to maintain an even keel during the most turbulent of times.

Settling there after World War II, he opened the store almost immediately, and managed to build his trade as much by his personality as by business acumen. A student of human nature, he quickly learned to deal with the high spirits of the shrimpers, as well as with their surliness. Their moods seemed to fluctuate with the season's catch, and lately it had been anything but good.

Halsey's openness of spirit had drawn Doc Roth to him. And since there was no pharmacy in town, Doc had gotten to know Halsey immediately. Medicine was ferried in by Halsey's delivery van. Prescriptions dropped off at the store were filled in Port Lavaca and returned the following day.

Halsey was the only man in town, besides Luke Darby, who had accepted Doc immediately. If Doc and Darby had become friends, it was partly due to him. He took everyone at face value, made no attempt to analyze, and judged people only by what they did. If somebody did something wrong, then he was a bad man. Like Darby, the storekeeper seemed to know everything there was to know about Witman.

Soon after Doc arrived, he noticed that most buildings were the same color. That was because there was only one color of paint available in Witman. Halsey didn't have room to stock much and said he'd be damned if he was going to try to outguess the ornery taste of Witmanites, or cater to it. *You want paint, I got it. You want something ain't white, I'm fresh out.* Since the hardware store didn't bother with paint at all, everyone worked with Halsey's limited palette. They were practical, and as indifferent as the sun and rain to anything as subtle as color.

31

Halsey developed a protective curiosity about Doc, watching him like a boy with a garter snake in a shoe box. Almost from the first, Doc would come into the store nearly every day with another question or anecdote, the nub of which almost invariably was his lack of understanding, either of Witman or of his place in it. Some concerned things of which Doc had been rudely made aware; others were so subtle that he approached Halsey out of mystification rather than injured feelings.

Local wisdom was muted on the question of why Doc had even come to Witman. *What in hell's he want with a place like this?* No one professed to have the slightest idea, a bafflement remarkable for a town that had a dozen explanations for why anyone did anything. Doc himself seemed uncertain at first, but as he struggled to establish his practice, he spent less and less time trying to answer that question. Although Witman's residents seemed to appreciate him, they were wary. Some, of course, were skeptical of his motives, but even they were glad enough to take advantage of his skills when word got around that he was willing to treat them on credit. Their needs and his seemed to coincide, and Isaac Roth, New York physician, was soon Doc to most of them. Oh, he was still the Jewboy to a few, mostly behind his back, but never when they were sick or hurt.

The poor Mexicans, a large contingent of the shrimpers, thought of him as a blessing sent from heaven. Having had their own difficulties with strangers and local prejudice, they were the most willing to accept him simply as a doctor, and being less prosperous than their Anglo peers, they knew that a doctor near at hand could mean the difference between the loss of a few weeks' pay and permanent disability. When it became known that Doc cared less about citizenship than affliction, new patients increased rapidly from among the illegal aliens who were tolerated among the shrimpers for their willingness to work hard and cheaply and, perhaps most important, for their vulnerability.

Doc's Spanish was worse than rusty, but he had a subtle, well-honed diagnostic eye, and so began to build a reputation that contributed mightily to his early practice, if not his bank account. It seemed finally, despite the sense of not belonging that haunted his more introspective moments, that he had found the kind of role that would help him forget New York and, less certainly, Rose.

What unsettled him was the impersonality of it all. No one had any special attachment to him, or reason to care about his feelings. If he could take the heat, all well and good, and if he couldn't, that was all right, too. During the first weeks, it was the solicitousness of Darby and Halsey that kept him going, the former with his logic, hidden behind a folksy veneer, and the latter with his no-nonsense humaneness.

He was hopeful that, in time, his uneasiness would fade, that mistrust would slowly be replaced by tolerance, then acceptance. He made a few acquaintances, through Darby and Halsey, and his burgeoning practice was a more effective tranquilizer here than it could ever have been in New York, so he kept postponing a decision on whether or not to stay on. Despite the incident with Pat Riley, he knew it was no longer a decision he would *have* to make. If he were to leave, it would be by choice, not because he had been driven out of town.

Doc's office was functional to the point of Spartan severity. He had decided that it should reflect the lives of those he would treat. Frills would have been out of place in Witman. It was a simple matter to design a clean, stripped-down environment for his new practice. Since he would live alone, it was sensible to set it up in a house, devoting two large rooms to waiting room and office and reserving the rest for living quarters.

The only concession to his earlier pattern was the magazines he scattered on the waiting-room tables. He'd brought along some back issues and advised the publishers of his new address. He didn't doubt he was the only subscriber in Witman for several of them. Luke accused him of having more books than the county library, but Doc wasn't sure. He'd brought so many with him, and his taste was so idiosyncratic, that he hadn't bothered to visit it. He avoided best sellers like the plague; his taste ran to Continental fiction, mostly nineteenth century. Luke disparaged the collection as "that mess of fat books," but had borrowed a few before they were all on their shelves. Mixed in among the fiction was a smattering of philosophy, mostly French and German, and several collections of poetry and drama.

If his reading habits weren't calculated to endear him to Witmanites, it was his taste in art that caused the most comment. He had kept a couple of the abstract oils that had hung in his New York office. These, he was beginning to suspect, contributed to his reputation for oddity. The Rothko and the Mondrian could stay, but he was increasingly uncertain about the large Munch portrait. More than one patient had asked nervously whether it was anyone he knew.

He had two appointments scheduled for this particular morning, the first not due for half an hour. He spent the time going through his mail, mostly regional circulars addressed to occupant, which he deposited in the wastebasket after skimming them. There was a letter from Rose's sister, which he put aside for later. Then he took a supply inventory. He had used little and was looking forward to the time when he would have to reorder. The bottled aspirin and ampules of antibiotics, assorted serums and samples of everything from ACTH to zinc ointment stood in neat arrays. Their number and variety were either pessimistic or optimistic, depending on whether they represented the future of Witman's health or of Doc's practice.

As he checked the last shelf of supplies, the bell over the door rang. He felt nervous, as he always did before the first patient of the day, and ran a hand through his hair to flatten it and restrain any stray locks. Clearing his throat, he went to the doorway between office and waiting room.

"Mr. Gutierrez?"

The patient nodded and closed the outside door.

"Would you come with me, please?" Doc turned and walked back to his desk. As he took his seat, he looked up to see the man standing in the inner doorway. "Come in, come in, please," Doc said, more loudly than he intended, gesturing with his hand. "Please, take a seat." He indicated the large leather chair facing his desk.

The man moved cautiously, looking around at the office as he approached the chair. He sat slowly, perched on the front of the cushion, his hands in his lap.

"What seems to be the trouble, Mr. Gutierrez?"

It had been this way with nearly all his patients. They seemed uncertain whether they wanted to be in his office at all, as if they were reluctant to entrust themselves to the care of someone willing to treat them. Doc understood their nervousness and controlled his impatience as he dealt with their problems. Someday, he hoped, they would be more relaxed, more natural, with him, and he could be the same. But it would be slow going.

Rodolfo Gutierrez had little English, so the examination took longer than he had expected. It was frustrating to deal with a simple case of flu with such agonizing slowness. As Doc removed his stethoscope and rerolled the crisp armband of his new sphygmomanometer, the bell rang again. Doc smiled, realizing that it was the first time since his arrival that he had had more than one patient in the office at the same time. It wasn't the traffic he'd known in New York, but it was a start.

When Gutierrez left, Kevin McIlhenny stepped into the office. This was a milestone. McIlhenny was his first Anglo patient. This time he could be expansive, spend a little time chatting. He would have to work on his Spanish, so he could do the same with all his patients, but that would take a while. At the moment, McIlhenny was a welcome relief. He, too, had the flu, and while writing out a prescription, Doc engaged him in conversation.

"You a shrimper, Mr. McIlhenny?"

"Nope. Own a boatyard. Two, actually, but only one's operating."

"What sort of work does that involve?"

"Pretty near everything you can think of. We build some, repair some. Engine overhauls, paint jobs. And we rent out space for drydock. Everything *but* shrimping. I had enough of that."

"I'd like to come down, sometime, if I could. I'd like to know more about what goes on around here."

"Sure, anytime. But you don't have to come to the yard to learn what goes on. You can stay right here. Everything that goes on goes wrong, once in a while. You'll learn all you want to know when the casualties come by for fixing. You're in the same business I am, Doc. I fix boats and you fix people, but there ain't much difference down here."

"I hope I'm here long enough."

"You ain't thinking of leaving already, are you? We sure could use a good doctor."

"Well, Mr. McIlhenny, like you said, we're in the same business. If I don't get the work, I can't very well *stay* in business. Unlike you, I can't build anything. I'm just in the business of repairs."

"You'll get it, Doc. Takes folks a while, but they'll come around. Next time I see you, you'll be telling me how much you need a vacation."

It was eleven-thirty when McIlhenny left, nearly time to go for the homecoming ceremonies. He was heartened by the morning, and hopeful that McIlhenny would be right. It would take some getting used to, but he was sure he could adjust. He was still far from certain that he wanted to, but it just might be worth a try.

4

THE Witman bus station had little to recommend it, and even less to distinguish it from most small-town bus stations in the Southwest. Inside a single large room was a small glass cubicle, a combination ticket window, information desk, and dispatcher's office. Outside, there was a row of gray slat benches against one wall, under a weather-whitened aluminum awning. Across a narrow sidewalk, between the parking area and the building, a row of concrete curbs was bolted to the asphalt. In front of each was an oblique rectangle of faded yellow lines. The only indication that the day wasn't ordinary was the strand of faded red, white, and blue pennants flapping in the hot afternoon wind and wan bunting dangling over one of the parking places. They had seen long, hard service in a town reluctant to indulge itself in community frills.

Three or four highway cruisers sat in the lot. As Doc

took a seat on the end bench, one of the buses started with a grind that grew into a slow rumble. As he watched, its destination roller slapped stiff, resistant paper against the glass before, with a sudden billow, settling on Brownsville as the bus backed out.

Trying to shrink back out of the heat, Doc wondered why he was the only one waiting. Even Kate wasn't here yet, and he began to think he had misunderstood the time for the parade. It crossed his mind that the pennants might be so bedraggled because they were always there, not just for the homecoming. There were no signs, nothing at all to connect David with the increasingly less convincing festiveness of the bus terminal. Doc was about to go inside, when Kate came around the corner with the same woman she had spoken to earlier.

They stopped abruptly when they saw him. Kate said something to the older woman, then resumed walking so quickly her pause might have been nothing more than the blinking of his eye. He stood as they approached, and Kate smiled a quick smile, nearly as illusory as her hesitation.

"Doctor Roth, this is my mother, Maggie."

"How do you do?" he asked. He scrutinized Kate's face, but there was no sign of lingering upset from their last meeting.

"Doctor Roth is from New York, Mother. He plans to stay in Witman."

"Doc . . . how are you? Why in hell would you want to set down roots in a godforsaken place like this?" Maggie demanded.

"Mother!"

"That's all right, Miss Riley. Your mother has a point. In fact, I was asking myself the same thing just before you arrived."

"What'd you decide?" Maggie asked.

"Mother, that's really none of your business. You'll have to excuse her, Doctor; she tends to be rather blunt."

"Why shouldn't I? I don't know what good there is in beating around the bush. Do you, Doc?"

"No, I can't say I do, Mrs. Riley."

" 'Maggie' will be fine, Doc. That's what everybody else calls me. If you're gonna stay around, you might as well get used to it. If you're not, it won't make much difference. And you might as well call her Kate, while you're at it."

"Maggie . . . I think I'll use it, if you really don't mind . . . maybe we should leave Kate alone. This must be a very important day for her."

"Mother, please make this one time in your life you follow doctor's orders." Kate flashed Doc a grateful smile.

"I don't see what makes doctors so special. All they do is charge a lot of money to tell you to go home and put something on whatever's wrong with you."

"Mother," Kate interrupted, "can we change the subject?"

"Kate, why don't you shush up. Every other word out of your mouth the last few minutes is 'Mother.' "

"I just don't think you ought to talk that way in front of Doctor Roth. You just met him. He doesn't realize you're only teasing."

"I haven't said anything bad about the doctor here. I don't know anything bad about him. That don't mean he's innocent, mind you, just that I don't know him to be guilty."

"Can we *please* change the subject?" Kate asked again.

"I don't mind, if the Doc here don't."

"Not at all."

"It's nice of you to come down and welcome David home," Kate said.

"Actually, I was wondering whether I had the right day. I didn't see anyone around."

"Oh, yes, it's the right day," Kate said. "But people around here don't like waiting. They usually show up with minutes to spare."

"I'm afraid that's not a good habit for a doctor to have."

"I'm not sure you're gonna make a go of it around here, Doc. If you get in the habit of hanging out by somebody's sickbed, they might get worried."

Doc was about to reply, when some newcomers turned the corner. They nodded to the Riley women. Halsey was with them, but he was the only one Doc recognized. He said hello, before taking a seat with his companions. They were followed by a few band members, who moved past with a clatter of instruments, and the grunting of a sousaphone player. Kate welcomed the interruption and moved off to organize them.

"Doc," Maggie asked, "why don't you and me take a seat, and leave Katie to her fussin'?" She took him by the arm, ready to march back to the bench. Her grip was strong, and her tug determined, so he followed meekly along at her side.

They sat quietly for a while. Maggie was watching her daughter intently, and Doc had the opportunity to examine the older woman's features in some detail. Her skin was taut and leathery. There wasn't a wrinkle, not even close to the hairline or around the eyes, which were bright blue.

The skin of Maggie's hands, too, was taut. Their backs were knotted with muscle, strong and flexible, not gnarled like the hands of an old person. They were the hands of someone who depends on them for a livelihood. Her mouth was firmly set, and she wore no makeup. She was dressed in faded denims, which had seen hard wear but were well cared for. On her feet were scuffed penny loafers. There was a small white blur on each instep, contrasting with the darker skin of her hands and face, as if she were used to a higher shoe. Her hands, although they lay still in her lap, gave the impression of restlessness. Doc was about to break his silence, when Pat Riley turned the corner and sauntered in their direction.

Doc wasn't happy to see him, but, much to his surprise, Riley's mother and sister seemed no more pleased by Pat's sudden arrival. He walked over to Kate, put his arm around her shoulders, and leaned down to whisper something in her ear. Kate tensed and turned to face her brother. Doc thought for a moment she was going to slap him, but Pat backed away, feigning fright, then laughed before coming toward Maggie.

He walked over to the bench and planted himself in front of Doc for a minute before speaking. When he finally opened his mouth, it wasn't to say hello to his mother, but, rather, "If you weren't such a stranger around here, and unused to manners, you'd probly get up and let me sit down next to my ma."

Before Doc could respond, Maggie said, "Pat, mind *your* manners. I won't have you ruining this afternoon for your sister."

"Now, Ma, you know I wouldn't do anything like that. I was just joshing the doc here. Him and me are old friends. Ain't we, Doc?"

"I don't know if I'd go that far, Maggie, but we've met. This morning, in fact."

Maggie grunted before answering Pat. "Why don't you just go on about your business and let those of us who want to be here do what we came to do?"

"Now what makes you think I don't want to do the same thing? I always was partial to Davey. I can't think of any-place I'd rather be."

"Try, Pat. Do me a favor and try." The voice, brittle

and razor sharp, belonged to Kate. She was heading toward the bench, glaring at her brother.

"Now, Katie, I mean it. I want to be here. It makes me proud to think my brother-in-law-to-be is coming home a hero. That's something I never would have believed."

"If you were so partial to David," Kate snapped, "you'd know he doesn't like to be called 'Davey.' You'd also know he wasn't partial to you. So why are you here?"

"To pay my respects is all, Katie. What's wrong with that?"

"Nothing, if it were true."

Pat laughed again and sat on the bench next to Doc. "All the same," he said, "I'm going to be right here when old Davey gets off that bus. You never know who might be coming home with him."

"What is that supposed to mean?"

"Well," Pat drawled, "you got a brother, don't you? Davey does, too, if I remember right."

Maggie stood up and stepped briskly in front of Doc to lean into her son's face. "Patrick, I don't care what you do when you're running around with those rowdy friends of yours, but I won't have you ruining this day for your sister. Or for David, either. Do you hear me? I don't care *who* gets off that bus with David."

"Ma! I don't believe what I'm hearing!" Pat said. "Do you want me to turn my back on my duty, just so my little sister can welcome her boyfriend home? You can't mean that!"

"I do mean it, and I'm telling you to get on away from here. And don't you grin at me like that, boy, or I'll box your ears."

"Well, I never heard the like of this, when a man has to choose between enforcing the law and obeying his own ma! What do you think, Doc?" He grinned at the physician.

43

"You leave the doc out of this and do what I tell you, boy!"

Pat made a show of getting slowly to his feet, grinning broadly, then shuffled off, elbowing his way through the gathering crowd.

Maggie stared after him, her face an angry mask. Kate's expression was even more forbidding. Her fury had completely erased the elation she had been struggling to control since her arrival. She sat alone on the next bench, gazing over the heads of the crowd, the muscles of her jaw knotting. She was fighting back tears.

"Doctor Roth," Maggie said, "you'll have to forgive my son. I'm afraid he doesn't have the manners he was born with. I'm sorry for the way he acted just now. He's just . . . I have to see to Katie. Excuse me for a minute, please."

The younger woman tried to reassure her mother, patting her hands to emphasize that she was under control. Doc noticed they had the same long, tapered fingers, which would not have looked out of place poised over a piano keyboard. He was impressed by the dignity Maggie conveyed, the strength of character that seemed to mantle her slender shoulders. Kate glanced in his direction once, and he smiled encouragement. She nodded slightly and turned back to her mother. Maggie reached out to stroke her daughter's cheek. Then she resumed her seat beside Doc.

"I apologize again for Patrick's behavior."

"No need for that, Maggie. I can't say I'm surprised at the way he acted, not after this morning, but you're certainly not to blame."

"Maybe not. But I *am* his mother, and I have to take some of the responsibility. I get scared, sometimes, just thinking about what he's like lately. Something's changed him. I look at him now and I can't even recognize him. Anyway, sometimes I wish . . . No, I don't wish that."

She trailed off. Doc guessed she was as close to crying as she'd allow in public. She wouldn't permit herself to excuse her son, or to disown him.

"John Halsey told me about your younger son. I'm terribly sorry."

Before she could answer, they heard the roar of the bus, and if she said anything, Doc didn't hear it. A buzz went through the crowd, grown considerably larger, just as Kate had said it would. A big, dusty Greyhound disengaged its gears and coasted to a stop, its tires flush up against the curb under the large bunting, which was billowed forward by the top of the bus and straining at the four lines that held it in place. The bus rolled back a bit, away from the curb, almost as if the tension of the banner were too much for it. Then, with a hiss of its air brakes, it came to a standstill. There was a hush of expectancy.

Someone in the back of the crowd started a rhythmic clap-clap-clapping, and, as if in response, the door of the bus swung open. For a moment, the clapping stilled, then started up again, more insistently than before, as more and more of the onlookers joined in. A man appeared in the door of the bus, the sun glinting off his peaked cap, and someone whispered, "There he is," only to be corrected a moment later by a neighbor, as the driver swung free and helped an elderly woman down from the step.

One by one, several other people straggled off the bus, and then there was a long moment when no one else left it. Doc caught a glimpse of Kate Riley, whose features were drawn taut, as if her skin had suddenly grown too small for the bones wrapped within it. As suddenly as the hush had fallen, there was an eruption of cheers. The clapping started again, more spontaneously this time, as a young man in a checkered shirt and faded jeans swung lightly through the bus door and landed soundlessly on the hot asphalt. His face was well tanned and leaner than Doc would have expected. The dark hair was cropped short, recently cut. The sleeves of his shirt were rolled above the elbows, and the young man's muscular forearms and compact six-foot frame implied that power accompanied his athletic grace.

"There he is, there's David," someone yelled, and others took up the chant, "There's David. Welcome home."

Kate looked stunned for a moment, then, squealing with delight, rushed forward to throw herself into the young man's arms. He grasped her in a tight hug and easily whirled her in a broad arc.

Kate squealed again, and he twirled her gently to her feet. He looked long and quietly at her face before, without a word, draping an arm across her shoulders and guiding her firmly away from the crowd. They moved briskly, the crowd too dumbfounded to do anything. The band, which had been waiting patiently, horns at the ready, struck up "The Stars and Stripes Forever," but quickly lost its way as the conductor turned to watch David and Kate over his shoulder, his baton twitching spasmodically.

Frank Willard, all set for the opportunity to deliver himself, as Halsey had predicted, of a "few thousand well-chosen words," looked after the couple helplessly. He turned to the townspeople, as if for a moment considering whether he might still speak. Then he slowly balled up his page of notes and tossed it to the ground, where it curled in a spidery dust devil. It skidded across the pavement, coming to rest against one of the massive tires of the bus.

"That boy's got more sense than the rest of us put together," someone whispered in Doc's ear, and he turned to see Halsey beaming after the refugees. "I can't say as I blame him none, either. Not after what he's been through. And not with a gal like Katie waiting for him."

46

"But it was Kate who planned this affair, wasn't it?"

"Sure, but so what? It could have been an icebreaker if he needed it, but he didn't, did he?" Halsey laughed. "Maggie, how are you?" he said, shaking her hand.

She nodded. "Well, I guess the party's over for now. I'll be getting on back to work. Nice meeting you, Doc." She took his hand, as well, squeezing it warmly.

"Ain't you going over to the school for some free food, Maggie?" Halsey asked.

"Nope. I got too much work to do to earn my own." She turned to thread her way through the thinning crowd and was soon out of sight.

Here and there, Doc could hear snatches of grumbling about "lack of appreciation" and "uppityness," and he had the uneasy feeling that this homecoming was not exactly what the people of Witman had been led to expect. Some of the more vocal members of the crowd voiced resentment, as if Hodges had somehow slighted them all.

Doc mentioned it to Halsey, who shrugged it off, saying that people got their feelings bruised pretty easily, but managed to forget just as easily. On reflection, he guessed most of them would see it David's way, even admit that they might have done the same in his shoes, or at least have wanted to.

"Feel like a beer, Doc?"

"No, I don't think so, John, thanks. I'll just head on home and take a nap. I didn't get much sleep last night."

"Well, don't go reading things into this little mix-up. There's a lot less here than meets the eye, believe me."

"It's not that, John. I'm just feeling a little tired."

"Why don't you come by later on? I think Luke was planning on playing a little chess this afternoon. What shall I tell him?"

"Say I'll likely be back later, after I see how I feel."

Doc's house was half a mile or so past the edge of town, and he thought a walk, despite the heat, would do him more good than the nap he suddenly didn't feel like taking. In the distance ahead he could see two figures, very close together, ambling along the dusty road.

5

THEY were reluctant to speak as they walked along the highway. David rested one hand on Kate's shoulder and glanced at her face from time to time. Kate couldn't bring herself to look at him. David sensed her reluctance and wondered about its cause. She had changed little, whereas he knew himself to be someone else. Whether she knew or not, he couldn't tell. And if she did, he wondered if it would make a difference.

That she understand him, and what had happened to him, was paramount. She *had* to understand, both for herself and for him. His acceptance of the ways he had changed would depend on her. If he was a mystery to her, he'd remain a puzzle to himself. In his private world, haunted by nightmares, hope was sustained, however tenuously, by reference to their common past.

He knew he was less flexible than when he had left. He

had become rigid in self-defense, steeling himself so often, against so much, for so long, he wondered if he'd ever be content again. It was a question he didn't want to ask. Not yet. It was too soon; too soon to answer and, especially, too soon to face the possibility that the answer might be no.

For more than two years, afraid of the telephone and the sound of her voice, he had been able only to write, and not often. There was so much she ought to know, so much he had to tell her. But he didn't know how. Each time he tried, it grew more difficult, until, finally, he dreaded the feel of a pen, the sight of blank paper. That pervading isolation had driven him to stay on, to reenlist as the war continued its deadly spiral into history. He had come to believe that he needed forgiveness, which only Kate could give him.

At night, the sounds of the war ominous, relentlessly approaching, he would lie awake staring into the dark. Sometimes he could hear mortar rounds thumping through the blackness, regular as the footsteps of a bored night watchman. The final round always seemed to fall a little closer than the night before. He visualized the shells, detonating in bursts of flame, closing a circle of which he was the center. Secretly he felt as if he were the focus of the war, the pivot on which it all turned. Eventually, the bright line of fire would reach him, the final round would not fall short, and as it blew the life out of him, the war would collapse inward on itself, ending not just for him, but for everyone. It was a conceit that awareness had done nothing to diminish.

Now, home at last, there was an unreality about the things he saw. They were too quiet, too perfect, the way only memories of a distant place could be. He had wanted this so much for so long that he was convinced it was not, and could not be, real.

He looked at Kate again and stopped, squeezing her shoulder to bring her to a halt. Then he walked into a meadow to the left of the highway and sat in the dry grass. He looked up at her. She seemed baffled.

"I just want to sit for a while," he said.

"Are you all right?"

"I guess."

"That doesn't sound so sure."

"I suppose not. . . . Look, Katie, I just want to be quiet for a while. I'm here, with you; that's all that matters."

He uprooted a handful of the tall, brittle grass and shook it roughly to dislodge the dry soil tangled in its roots. When it was clean, he tapped the clump of yellow-green against his shins in a slow, gentle rhythm. He ran his fingers through the sandy earth where the grass had been, then eased backward.

Overhead, there was a bright sheen of yellow-white between the earth and the deep blue of the sky. He hooded his eyes to look up at Kate and patted the ground with the clump of grass. Kate sank down beside him. He cradled her with one arm, and she looked at the sky as if to see what he studied so intently.

"I've been away a long, long time," he said.

"I know. . . . "

"No, you don't know."

"I do. I missed you, David. I bought calendars. I counted days, weeks, months. I know how long you've been gone."

"No," he said again. "You know when you saw me last. That's not the same thing."

David raised up to brush away a lock of hair that had strayed across her brow. For a moment, she thought he was going to say something. His lips moved slightly, and he started to smile. She watched him so intently that the slightest movement seemed magnified a hundred times.

Scrutinizing him made her self-conscious. Turning away, she rubbed her free hand through the grass, as if ruffling a horse's mane. Each blade felt stiff, unyielding, unnatural, like her own movements. Afraid she would seem as awkward as she felt, she resolved to lie still. David lay back beside her.

"David?"

When he didn't answer, she turned back to him. His eyes were closed against the sun. She said his name a second time, again as a question. "David?"

This time, she realized he had fallen asleep. His breathing was quick and shallow. More bewildered than hurt, she carefully got to her feet and stood looking down at him. He slept as if he were a coiled spring poised precariously on the edge of its own tension.

She lay down again, this time on her stomach, propping her head to watch him sleep, but not so close as to intrude on his fitful solitude.

She wondered how long it would take him to resume a normal life, or whether he would even be able to. She had been troubled by his sporadic correspondence and, now that he was home, she wanted to know what lay behind it. She knew him well enough to know he must have had his reasons, and loved him enough to let him tell her, in his own good time, what they were.

All she could do for the moment was wait. While she watched, he opened his eyes, but she didn't notice. "What are you thinking about, Katie?" he asked, startling her.

"I don't know . . . just, you know . . . wondering."

"Wondering what?"

"What it's been like for you. How much you've changed. Things like that . . . "

"Just wondering, or were you thinking I have changed, and wondering why and how much?"

"Both, I guess."

"Well, I have changed. I don't think I know how much. But I will. And when I put all the pieces together some way that makes sense, I'll tell you."

"I can't help then, can I?"

"Not just yet."

"You'll let me know . . . ?"

David nodded, as if he had run out of words, then closed his eyes and lay back in the grass. She kissed him softly on the forehead and whispered, "I love you, David. Whatever else you might doubt, don't doubt that."

He pulled her to him. Spreading his fingers wide across her back, he began to rub in broad, slow circles, just as he always had. Just as he had done the last time they had been together. The warmth was so familiar, so comforting, that for a few moments Kate thought maybe, after all, nothing had really changed. But unlike that time, now he said nothing, and soon his hand ceased its movement. Kate didn't want to know why.

On Decker Street, which had the reputation of being the rowdiest street in town, was a string of bars, which had done the most to create that reputation and seemed at times to be going out of its way to embellish it. The Double Header was no worse than most, and better than some. Like the others, it catered mostly to local bay fishermen and long-hauling Gulf shrimpers. Like the others, it smelled as much of the sea as it did of alcohol. It was dark, which most of its patrons seemed to like. They could drink without being reminded by the full-length mirror behind the bar that they had not yet shaved after a two-week run. It was simply furnished, but the regulars didn't mind, and the visitors were more likely to be thirsty than observant.

Other than hidden lamps that backlighted the bar, the

primary illumination came from a shaded lamp dangling over the pool table tucked into one of the rear corners. A wash of color was thrown over those tables nearest the jukebox, which featured everything from Bob Wills and Hank Williams on. In recent years, salsa and Tex-Mex tunes had found their way onto the machine, a concession to the growing number of Hispanic shrimpers who frequented the place. The volume on the box was loud, unless someone objected, usually to complain that it wasn't loud enough.

There was much speculation about how the bar had gotten its name. Explanations were long on invention and scanty on substantiation. Theories ranged from the minor league baseball accomplishments of its owner to the house custom of a free refill for each patron after the first drink. In fact, the place originally belonged to a pair of disenchanted shrimpers who had pooled their resources after deciding they were sick of shrimping. Having made enough to escape the sea, they earned enough from the bar to escape Witman altogether, sold out and moved on. That was two or three owners back, and the current proprietor was as ignorant of the origin of the name as the patrons who argued about it.

The one thing that distinguished the Double Header from the other bars on the strip was the fact that it was the favorite watering hole for most of the local lawmen. Even the sheriff, a near teetotaler, would stop in for an occasional beer. It was the first place anybody looked for a couple of the deputies when they weren't on duty, and sometimes even when they were. Pat Riley was one of the regulars, and usually stopped in every day after his shift. The morning he had stopped Doc Roth was no exception. When he got off duty, he wandered over to the Header for a little refreshment, and not coincidentally to spend a little time with his current girlfriend, Louise Dryden, who was a waitress there.

When Pat ambled in, he headed to his favorite table, in the shadows near the pool table, where he could watch the door without having to watch his back. It also gave him a good look at Louise when she bent over to get something under the bar. She knew it, and although she wasn't thrilled with the idea of someone looking under her dress, if it had to be anyone, it might as well be Pat. Soon after he took his seat, Louise stopped by to sit while he decided what he wanted to drink. He always took longer than necessary for his first order. He knew the place would get busy in a half hour, and Louise would be hopping from table to table, so he held onto her for a few minutes longer than necessary.

"Louise, honey, I think I'm just gonna have a ginger ale, today."

"Anything wrong?"

"Nope."

"You sure?"

"I'm okay . . . just a ginger ale."

Louise moved off to get the drink, glancing once over her shoulder to see whether Pat had been kidding and was ready to call her back for a more usual drink, but he was watching a game of eightball. She got the ginger ale and hustled back to the table, bringing one for herself. Sitting down, she poured it into two glasses, the fizz bouncing onto the back of her hand as the soda hit the ice.

"Thank you, darlin'." Pat smiled without taking his eyes off the game of pool.

"Pat, you sure there's nothing bothering you?"

"I'm all right, just a little off kilter's all. Don't worry about it."

He glanced up as the front door opened and got to his

feet as he recognized a couple of his regular drinking partners. "Afternoon, boys," he said, in an exaggerated drawl. The newcomers peered about to see who called them, standing in the doorway blinking away the bright afternoon light. "Over here, you assholes."

The taller of the two turned in Pat's direction. He grinned and nudged his companion in the ribs with an elbow. Jimmy Johnson and Roger Drake were sometime shrimpers, taking rigging jobs when they could get them, which was seldom, and signing on as headers when they had to settle for the lesser job, which had been more and more frequently of late. Jimmy, at six one and one hundred ninety pounds, was an inch or so shorter than Pat and thirty pounds lighter. They had known one another for most of their lives, though Pat had not seen Jimmy with any regularity until he returned from his tour in the Marine Corps.

Roger was a few inches shorter and proportionately slimmer. Their dress was so similar that Roger might have been taken for a copy of Jimmy, reduced in size by some miraculous scientific procedure. Each wore a pair of sun-faded jeans and a cotton work shirt, sleeves rolled up past the elbow. Both had the nearly universal sandy-colored hair of men who are fair and spend a great deal of time in the sun.

"Patrick, you son of a bitch, how you doing?" Jimmy said, sliding into a chair at Riley's table.

"All right, son. How's yourself?" Pat said, kicking another chair away from the table for Roger. "I thought you boys were going out this week."

"We were," Roger said, "but there ain't much out there the last few months. Eric Swenson had to work on his boat before going out, so we're just hanging around."

"Nothing major, I hope. Eric's a good man, and with all them kids, he can't afford much dead time."

"Naw, no big deal, Pat. But it still hurts. Half the time, you don't catch much anyhow, so you got to go out more, instead of less, just to stay even. And Eric don't need the money any more'n I do." Jimmy laughed.

"You boys want a drink?"

"You buying?" Roger asked.

"The first round . . . "

"All right, then. Just a beer," Jimmy said.

"Make it two."

Pat caught Louise's eye. "A couple of Lone Stars, honey," he said. "These boy's don't know how to use glasses, so you can just bring the bottles."

Before Louise could answer, the front door opened again. Randy McHale walked in, stopping long enough to shake off the glare. As soon as he spotted Pat, he headed straight for his table. When he reached the group, he nodded to Louise. "You boys mind drinking at the bar?" he asked, looking at Jimmy and Roger. "I got something I want to discuss with Pat in private."

They got to their feet with a scrape of chairs. "Nothing wrong, is there, Sheriff?" Jimmy asked.

"Nothing much. I don't want no interruption, that's all."

"Okay by me, Sheriff," Jimmy said, looking curiously at Pat, who shrugged to signify that he was as much in the dark as Jimmy was. When his friends reached the bar, Pat pushed his hat back and leaned forward, placing his elbows on the table.

"Something on your mind, Randy?"

"Pat, don't play dumb with me. I ain't in the mood for it."

"Chrissakes, Randy, let me know what the hell you're talking about before you go chewing me out, would you?"

"You know damn well what's pissed me off. Where were you all day?"

"Oh, around. Here and there."

"The way I hear it, you were bothering folks who didn't need no bothering. I hear you were working real hard at being a pain in the community butt. That's what I hear."

"Come on, Randy. You know how it is. You try to do your job, and there's always somebody who don't like it."

"Like . . . ?"

"Well, I had a real smartass this morning, Randy," Pat said, taking a sip of his ginger ale. He peeked at the sheriff around the rim of his glass. "Some doctor. Jewish guy. He was speeding. I gave it to him real good, though."

"How fast was he going?"

"Thirty-seven."

"Thirty-seven? You call that speeding? What the hell's wrong with you, Pat?"

"Well, now, Sheriff, it was a thirty-five zone." Pat laughed.

"A couple miles over ain't hardly criminal. Not around here. When's the last time you did thirty-five in a thirty-five zone?"

Before Pat could answer, Louise was back. "Can I get you anything to drink, Randy?" she asked.

"No, thanks, Louise."

"I could use a shot and a beer, honey," Pat said.

Louise went back to the bar, and Pat watched her for a moment, before turning back to McHale. "I don't see what you're all upset about, Randy. Shit, all I did was holler at the guy a little. You know, to make sure he got my message."

"What message was that, Pat?"

"Not to fuck with me."

"What makes you think he would?"

"I don't know. Just something about him's all. I could feel it. Don't think he liked me none."

"I don't think I'd like you, you did that to me. Fact is, there are times when I'm pretty sure I *don't* like you. Seems to me that you let that badge of yours go to your head."

Pat stared at the sheriff for a minute, then took another pull on his ginger ale. "Louise, honey, get a move on with that drink, won't you?" he hollered, glancing over at the bar. He didn't think McHale was joking, but decided to take the chance that he had been.

"Shit, Randy, you can always fire my ass, you feel like that."

"Naw, Pat. I'd never do that."

"Why not?" Pat asked, grinning.

"Well, I'll tell you. The way I figure, it's a hell of a lot easier keeping you in line on my side of the badge. I don't know but what I might have to lock you up and throw away the key if you wasn't," McHale said. Pat was now certain that he wasn't joking. There was an edge to the sheriff's voice. His lips just barely tugged upward at their corners, and his eyes didn't smile at all.

"Aw, come on, Sheriff, I was just having a little fun with the Jewboy."

"Pat, let me tell you a couple things," McHale snapped. "Number one, I don't care for your attitude about the man's religion. Number two—and I want you to think real hard on this one—doctors is scarce down here, and deputies is a dime a dozen. I ain't gonna sit back and watch you, or anybody else, try to hide behind the badge I give you. I ever hear you done something like that again, I'll do more'n fire your ass; I'll roast it over an open pit. And while I think about it, stay away from David Hodges. You hear me?"

Before Pat could answer, McHale pushed back his chair and stood up. He stared at Pat, who continued to look straight ahead, as if the other man had not gotten to his feet. Slowly, he reached up and took off his sunglasses, then turned his face toward his superior.

"It's a damn shame you ain't got no sense of humor, Randy," he said. "In our line of work, it helps make the day pass a little quicker."

"You just remember what I told you." McHale turned and left the bar, while Pat scowled after him for a moment before putting his sunglasses back on.

"Louise, darlin'," Pat called the waitress, "make that shot a double, would you, honey?"

6

ONCE introduced by Halsey, Lucas Darby quickly became Doc's closest friend in Witman. Their friendship was founded as much on Luke's desire to make Doc feel at home as on any natural kinship the two men might have felt. Discovering they had chess in common, they met at Halsey's for a game once or twice a week. Luke said Doc was the only man he knew who didn't insist on playing Texas rules. Doc had never heard of Texas rules, but had been playing chess long enough to doubt there was such a thing, until Luke explained that Texas rules meant that there *were* no rules. Doc still didn't know if Luke had been kidding, since he hadn't met anyone else who played chess. The preferred game in Witman was checkers, which he often played with Halsey, and for which Texas rules certainly *did* apply.

Doc was grateful for Luke's friendship. Luke knew

everyone in town, and was one of the few in Witman who believed there was life outside the state of Texas. He had gone to law school at the University of Pennsylvania, and had spent two years working for a Wall Street firm before returning to Witman, where he felt less vulnerable. He could help Doc fit into Witman because he understood New York.

The lawyer stood well over six feet tall. He had the bulk of an interior lineman, but it sat lightly on his large frame. His white hair, with which his hands were constantly at war, tended to go its own way, usually adding an inch or more to his height. Soft brown eyes, which would ignite when he was agitated, peered through heavy, horn-rimmed glasses. He used them mostly for reading and had several pairs, due to his habit of leaving them anyplace he stopped for more than a few minutes. Rather fair, he avoided the sun as much as possible. He regarded the tan on his left arm, a consequence of the time he spent behind the wheel of his dun-colored Buick, as a nuisance, since he had to work hard to get as much color on his right arm, claiming he felt "unbalanced" if the arms didn't match.

Luke had watched most of the town grow up. He had known the Hodges boys all their lives, and the Riley kids, too. He had been present at all of the christenings and all of the funerals. Events that had not required his skills as an attorney had attracted his natural inclination to observe. The years had convinced him that there was more to Witman than the casual observer, or the newcomer, could understand.

Luke's living depended on his knowing people better than they knew themselves. He'd been the only lawyer in town for the last thirty years. During that time, nearly everyone had been to see him. He always made clients tell him what he needed to know to do his job, and to some of the more reluctant he sometimes seemed more like a prosecutor, or an inquisitor.

He wasn't the least bit backward in warning them. He always opened up with a little speech, and although the text varied to suit the circumstances, its message was always the same. I am your lawyer. I am not your minister. You can tell him what he wants to hear and, most of the time, he'll be satisfied. You'll feel better because he tells you what you want to hear. But a lawyer's different. He's got to know everything, even things that don't seem important or to mean much. You have to tell me what I want to *know*, not what I want to hear. And what I want to know, friend, is the truth, plain and simple. If you want your money's worth out of me, I'm the boss, and you answer my questions. Then you shut up and do what I tell you.

One aspect of Doc's personality fascinated Luke, who recognized the physician as a complex, even contradictory, man. He suspected that Doc had deliberately chosen to live with doubt and contradiction. To Luke, he seemed to have been tailor-made for ambiguity, to relish uncertainty, thriving in it as a natural condition. In this, Doc reminded him of David Hodges. The problem of David Hodges threatened to be the most challenging he had considered in a long time. And he was counting on Doc to help him with it, or, at the very least, to be a laboratory. By observing Doc, he hoped to gain insight into David.

Except for Kate, no one saw much of David for a while. Given his perfunctory arrival, no one really expected to, but some seemed to take it personally. Luke knew David would have to ease back into home life a little at a time. He was spending most of his free time with Kate, working around his house, and, without a job, his free time was considerable. It was summer, school was out, so Kate was available. Everyone knew she hadn't waited all that time for no reason.

Kate had never been one for patience, and Luke had wondered, even before David had gone away, whether he might not be too deliberate for her. David never seemed to do anything without considering every angle, a habit he shared with Doc, but which Luke found odd in so young a man. He thought David ought to be more spontaneous. He could have learned from his brother, Peter, who was spontaneous enough for any two people. True, if someone pushed David, it was a different matter. He'd react explosively, without thinking. At least, that's the way he had been. He was so little in evidence, Luke didn't know if he was still like that, but he suspected David wouldn't have come home at all if he wasn't.

Visible or not, David was the main topic of conversation. Everyone seemed to have an opinion about him, whether it was about what he did in the war, why he went, why he came back, or, most frequently, why he didn't at least go through the motions the afternoon he came home. A lot of people seemed to think it was the least he could have done, under the circumstances, although what they meant by "the circumstances" wasn't clear. They seemed less interested in accepting what had happened than in trying to explain it to one another. Luke was irritated by the gossip. He thought it told more about the talker than the talked about.

Over a hand of poker in the back of Halsey's store one night, one of the town's more gifted mythologists began exploring the notion that David wasn't David at all, just somebody who looked like him, and not all that much, either, come home in his place. The story died a painless death when Luke defied the alcoholic Homer to give a plausible reason for such a charade. Despite having dispelled it so easily, though, the story troubled him. He wondered how many other outlandish notions were circulating, all because a man who had been through hell chose to keep to himself for a bit.

What upset Luke most was the fact that, as he put it to Doc one afternoon, "the biggest mouth, doing the most flapping," belonged to Pat Riley. Since David saw more of Pat's sister than he did anyone else, people assumed Pat knew what he was talking about. They all knew Pat themselves and should have known better than to take him seriously, but that didn't seem to matter.

Playing chess in his office with Doc, Luke got angry just talking about it. He needed a break. Standing up to stretch, he stared down at the board for a moment, then went to the window to pull aside the curtain and stare out at the street, nearly deserted in the hot afternoon sun. "Feel like a beer, Doc?"

"No, thanks, Luke. I'll take some ice water, though."

Luke went into the next room, where a small kitchen was tucked into one corner, and returned with a beer and a juice bottle full of water, its pebbled skin beaded with condensation.

"Luke, it seems to me you're making more out of this nonsense than it deserves."

"You may be right, Doc, but I got a funny feeling. I can't shake it, and I don't like it."

"Well, then, what does it all mean?"

"I don't know. But I do know thinking seems difficult for most folks at the best of times, which these ain't."

"Maybe you're just expecting too much."

"Maybe so, Doc. Maybe I am. I guess it's easier just to credit old Pat and pass the word along, touching it up now and then to make it sound like you know what you're talking about. What I could never figure, though, is why those boys didn't get along any better'n they did. Donald Riley and David were best friends, and David and Katie have been keeping company since high school. It's almost unnatural, don't you think, for there to be so much animosity between an older brother and the man who's so close to his own kin?"

"Not necessarily, Luke. It happens."

"Doc, you have to understand how it is down here. Friends of kin are friends of yours. Period."

"Always?"

"Close enough to always that it means something if they ain't. That's exactly what I'm saying!"

"Did you ever ask them about it?"

"Yup! I asked David once. But he didn't have much to say, and I didn't press him. He seemed to tense up when I mentioned it. I think sometimes David just goes out of his way to ignore Pat, because of the way he feels about Katie."

"Riley was in the Marines, too, wasn't he?"

"Yup. And, come to think of it, that was really the beginning of Patrick changing from ornery to ugly. Most of the boys around here are roughnecks for a while. They mostly outgrow it, though. Some don't, I guess is all there is to it. But I swear it doesn't seem that simple."

Luke twirled the beer bottle in his hand, staring into its open mouth, then rolled it, label out, across his brow before setting it down on the edge of the marble chessboard with a crack.

"You know, Doc," he said thoughtfully, "I never was too fond of Pat, and I got to like him less and less after he started bullying folks from behind that badge of his. The funny part of it is, I don't think he's a bad man. Not all bad, anyhow. It's more like he's got something goading him, like he can't control himself. There ain't a whole lot you can do to change a man who doesn't want to change. One thing I do know, though, is that he never did like David's brother, Peter. I hear he was down at the bus depot the day David came home, asking around for Peter, like he expected him, too."

"Yes, that's true. But I don't think he really expected Peter. Seemed to me he was just trying to give the whole thing a sour flavor."

"Well, he's good at that; that much I'll give him."

"Where does Peter figure in all this?"

"Hell, Doc, I don't know. Peter was always a hell-raiser, just like Pat. More than once, even after, maybe especially after, David and Katie got sweet on one another, David had to pull Pat off Peter. As often as not, he needed Donald's help. Katie stood there the whole while, her hands over her ears, screaming at the pack of 'em. Their father died when Patrick was fourteen, so maybe it was just a case of Patrick getting out of control early and staying there. I don't think it's much use trying to figure it out. What we got to do is put a stop to it."

"How is David adjusting? I've seen him only a couple of times. Haven't even been introduced."

"I don't think he's really home yet. Katie says there's something bothering him, and he won't talk about it. She leaves him be as much as she can, to let him get used to things again. Peter being away doesn't help any, either."

"Where is he?"

"Toronto, I think. Someplace in Canada, anyhow. I guess he might come home now, especially if he knows David's back. Leastways if that talk of amnesty means something.

It'll be tough on him, though. I feel sorry for them both, Doc. They're good boys, both of 'em, and they did what they thought they had to do. I admire that. You don't see too much of it anymore. But I'll tell you what—I think it was as hard for David to do what he did as it was for Peter to go to Canada. It took guts to go either way."

"How so? Don't you think Peter's choice was the right one, and the most difficult?"

"Oh, hell, Doc, I don't know. And you don't either, really. It's so damn easy to sit here and say this is moral and that ain't. Life ain't that simple, and living it's tougher still. Sure, going to Canada was harder to do if you're talking about how folks around here would react. I'm not talking only about that. I'm talking about facing yourself, and that was no easier for David than it was for his brother. Peter was more book smart than David, always reading philosophy and such, but David had something Peter didn't. He understood people better'n Peter. Almost like he was born grown up. No way he didn't go through hell making up his mind to enlist in a shooting war. He knew what bullets do to people."

Luke sat and stared at the bottle. In the silence, Doc could hear the large old wall clock whirring, its gears wheezing and springs pinging intermittently. He looked up at it, and the sound seemed to diminish, as if the clock was reluctant to call attention to itself. The tarnished key used to wind it dangled from a chain and swayed gently in the hot breeze coming through the open window.

"That's quite a clock, Luke," Doc said, getting up to examine it more closely. "It must be old."

"Forty years, maybe more. I've had it for quite a while now. Got it from Maggie Riley. Used to be on *Sundancer II*, the old trawler Maggie and her husband owned. Matt said that clock kept him sane out in the Gulf. When Maggie sold *Sundancer*, I bought it from her. Keeps *me* sane, now. Just listening to that old thing grinding away is a comfort."

If time was a comfort for Luke, Kate Riley was finding it a cruel enemy. Though she and David had been spending time together, little of it was the passionate making up for time lost that Kate had imagined. David was affectionate, and she had no doubt he still loved her, but his reserve toward her was a disappointment. There were moments, when they were alone, when it seemed he would finally break through the wall between them. His eyes would search her face, as if looking for some way in. She wasn't even certain whether the wall was around him or around her. That it was there, she knew.

Now and then, they would lose themselves in a frenzy of sexual activity, and the tensions, whatever their cause, would recede. Each time, Kate hoped it would be for good, and each time they returned. David knew her frustrations and knew, too, that she would not tolerate them for long, but he was as helpless as she to explain what was happening to them. No less confused by the contradictory emotions that assailed him, he was no more able to control them. In bed with Kate, he felt released, then at peace, as he did at no other time, but the sweaty contentment never lasted more than a few hours, and often was gone before one of them had risen for a cup of coffee or a cigarette.

Once, reaching out for her, he had stopped short, his hands, like stricken birds, hovering over her breasts. He wanted to touch her, and was afraid he could not. Finally, no longer able to endure the strain, he had thrown himself upon her, but, rather than making love, had buried his face in her shoulder and moaned, a terrifying sound unlike anything human Kate had ever heard. She wanted both to comfort him and to push him from her, as if he and the sound were different entities. Instead of doing either, she lay in stunned silence, her breath racing through her lungs in shallow gasps.

When the panic was over, David sobbed, and Kate cooed to him as she would to a child. Slowly, he regained his composure, lifted himself from her body, and rolled to one side, to lie on his back. The blinds were down, but not tightly drawn. Bands of light striped his face and chest like some ghostly war paint, the contrast darkening the shadows around his eyes, contorting his features beyond recognition. Kate sat upright, pulling the sheet over her breasts as if the man beside her were a stranger. She went into the bathroom still draped in the sheet. Sitting on the cold enamel of the tub for several minutes, she wondered whether he would call her back and, if he did, whether she would have the courage to go to him.

The man in her bed couldn't be David, and making love to him would be worse than infidelity. She couldn't bear the echo of that unearthly sound and was thankful that, for whatever reason, they had been unable to consummate an act that would have been unrecognizable as love. And yet she needed something, some physical contact, some affirmation of the feelings she had controlled for too long. She needed release, and so, clearly, did David. Maybe they needed one another more than either of them knew and in that need they had been transformed. How could she know, how could she be sure, unless she went back to him, opened herself to him as freely as she wanted him to open himself to her?

Kate was frightened. Her hands were shaking, and the more she strained to control them the more violently they shook. She was crying, the tears gathering in the corners of her eyes, as if afraid to fall.

As she continued to sit alone, the closed door imprisoning her uncertainties, she hoped she could find the strength to go back to the bed. Failing that, she knew David would eventually come to her, the David she knew, and lead her back. He would make it all right, as he always had. Maybe waiting had been enough, maybe she had done her part, and he would do his, however difficult it was, and however long it took. But when at last she opened the door to call him in the semidarkness, he didn't answer. She hadn't heard him get out of bed, hadn't heard him dress. Now she knew he had gone, and she wasn't sure of anything at all.

7

WHEN Peter left for Canada, Alice Hodges was all alone. She hadn't wanted David to go, but accepted it because she had no choice. With Peter, it was different. He was her baby. The war didn't need him. Surely he could stay home. But for Peter, it wasn't that simple. He could have stayed, taken his chances on Nixon's lottery, but he wanted to make a gesture, express his own view of the war. Without discussing it, he made up his mind to leave, and he left. One day he was there; the next he wasn't. Its surgical simplicity, its elegance, appealed to him. But it nearly killed Alice. Luke thought it had.

Alice was different after Peter left. Everyone noticed how withdrawn she had become, but she wouldn't let anyone come close enough to learn what was really going on. Peter's departure had hurt her, subtly but deeply. She had wanted to keep him close, as much for her comfort in

David's absence, as for his safety. She lost interest in everything except television. Every night, she would watch the news of the fighting, the slow, obscenely solemn crawl of the casualty list. When it was over, she would turn off the set, make a cup of tea, and go to bed. Luke visited occasionally, but her slow, steady slide into depression upset him. He wanted to scream at her, or shake her until her teeth rattled, but he didn't have the courage.

Her health deteriorated slowly during the first few months, then seemed to level off. Luke hoped it was just a plateau, a place where Alice had chosen to rest, to marshal her resources for a climb back into life. Her condition wasn't serious enough to bother David about; he had enough on his mind. And Luke didn't know where to reach Peter. So, instead, he took up nursing, visiting every evening. He made it a point to be there during the news whenever possible. The last thing he wanted was for Alice to see her worst fears realized with no one to turn to. Then, too suddenly for anything to be done, she deteriorated in one final plunge into the abyss of her own despair. She was dead before David could be notified of her condition. Peter was still keeping himself incommunicado. Luke buried her alone.

With the boys away, Alice's brother, Wesley Roberts, who lived in Palacios, had been looking in on the house. He stopped by at least once or twice a month and spent a week now and then, to do some fishing. Luke had been the local caretaker, since Alice had asked him to look after the boys. It wasn't a formal arrangement, but she wanted to be sure somebody kept an eye on them when they came home, although Luke suspected she never believed either one of them would. If she had, she'd have made more careful arrangements.

Though the house had been watched over, it had received only the scantiest maintenance. No one believed there was any reason to keep the place up. Even Luke, who was more fastidious than most would have been, didn't believe there was a point to much effort. So, when David came home, the house needed fixing. He had immediately set up housekeeping there and, when he wasn't with Kate, had been making repairs and alterations.

The first thing he'd done was add a back porch and screen it in. He poured himself into the job, as if building more than a porch. When it was done, and Luke saw it for the first time, he understood just what it was David had made. He remembered Alice had always wanted a place where, at night, free of troublesome insects, she could lie on a chaise longue and read after Joe and the boys had gone to sleep. Joe never had the time, and there hadn't been money to pay someone else, so the porch never got built. Now, tucked into one corner, up against the aluminum screen, was a white chaise longue, a small table, on which stood a small lamp with an imitation Tiffany shade, and a waist-high walnut bookcase full of paperback mysteries, mostly Agatha Christie and Ellery Queen, Alice's favorite authors.

After this first burst of renovation, David's pace slowed. He was seeing a lot of Kate and had less time to spend at, or on, the house. He continued to make changes, but more deliberately, as if the feverish explosion that resulted in the porch had drained him, or as if, in building it, he had accomplished most of what he wanted to do and the rest was cosmetic. He turned next to the kitchen, and when it was repainted, the cabinets stripped and revarnished, and a new floor installed, he invited Kate to dinner. He wanted to celebrate, and it seemed the perfect way to do it.

Kate was impressed with the amount of work he'd done, but the meal was another matter. Once they sat down to eat, David spent most of the time staring into space. While Kate watched him discreetly, pretending to concentrate on her meal, he picked up the salt cellar and stared at it for a while, then ran his fingers over it, gently feeling the holes in its top, one by one, and sliding the tips of his fingers along the grooves in the side of the glass. He did that for about ten minutes, and Kate kept silent, watching him. It was as if he'd never seen it before or was baffled by something he'd used a thousand times. Finally, she couldn't stand it any longer. She wanted to laugh, or cry, do something, anything that would release the emotions swirling inside her. She asked if anything was bothering him, knowing there was but hoping he wouldn't know she knew.

"No, nothing's bothering me. I'm just trying to get back something I don't seem to have anymore."

"My God, you're sitting here like a goddamned zombie. Why don't you *say* something, David?"

"I'm sorry."

"Look, if it's about me, if you don't love me anymore, just say it."

"Of course I love you! It doesn't have anything to do with you. Not directly, anyway."

"What is that supposed to mean?"

"What it means."

Kate knew he needed to talk as much as she needed to listen. And she knew he wasn't being deliberately difficult. But there were times when he would fade out on her. At other times, he would badger her to walk. They walked all over, but never in town. She knew, without being told, that he wasn't in the mood for seeing anyone but her. He didn't look up old friends. She started to think it might be they, most of all, he didn't want to see. She was astute enough to know that her wisest course was to sit and wait, not try to press him. She didn't stop trying to understand him, but she stopped trying to interrogate him.

Initially, she thought it might be what he had seen, maybe what he had done. She had no idea at all how to talk about something so far removed from her experience. But eventually she decided it had to be some particular thing. She didn't know why. There was nothing obvious in his manner, or the few conversations they did have. But his insistence on being with her, from morning to midnight most days, must mean it concerned her directly. The only connection she could make was through her brother Donald, but it was a connection whose poles were blanks. She didn't know what was connected to what, only that Donald was somehow central.

The more she thought about it, the more persuaded she became that she was right. It was logical, and it was convincing, or so, in the absence of real information, it seemed. Donald, after all, had been David's best friend. They had enlisted together, gone through boot camp together, and gone to Vietnam together. David was there when Donald was killed, and he had told Maggie in that letter that Donald died in his arms. It was the only letter he'd written to Maggie the entire time he was away.

And it was after that letter that Kate heard from him less and less frequently. After the cease-fire, he'd stayed on in Saigon with the small detachment of Marines guarding American installations. She'd been stunned by his decision, and there were times when she'd been tempted to believe he no longer wanted to come home. It had begun to seem that he never would, but she didn't give up on him, or on the idea that he would come home, and to her. Somehow, she knew, even then, that he had something on his mind, and understood his need for silence, if not its cause. In a way, the protracted periods of silence now were little more than a continuation of those long letterless times,

and his presence at her side seemed to have brought him
no closer to home. What little conversation he made was
as hollow and meaningless as echoes in a shell. She was
still waiting.

One night they took a drive down along the Bay, to the
edge of the Aransas National Wildlife Refuge. It was nearly
sundown, and little lay ahead of them but sand and water.
They left the car and walked into the dunes. There was
no sign of civilization, no evidence that anyone had ever
walked through the dune grass or down along the beach.

The shore birds ignored them, moving only to watch as
they passed. Once, they heard the deep bass horn of a ship
passing by on the Intracoastal Waterway, but it was so far
off in the twilight they couldn't see it. After twenty minutes, they crested a high dune above a jetty. The tide was
out, and they could walk well out onto the rocks without
getting wet. The few waves that reached into the stones
spent their energy in the climb and had none left to splash.

Sitting at the outermost reaches of the jetty, they dangled their legs over the gentle swells. The sun, setting
behind them, dyed the water a deep, bloody red as far as
they could see. David was staring out over the darkening
water, the low hump of Matagorda the only obstacle between him and Yucatan. He put his arm across Kate's
shoulders and rubbed her back with his thumb. He sighed
heavily, then said, "It's funny. . . . "

"What's funny?"

"The Mayas. One day they're there and then, poof, they're
gone. Everybody has an opinion, but nobody knows what
happened to them. I'd like to see some of those ruins
someday, but I don't guess I will."

"Why not?"

"Oh, I don't know. You know how it is. Things fascinate
you, but you really don't want to get close enough to see

too clearly. The mystery, you know, sometimes that's better than knowledge. It's something to believe in, something to be awed by, frightened of."

"You think so?"

"Yeah, don't you?"

"I don't know. . . . No. I don't think so. Not always, anyway. I guess there are some things we don't really want to know, but I don't think it's because we want to be afraid. There's enough to be scared of as it is. We just don't want our illusions destroyed. I think I'd always rather know than not."

David turned to look at her, peering as if over glasses. Then he smiled and laughed softly. When she asked what was funny, he shrugged and returned to his silent contemplation. Under their feet, the shallow water was so dark now, the red almost gone, Kate had the feeling that if she were to fall in, she might sink a long time before hitting bottom.

David said, "You're up to something, as sure as I'm sitting here. What is it?"

"I want to know what's bothering you, that's all."

"We've been through that. Nothing's bothering me."

"There is. I know it. You sit and don't say anything. You stare at things like you've never seen them before. And that look in your eyes sometimes, like you're a thousand miles away. It frightens me, and I want to know why it's there."

"Just getting used to things, that's all."

"No! No, that's not all. There's more to it than that. I know there is. It has something to do with Donald, doesn't it?"

David flinched, but didn't answer. He didn't argue, either. Instead, he got to his feet, stretched his hands over his head and turned toward the west, where the last dark sliver of the sun was like red fire sliding down behind the hills of sand.

"You're not going to answer me, are you?"

"Nope!"

"Why?"

"Because I need a job, and that's the only thing that's on my mind, I swear. When I get back into a regular routine, I'll be as amusing and talkative as you remember. And you'll probably feel just a little foolish."

"Why? I only want to know if I can help you. That's no reason to feel foolish, is it?"

He stared at her, his eyes glazing over for a moment before he reached down, almost absently, to tousle her hair and whispered, "No, Kate . . . no, it's not."

Kate knew then, though convinced there was something he wanted, even needed, to tell her, that it would be a long time before he would.

She turned to look out over the water. Matagorda was invisible in the darkness. "You know, it isn't Yucatan that's mysterious. Not really."

"No? What is, then?"

"The gulf between here and there, between us and the Mayans."

"And between you and me?"

"Yes, that, too, most of all."

She said nothing further, and they walked back to the car. He didn't say more than ten words the entire time, or in the car on the drive home, and when they reached Kate's door, he kissed her on the forehead and left immediately, instead of staying for an hour or two, as he usually did.

Luke loved the smell of bay rum. He didn't know why, but guessed it had something to do with his childhood. Sometimes, like a junkie scoring at any cost, he'd drop into the barbershop to sit and breathe the sweet, narcotic fragrance for an hour. Dan Alvarez, the barber, swore that Luke was so fastidious about his hair, he'd come in twice a year, whether he needed a trim or not. In truth, Luke wasn't that negligent, but he was in the shop more often for a whiff of bay rum than for actual service. Dan was used to it and treated him with the wry benevolence usually reserved for a wayward but beloved pet.

Saturday was Luke's favored day for a trip to the barber's, and he found himself wandering there by rote rather than purpose once or twice a month. This morning, the heat had broken, and the day was more like late autumn than midsummer. Sitting in the corner chair, Luke passed the time reading magazines while Alvarez worked and chatting with him between customers. Dan had a generous supply of *Playboy*s and *Swank*s, reserved for regular customers, which he kept with the towels. Since Luke wasn't interested in flesh he couldn't touch, he tended to bring along his own reading, in case Dan's *National Geographic* was missing. Absorbed in a lengthy essay about silkworms, he didn't notice the door open. By the time he looked up, Roger Drake was already in the chair.

"Nice and short, Danny," Roger told the barber, hunkering down in the squeaky leather chair while Alvarez pumped it up a notch for comfort. "Lucas, how you doing?"

"Not bad, Roger. Yourself?"

"Oh, things could be better, I guess, but I'm not complaining."

"Since when?" Alvarez wanted to know.

"Come on, Danny, I don't complain that much, do I?"

"Not compared to an old maid, you don't."

"You're lucky you're the only barber around here, Danny. If I had a choice, I might not put up with the abuse I get in here."

"You want to talk about abuse, let's talk about what that wire you got up here does to my clippers."

"It ain't that bad, is it?"

"Not anymore. Then, you got less'n you used to, ain't you?"

"Luke, can I sue him?" Roger asked.

"Sure you can."

"Hold on there, Luke, whose side are you on, anyway?"

"Didn't say he'd win, Dan," Luke said with a laugh. The others joined him for a moment.

Alvarez got down to business, humming, as he usually did when absorbed in his work. Luke went back to his article, lulled by the sound of the scissors. Roger watched the street traffic, working hard at keeping still, to preserve his ears.

When Alvarez had finished the haircut, he unfastened the apron around Roger's neck and shook off the clippings. Next he cranked up his lather machine to get a handful for Roger's neck and sideburns. As he dabbed on the aromatic cream, Roger asked, "You see much of Davey Hodges, Luke?"

"When he's in town, I see him. Why?"

"No reason. Just wondering if him and Pat patched things up, that's all."

"Roger, I know you're friendly with Pat, but I don't think there's anything *to* patch up. Pat don't seem like he'll ever change, and since David don't have no reason to, I reckon things'll stay pretty much like they are."

"It's a damn shame. Those guys got so much more in common than most around here, you'd think they'd be friends. They was even both in Nam. Nobody else seems to give a shit, so you'd think the vets would stick together. But it don't seem that way. Pat seems to have a grudge

81

against Davey, but I'll be damned if I can figure out what or why."

Roger was riffling the pages of a magazine while he talked. Suddenly he stopped and held it before him at arm's length. "Well now, look at that. Miss February. Hellooo, darlin'." He whistled and held the magazine up for Alvarez to see over his shoulder. "How'd you like some of this, Danny?"

"Not me, son. I got a bad heart."

"There's worse ways to go."

"I guess."

"Luke, check this out, will you?" Roger turned the magazine and held the centerfold toward Luke's corner chair. "Ain't she something else? Kind of looks like Kate Riley, don't she? I sure wouldn't mind fishin' *them* waters."

"Pat ever heard you say that," Dan said, "it wouldn't be a heart attack killed you. That I can promise you."

"Nah, he don't care. They ain't getting along anymore'n Pat and Davey are. He don't like her hanging around with old Davey."

"Pat might not care, but if David ever heard you talk like that, we'd be finding bits of you for a couple of months," Luke said, as if he wouldn't mind.

Roger winced as Alvarez nicked him with the razor. "Take it easy there, would you, Danny? I only got two ears." The barber winked at Luke, who smiled in spite of himself. He wiped the last of the shaving cream off, snapped open the lid of his towel steamer, picked one that smoked, and slapped it over Roger's eyes and mouth with a certain quiet satisfaction. While he massaged the towel into Roger's face, the door opened to admit another customer.

A short, dark-skinned man, obviously Hispanic, stepped in and smiled at Luke as he took a seat against the wall. Alvarez nodded as he removed the still-steaming towel with some regret. The newcomer sat with his hands in his lap, then, glancing at the table next to him, reached out to flip through a few of the magazines, but chose none.

Roger sat forward in the chair, touching his cheeks, which were somewhat pink. "You near boiled me like a lobster, Danny. Jesus!" He patted his cheeks gingerly and took his fingers away gently, as if afraid his skin might come with them.

Getting out of the chair, he reached up to remove the apron himself and brushed the hair from his jeans. He spotted the new customer and spoke to Alvarez over his shoulder. "You doing poodles now, too, Danny?"

"Huh?"

"You got a chihuahua over there."

"All right, Roger. That's enough of that kind of talk," Luke said.

"Come on, Luke, I was just joking. Besides, Danny don't mind, do you, Danny?"

"You sit down here again, while I get my razor, and you think about it, okay, Roger?" Alvarez reached for the strop and rubbed the blade deliberately, smiling at Roger while he did so.

"What the hell you so touchy about? I was only joking, for Christ's sake." He pulled out his wallet and handed Alvarez a five.

"Uh-huh." Alvarez nodded. "Sure you were. Me, too," he said, giving the strop one final swipe with the blade.

"See you guys later," Roger said, nodding to Luke as he left the barbershop.

"Dan, there's times when I admire your self-control," Luke said.

"Oh, hell, Luke, a razor ain't nothing. A gun, now, that's something else. I'm glad I don't own one."

"Roger isn't a bad sort, really," Luke continued. "But I

don't think he's got the brains of a newt, sometimes."

"Funny, sometimes I think that's *exactly* what he's got, Luke." Alvarez laughed. "He could keep better company, though."

"Yeah, he could do that," Luke said.

"You're next, partner," Alvarez said, nodding to the new customer.

The man got to his feet, rubbing his hands as he walked toward the huge chair anchored to the middle of the floor in the small shop. "That son of a bitch calls me a chihuahua again, he'll wish I was one," he said, taking a seat.

"See what I mean, Luke?" Alvarez asked.

8

THE first time David asked about a job with Maggie, Kate thought he was trying to avoid answering her question. But when he brought it up again two days later, Kate realized he was serious. It wasn't unrealistic, because he'd spent three summers working as both a header and a rigger. When his college classes were in session, he worked evenings in the fish houses, sorting and packing shrimp. He knew most of what he needed to know, even if he wasn't a seasoned professional. Reluctantly, Kate agreed to ask Maggie.

David didn't realize how the industry had changed since he last worked the fisheries. Even though, due to tradition, the old-fashioned way, or simple inertia, it altered reluctantly, and only when unable to find an excuse not to, the economics of the business continuously changed under a variety of pressures, pressures that were relentless and inescapable.

Every now and then, Luke spent an afternoon sitting at the docks. Afterward, he'd swear he'd never heard such foolishness. He didn't think shrimpers were ignorant, but they were so caught up in shrimp they couldn't talk about anything else. He knew how dependent on the creatures they were, but he wasn't quite sure who really caught whom. And they were too superstitious by half. They had an explanation for nearly everything that happened. And it always had to do with shrimp.

He knew, of course, that many of the superstitions were rooted in the background of the Chicanos and Mexicans who made up a large, and growing, percentage of the shrimpers. Luke was skeptical of religion, and held a particularly jaundiced view of Catholicism. Doc offered a half-hearted defense one afternoon, when the two men were discussing the matter, but Luke laughed it away.

"I never saw a religion to beat the Catholics for explaining things. Why, those people have somebody to pray to for every little thing that goes wrong. I never saw that praying did anybody all that much good, you know, at least not for anything personal. If you watch some of these Spanish guys cross themselves when they step up to the plate, you'd think God wasn't much more than a .220 hitter with a good glove. I don't know about you, Doc, but I want more than a good-field, no-hit shortstop in my corner."

"Come on, Luke, isn't that an overstatement?"

"Course it is. Yet and still, that doesn't make me wrong. Why, we even have a special ceremony over at the Bay every year just to bless the boats. Every year it's the same damn mumbo jumbo, but they don't catch the same number of shrimp every year. Why is that?"

"You can't really say whether the prayers work or not, can you?"

"Sure I can. And they don't. It doesn't make a whole lot of difference who said what prayers to whom. The orneriest cusses catch the most shrimp, year in and year out. That means the less you pray, the better you do. Maybe they ought to give up the prayers one year, just to see what happens."

"Well, after all, there's more than prayer involved."

"That's what I'm saying! Al Rodriguez says it's pollution coming down from Galveston, refineries, chemical plants, and such, and that even God can't catch what ain't there. Al, by the way, is the local Catholic priest. He's one of the sharpest guys around, except when he gets all starry-eyed about changing things nobody can change.

"Anyhow, either I'm wrong about God, or he ain't all that interested in shrimp now that folks don't have to eat fish on Fridays. Fifteen, twenty years ago the big trawlers in a couple of weeks netted enough so everbody had something to show for it. Hasn't been like that for a while now. It ain't uncommon to work a whole day for nothing but a good tan and a sore back. Now, a lot of boats sit in dry dock half the year, or, worse still, rot where they sit in the water. Seems like every year somebody else's sold his boat and tried to hire on with somebody luckier. Or smarter. With the price of shrimp going up all the time, it brings a lot more in. Trouble is, a lot more goes out now, too. Diesel fuel ain't cheap, even here. Nothing's cheap when you have to have it."

Maggie Riley could have been a textbook example of Luke's argument. Like most people in Witman, she and her husband hadn't known any way to make a living that didn't have something to do with shrimp. Everything they had was either for catching shrimp or bought with the money earned from shrimp already caught. When Matt died, Maggie inherited everything, but it wasn't much to begin with, and was getting to be less by the month. She did own a small trawler, but increasing costs forced her to trade down in size, which led to smaller catches, less money, and so on. To Maggie, life often seemed an ever-tightening spiral into bankruptcy. And if her shrinking resources weren't trouble enough, she also had to cope with the declining catch. The most frequently heard complaint in Witman was that every year there were fewer shrimp and more people after them.

She was widely admired, and conceded by the shrimpers to be the toughest woman they had ever known. If she wasn't quite as tough as her husband, she was still tough enough. Most shrimpers made fishing a family affair, but with Pat more interested in his personal vision of the Wild West, and Donald in the Marines, she had to hire help to keep what was left of the business. Since she'd been forced to sell off *Sundancer II*, she hadn't been the same.

It had been a shock to her. She loved the old boat as much as Matt had. Selling it was selling the last piece of him she had, and letting it go was like letting him go. Luke had handled the transaction for her and knew how hard a thing it was. Until she'd finally arrived to sign the papers on the morning of the sale, Luke hadn't believed she'd be able to do it. It had made business sense, and she had no choice, but still she'd been nearly an hour late. He'd been about to postpone the formal proceedings when she'd come dragging in.

She claimed she'd had a flat tire, but Luke hadn't been convinced. Maggie hadn't said a word to the fleet owner acquiring *Sundancer II* and had refused his hand when he offered it. When Luke had walked her to the car afterward, he'd helped her move some things into the trunk. He couldn't help noticing the spare tire was a new one and had never been on the ground, let alone driven on. He'd realized Maggie wanted him to know she'd been lying about the flat. And to know without having to tell him, as if she couldn't stand to put into words what selling the boat meant to her, but couldn't stand for anyone else to know, either.

Although any reasonable assessment of Maggie's current situation suggested the contrary, Luke wasn't convinced it was a good idea for David to work for her. He also knew David well enough to understand that he gave no thought to such things. Or, if he did, it was Kate he was thinking about, and Maggie, not Pat.

Luke didn't want to interfere in David's affairs, or Maggie's either, so he didn't try to talk David out of it. It might help, he thought, if he made David aware of a few things he may have overlooked, probably conveniently, but he wasn't prepared to go further than that. One afternoon in Halsey's, Luke got his chance. Uncomfortable with meddling, he went straight to the point.

"David, I hear you're hiring on with Maggie."

"Yeah, that's true, Luke. Why?"

"No reason. Long time since you been out there, ain't it?"

"Five, six years, maybe. I'm not sure."

"Things have changed some, you know. It's not like it used to be. Ain't often much reason to celebrate when you get in."

"Luke, I'm not interested in celebrating anything. I need work, and Maggie needs help. It's that simple."

"You know, son, what you probably need more than anything right now is to get used to being around people again. It gets awful lonesome out there. And Katie's waited a long time to get you back."

"Luke, you think I don't know what I'm doing, don't

you?" David asked, almost demanded, in that sudden off-hand way he had, his voice so soft it was barely audible.

"Now, I don't think I'd put it exactly that way, David," Luke said, caught off guard.

"All the same, it's what you think. I know that. I also know it doesn't matter."

"Course it matters, son. How could it not? You're too smart to be that dumb."

"It isn't what you know. Sometimes, it's what you have to do, no matter what you know. And I have to do this."

"You're not making a whole lot of sense just now. You know that, too, don't you?"

"I don't have any choice. Besides, I owe it to somebody."

"You owe what? To whom? What the hell are you talking about, son?"

"Never mind. You wouldn't understand. Luke, you can't change my mind. I don't want to change it, and even if I did, Maggie needs me. Helping Maggie is good for Kate, too, you know."

Luke cleared his throat and looked out the front window of the store before continuing. "How you getting on, otherwise?"

"Luke, why don't you come out and say what you want to say? That way I can say no, and we'll both be more comfortable."

Luke laughed. "You're right, son. It ain't my business. Good luck is all I want to say, I reckon."

"Thanks, Luke. Listen, I have to pick up a few things and get out to the house. Bye." David hesitated, as if considering whether to continue the conversation, then reached for Luke's hand, shook it, and moved down the aisle.

Luke surrendered to the inevitable, knowing that David didn't want to be persuaded, and hadn't been. His failure came as no surprise. He knew David was unpredictable, even rebellious on occasion. Like Luke, David believed there were things you couldn't change, no matter what you thought. He'd get used to David working for Maggie.

So David took the job. Maggie wanted to pay him a salary, but he declined, insisting he'd make do with a cut of the take, like everybody else. She tried to argue with him, and when that didn't work, she tried to get Kate to argue for her, but Kate refused. Even his willingness to work hard, for no special consideration, didn't immediately improve things for Maggie. David or no, there were only so many shrimp in the Gulf. And he didn't have the easiest time of it. On his first trip, he was a header, and the long hours bent nearly double from the seat of a low stool, sorting through the trash fish, crabs, and garbage to find the shrimp, left him stiff and bone tired. The rest of the crew, unsure why he was there, were wary of him, but that suited his need for solitude, and the concentration required for heading the shrimp and packing them in ice was a convenient cover for his disinclination to talk.

The boat brought in its share, but no more, and David worked with a determined, if somewhat rusty, proficiency. It would take him two or three trips before his muscles were attuned to the work and his movements as fluid and mechanical as they ought to be. He did what he was supposed to, and better than most expected, including Maggie.

Late one night, toward the end of the first week, David was on deck, leaning against the cabin smoking a cigarette. It was so dark away from land that the only lights visible were the boat's own running lights, the stars, and a faint glow from the wheelhouse. As he flipped the butt over the rail, the tip fanned into a bright arc across the water. He lit a second, inhaling deeply, and sighed the smoke into a small cloud. Juan Ramirez, the rigger on this trip, stepped on deck and walked toward the stern, where he lit his own cigarette and leaned over the rail to watch the algae stirred into a bright glow by the passage of the boat. After flipping his dying butt into the wake, he headed forward, toward the cabin, and spotted the glow of David's cigarette. He paused, as if debating whether or not to approach the new hand, then walked over to sit down beside him.

"It's a beautiful night, eh, amigo?"

"Not bad," David agreed.

"How you like it so far?"

"Okay. It hasn't changed much since the last time I was out. Fewer shrimp, but that's about the only difference."

"Better than the war, though, no?"

David didn't answer, and Ramirez changed the subject. "You gonna do this for long?"

"I don't know. Maybe."

"Maybe yes, maybe no, huh?"

"I guess."

"This ain't a bad boat. Maggie's all right to work for. You know? I like her. She's not like most women around here, but I think I like her pretty good. She's fair."

"I know."

"You know her a long time, huh?"

"Look, Juan," David said, "I know you're just trying to make me feel comfortable and all, but I'd just as soon be by myself right now, if it's all the same to you. Okay?"

"Sure, no problem, amigo. You got a lot to think about I guess, huh?"

When David didn't answer, Ramirez got to his feet. "Buenas noches, amigo. See you tomorrow."

"Good night, Juan. No offense, okay?"

"Okay with me. Nobody gotta talk to somebody if he

don't want to. I don't talk much myself, most times. I understand."

Pat Riley sat in a rocking chair and stared at the rumpled sheets from which he had just risen, as if the bed were something from which he had narrowly escaped. His face wore the puzzled frown of someone trying to read an unknown language. In the bathroom, Louise was humming softly, barely audible over the running of her bath. Now and again an angry buzz sounded in his ear as the rocker tipped back toward the open window. Each time, it got louder, but he wasn't sure whether the insect was getting angry or he was growing more conscious of its sound.

Dressed only in khaki jockey shorts, he looked bulkier, more ungainly than he normally appeared and than he was. He was powerfully built, but there was a hint of softness or uncertainty, or perhaps both, around the corners of his mouth, which was more childlike than one would expect in so large a man. There was a bright red U on the upper part of his chest, more consistent with his fair skin than the bronze of his forearms and neck. His face was fitfully illuminated by the dull glow of the Hotel Witman sign, across the street from the boardinghouse where Louise lived. It was her bedroom into which the angry mosquito sought access.

Early August. The summer had hit its stride at last and had been baking the Gulf coast for the last month. As the sun went down each evening, it left a bit more of itself behind, and every morning the mercury leaped out of the bulb from a higher springboard, topping 100° just as often as it failed to. Pat had gotten angrier with each passing day, and each day had been less certain of the cause of his anger, though more sure of its focus, David Hodges. He had argued with his mother on several occasions about her hiring David, but Maggie had refused to listen, either to reason or to bullying. Kate, too, seemed to have turned on him.

Not inclined to self-analysis, Pat had nevertheless scrupulously examined his motives in opposing David, and his mother's wishes, but came away no more enlightened than before. It had been bad enough that Donald had preferred David's company to his own, and now the rest of his family wanted to welcome him into the family. The very idea that David could be his brother *and* Kate's husband made his gorge rise.

Getting up, Pat slipped in behind the rocker, pushing it away with one hip, and pulled the filmy curtain aside to look out the window. It was nearly midnight, and the street was deserted. Across the way, all but one window on a high floor of the hotel was dark. In the one exception, a woman, who might have been Kate if her hair were longer and darker, was reading a magazine, her body positioned uncomfortably to make the most of the available indoor light and the breeze from without. As he watched her, she looked up for a moment and seemed to be staring back at him, although he knew she couldn't have seen him.

Absorbed in the night and its silence, Pat gasped when Louise placed a cold hand on his bare back. He glared at her over one shoulder and turned his attention back to the street. Louise squeezed in beside him, sliding one arm around his neck. When he still failed to acknowledge her presence, she asked, "Anything wrong, Mr. Riley?"

"Nope!"

"Uh-uh . . ."

"What's that supposed to mean?"

"It means don't bullshit a bullshitter, honey. You forget I work in a bar and I've heard every version of every line imaginable. I *know* when somebody's pulling my leg, especially if it's a man."

"So?"

"So, I want to know what's bothering you. You ain't been right since David came home."

"If that's what's bothering me, then I ain't been right a lot longer'n that, darlin'."

"Pat . . ."

"Louise, I'm telling you now, there ain't no reason for me to be upset, because I *ain't* upset. Now, if you want me to make something up, just so you can feel like your years in a gin mill ain't been wasted, I'll try to oblige."

"Damn you, I'm only trying to help."

"I'm sorry, honey," Pat said. He draped an arm over her shoulders and slid one hand down over her collarbone and into the bodice of her slip. "I'm a little edgy, I guess. But that's all, I swear. I'm thinking too much. It makes me crazy. You ought to know that by now. Course, if you really mean you wanna help, we can get back to doing a little more of what we *was* doing. That'll help some."

"What do you mean, *some*."

"Well, I don't want you getting a swelled head, is all."

"I'll make you a deal. You tell me what you were thinking about when I came out, and . . ."

"And what?"

"And we'll see."

"Darlin', you sure do drive a hard bargain."

"I just don't want you to think I'm easy. At least, not *too* easy."

"Honey, there ain't no such a thing as too easy. But I'll take the deal, anyhow. I was just wondering how come I didn't get no parade when *I* come home. I mean, *nobody* gets a parade for that fucking war. Not me, not anybody

I know. Nobody even wants to admit they went. People look at you like you're a little crazy, or something, like they don't want you standing behind 'em. Now, what's so damn special about Hodges?"

"I guess you'll have to ask Kate that, won't you?"

"Well, hell . . . I'm her *brother*, for crying out loud. Don't that mean nothing?"

"Of course it does!"

Pat turned back to the window. The light across the street was gone. There was nothing out there but the flickering blue glow from the hotel sign, flashing on, then off, then on again. Without looking at Louise, he said, "Well, it don't seem like it. Not to me, it don't."

As he spoke, he replaced his hand, working it deeper into her bodice, rubbing one breast with more earnestness than finesse. Turning to face her, he slid the straps from her shoulders, let the slip slide to the floor, and stepped back to appraise her. Nodding his approval, he asked, "Now, how about *your* end of the bargain?"

9

A FEW days after David's first fishing trip, Kate enlisted
Luke's help. She wanted to have a barbecue, something to
help David relax and ease back into the life of the town.
Luke persuaded him to come by promising there would
be only a few people. David's consent, though grudgingly
given, seemed like a small victory to Luke and Kate. Luke
particularly looked forward to the opportunity to introduce
David to Doc. He was certain they would hit it off.

But Luke soon found it more difficult to arrange than
he had expected. It wasn't easy to make up the guest list.
There weren't that many people who were friendly enough
with one another, and with David, to spend a few hours
in the same spot, at least not many with whom Luke would
enjoy spending the time, and when he eliminated those
who wouldn't appeal to Doc's limited social inclinations,
the number was small indeed.

He spent a week putting together a group who would tolerate one another and who were tolerable to himself and David. He was soon so concerned with the theoretical chemistry he forgot the human element. After several days, it dawned on him that he was just making Kate's welcome-home mistake all over again. He was trying to create something with people who didn't want to be part of anyone's creation. Eventually, the process of refinement abandoned rather than completed, he drew a few names out of a hat and sent out the invitations.

The barbecue seemed off to a good start, but Luke knew it was only too tempting to think so when everybody you invite decides to show up. After all the guests had arrived, and the initial round of greetings had died down, a silence fell over the gathering. Everyone seemed to be wondering either why he was there, why the others were there, or both. Aside from Kate, Maggie, and Doc Roth, those present included Bob Olson, Maggie's captain, Juan Ramirez, John Halsey, and a few fishermen with whom David had been friendly during the summers he spent shrimping.

Amid throat clearing and idle chatter, Luke suddenly started talking louder than he should have and acting jollier than he had begun to feel. Finally, he just confessed his misguided intention and went out on the back porch to have a drink. He was feeling sorry for himself, which made everyone else feel bad on his account. He had his feet on the rail and was swirling the ice in his glass, listening to it clink, and watching the dew gather, when Kate came out to join him.

She stood quietly for a moment, looking out over the yard, really more of a meadow, shading off into the sandy grass toward the Bay. Inside, he could hear everyone talking as loudly as he had, trying to be funnier than they were able. Since he had nothing to say, he just watched her staring off into the distance. When she glanced at him over one shoulder, he looked sheepish, and she smiled.

"Now, Luke, it isn't all that bad, is it?"

"I guess I tried a little too hard. Feel like a damn fool."

"But why?"

"I saw what happened to your little celebration. That should have woke me up, don't you think?"

"It was my idea. Besides, once everybody stops trying so hard, they'll have a good time."

"I suppose." Luke sighed.

"Still . . . I'm worried about David."

"Why? He said anything you wouldn't expect after going through what he's been through?"

"No. It's what he hasn't said that worries me. Why won't he talk to me?"

"Have you asked him to?"

"Yes, of course!"

"And what does he say?"

"Nothing. He just changes the subject. I don't think he's hiding anything from me, nothing like that. But it makes me feel . . . oh, I don't know, so . . . helpless."

"Look, Katie, there are some things you can't tell anybody, especially those close to you. You can't take the chance they might not understand. Some things are so intense, so . . . private, there's no way in hell you can put 'em into words. War is like that. And death is like that, too. God knows, David's seen his share of both."

"I don't understand."

"He hasn't told you anything because he can't. He won't refuse, because that's conceding defeat. It would mean he couldn't count on you to understand. Like his not being able to tell you was your fault. But he doesn't think that, and he doesn't want to take the chance that he might *start* thinking it, either."

Luke knew he wasn't making himself clear, because Kate's face was blank and bewildered. While he pondered a new approach, he realized how much like David's situation his own had momentarily become. The screen door squeaked, and David joined them on the porch.

"Luke, Katie . . ." He nodded, grinning at each of them in turn.

"What's so funny?" Kate demanded, her hands on her hips.

"Oh . . . nothing."

Luke chimed in. "Come on, now, David, what's so funny?"

"Nothing, really. Just the two Elsa Maxwells of Witman hiding out from their latest disaster."

"David! How can you?" Kate was feigning outrage, and the more David grinned, the less effort it required. Luke started to laugh, because he knew David was right. And he could tell by Kate's trembling lip that she knew it, too.

"Never you mind, Katie," Luke consoled her. "He thinks he's right, and he may be, and he also thinks he's funny, which he ain't. But I'm not licked yet. Let's you and me go on inside and get things going. He can stay outside and laugh all he likes."

"Hell no, Luke! You don't think I'm going to stay out here and miss all the fun, do you? Why don't you see if you can get up a game of pin the tail on the donkey? I got a couple of targets for you."

David bowed with a grand flourish, holding the screen door for Kate. He reached out to swat her bottom but stilled his hand in midair and winked at Luke instead. Luke thought it David's most spontaneous gesture since his return.

As Luke entered, he noticed David's grin fade. Grabbing his arm, Luke hauled him over to a couch in the corner of his study, where Doc was sitting with John Halsey. He motioned David to take a seat. Pulling up a chair for himself, he turned it around and sat with his elbows on its back, scrunching his cheeks down into his hands.

"Luke." Halsey nodded, preparing to engage him in an argument of some sort, Luke guessed. Halsey loved to provoke others to debate without revealing his own opinion. "What do you think of the Rangers' chances this year?"

"Hold on there a minute, John. I want to introduce David to Doc, here. Doc, this here's David Hodges, the young fellow I'm always talking about. David, this is Doc Roth."

The two men nodded, and David explained that they had met, although informally, so there was no need for ceremony.

"Never mind, David, he ain't no more polite than anybody else around here," Halsey said. "He just don't want to answer my question, that's all."

"What *was* your question, John?"

"About the Rangers, and how they'll do this year."

"Hockey's over for the year, John. That's a pretty dumb question."

The others laughed, while Halsey tried to explain. "I'm talking about the Texas Rangers, Luke, and you know it."

"Course I do, John. I know it. You've always been a law-and-order man. We all know that."

"Sounds like you struck out, John." Doc laughed. "I don't think Luke wants to talk about baseball."

"You guys are no fun anymore," Halsey said, doing his best to sound dispirited.

"Why don't we change the subject?" Luke asked.

"Heard from Petey lately, David?" Halsey asked.

"As long as we're changing the subject, why don't we move on to the next one, Mr. Halsey?" David said.

Halsey raised an eyebrow and looked at Luke, who just

shook his head. They chattered aimlessly for a while, and Luke noticed that David was starting to relax. Every now and then he'd look over at Luke to see whether the older man was gloating, but Luke didn't let on he was aware. Eventually, David lost sight of him altogether, as people started to wander around. Pleased that the little gathering hadn't backfired, after all, Luke, too, started to relax. He drifted from group to group, like a monitor in high school study hall. He looked for Kate once or twice, but didn't see her. It was too hot to go searching for her, so he finally just sat back in a corner, taking over Doc's seat when he and David went out to get some air.

Once in a while, Luke got up to check on the ribs and chicken marinating in the kitchen, and to throw a little more beer into the ice-filled, galvanized tub serving as a cooler. As he eased back onto the sofa after his latest trip, the front door squeaked open. Conversation stopped as everyone turned to see who was arriving so late. Luke was the most interested, since everyone he had invited was already there. When he realized the newcomer was Pat Riley, he was annoyed, more than surprised, and got more so when he realized Pat wouldn't need any of his beer to get drunk. The deputy half stumbled and half strutted over to stand in front of Luke, blinking against the bright sun coming through the window behind his involuntary host. He was slowly shifting his weight backward and forward, always just a little too late to come to rest in an upright position.

"Luke, how you?" Pat mumbled.

"Pat . . . I'm all right. What can I do for you?"

Pat was still wearing his uniform, and Luke hoped he wasn't on duty. As an officer of the court, he'd have to report Pat's condition. Luke didn't much relish the idea. He'd reported him for similar behavior twice before, and each time Pat had been nasty with just about anyone who crossed his path for a couple of weeks after Randy McHale chewed him out. McHale was a decent man, and a good sheriff, but Luke couldn't understand why he put up with Pat. He was willing to concede that the man had his reasons, but he hadn't a clue what they were.

"Katie here?" Pat asked.

"Yes, she is. At least, she was. I haven't seen her for a half hour or so. Anything I can do for you?"

"What about Hodges? He here? Where is he?"

"Now hold on a minute there, Pat. Why don't you let me answer one question before you ask the next one? The shape you're in, I think you'll have to go slower than you usually do."

"I ain't drunk, Luke, so don' go tryin' to change the subject. I wanna see Katie. Now is she here or ain't she?"

"I already told you she was." Luke looked at him for a few seconds, trying to figure out what was on his mind. Pat didn't seem to think like ordinary people, and his speech tended toward the elliptical. Luke decided he had no choice but to answer the earlier question, too. The deputy was in a foul mood already, and there was no need to make it worse. "David's here, too. I think he went for a walk with Doc Roth, though."

"That Jew here, too? Christ, Luke, I swear to God I don' understand you. I swear I don'!" He wagged his head from side to side, as if Luke's conduct were incomprehensible.

"Pat, why don't you go home and sober up? I'm not gonna sit here and listen to that shit, especially about my friends, even if you are half my age."

"Now hold on, Luke. I ain't got no quarrel with you. Jus' hold on a minute . . ." Before he could explain with whom he did have a quarrel, David and Doc came into the study, Kate right behind them. Pat turned as they entered, and it looked like he was reaching for his side arm, his hand clenched just above it. He staggered toward the trio, reached out to push Kate to one side, and planted himself unsteadily in front of David.

"Patrick! What do you think you're doing!" Kate exploded.

He ignored his sister to concentrate on David, glowering at him from his height advantage.

"I don' know why you come back here, Hodges, but you'd better stay the fuck away from my sister. I'm sick of you hangin' around. And keep your ass off my ma's boat, if you know what's good for you."

David looked as if he were about to start laughing at Pat's manner, which was that of a spoiled little boy. Instead, he just grinned slightly at the taller man.

"You hear me?"

"I hear you, Pat," David said. His voice was barely a whisper, but they all heard him. Pat's outburst had stilled all other conversation. "But you don't have anything to say about it."

"Like hell I don't! You go near her again, and you'll have to deal with me."

Kate stepped between the two. "Pat, why don't you . . ."

Pat brushed her aside before she could finish. He squared off against David, whose grin was now wider and more menacing than Pat seemed to realize.

"Fact is, Pat," David said, "it's up to Katie and me whether we see one another, and it's up to Maggie to hire who she wants. When *Setting Sun* belongs to you, you can fire me if you want, but until then, I'll work for Maggie as long as she'll have me."

Pat reached out to grab the front of David's shirt, but David smacked the hand away before it made contact with the fabric. In the quiet, it sounded like a gunshot. Luke flinched in spite of himself. Pat snarled, grabbing the wrist in his other hand and rubbing rapidly to ease the sting. "You touch me agin, I'll kill you," he shouted.

"Mr. Riley," Doc interjected, "why don't you go home and sleep off what is obviously a case of intoxication."

"Why don' you min' your own fuckin' business, Jew-boy?"

Luke flinched again. Pat's remark had sounded more violent and more malignant than the impact of flesh on flesh that had preceded it. Doc, though, didn't seem to notice. He just shook his head and continued to stare at the angry deputy. Before anyone could say another word, Kate grabbed Pat by the arm and started to drag him toward the door, hoping to get him away before things got totally out of control. She didn't know what had come over him, but things would only get worse if he stayed. Pat gave her a shove, and she fell backward, slamming her head against the base of the sofa at Luke's feet. Maggie, who had been on the back porch when Pat arrived, was just stepping through the door, to see why things had gotten so suddenly quiet, when Kate fell.

"Oh, my God, what's . . . ?"

Before she could finish, David moved, so quickly that Luke wasn't sure he saw it begin. Springing forward, he landed a flurry of punches on Pat's face and midsection, and the deputy, too, fell backward, landing in a heap beside his sister. He wiped the back of one hand across his chin, and it came away bloody, a bright smear of red shading into the brown of his wrist.

"Motherfucker, you'll pay for that," Pat said. He struggled to get to his feet, only to lose his balance and collapse back onto the floor.

"I suspect maybe I already have," David said quietly,

105

"but not in any way you could understand. Why don't you get the hell out of here before somebody has to carry you out?" David looked at Maggie then, before helping Kate to her feet.

Again Kate grabbed her brother by the arm, this time to help him up. He didn't resist, and allowed himself to be pushed toward the door, looking helplessly at David over Kate's head. Kate, too, was looking at David as she blindly shoved Pat farther away from him, her face angry and bewildered. Then they were gone, and the screen door closed with a bang.

"What in hell was that all about, David?" Luke asked, breathing normally for the first time since Pat arrived. He turned to Maggie and Doc Roth. "I'm sorry you had to get dragged into this, Doc."

"Dragged into what?" Maggie demanded. "What's going on here?"

"Never mind, Luke," Doc said. "I've met his kind before. Besides, it was my own fault for opening my big mouth. It doesn't matter, anyway."

"Oh, it matters, Doc," David said. Again he looked at Maggie, who could only stare back at him in silent amazement. "It may not bother you, but it sure as hell matters."

10

SEVERAL months later, there was another homecoming, this time without a crowd. He wasn't expected, but, before long, everyone knew Peter Hodges had followed his brother home. Luke was the first to know, because Peter went to his office right off the bus.

"Peter, I'm glad to see you. Welcome home."

"Lucas, it's good to see you, too. I'm not sure why I'm here, but I guess I want to know what you think about it."

"I don't know, son. Some folks are gonna be a lot more surprised than I am. And a whole lot less happy. Then again, I don't guess I'm telling you something you don't know."

"No, you're not. I know I'm not too popular around here, but I think I can handle it."

"It ain't just a question of being popular. Some people think it was guys like you who lost us that war. They sure as hell ain't gonna make you glad you came home."

"You know, Luke, if anybody tried to understand how hard it was for me to go, he might have to admit that what I did took courage. They might think I'm a lot dumber than David, but that's okay. Maybe I am. I just don't want anybody to think I'm a coward."

"Petey, it may not be that simple to some folks."

Peter nodded. He stood up and walked over to the window. "It's still hot as hell in the summer, isn't it?"

"Some things never change. What're you gonna do now, son?"

"I guess I'll go on home."

"David know you're coming?"

"No . . . I heard he was home, but I haven't had the nerve to call him."

"Why in hell not?"

"I don't know. . . . I . . . I thought it might just be better if I sprang in on him in person. I'm not sure how he'll take it."

"Hell, he's your brother, ain't he? How's he supposed to take it?"

"Luke"—Peter sighed—"if I knew that, this would be a lot easier than it's going to be."

"You want a ride out to the house?"

"Yeah, thanks. Just let me run down the street to pick up a couple of things. Halsey's is still there, isn't it?"

"Like I said, some things never change."

"I'll be back."

As Peter stepped out the door, Luke sank back into his leather chair to mull over this unexpected development. Whether Peter realized how much of an irritant his presence might be, Luke wasn't sure. But, since Peter seemed convinced it was more important to be home than to be welcome, he'd do what he could to help. Luke understood

Peter's determination not to be thought a coward. And he knew it was that which threatened him most. He'd fight just to prove he wasn't afraid. Once he decided to do something, he couldn't be talked out of it. He'd been that way about going to Canada, and would be that way about staying.

On his way to Halsey's store, Peter took his time, stopping occasionally to look around at the town to see what had changed. Anyone watching might have thought he was appraising the place with an eye toward its purchase. In a way, he was. He had bought Witman a long time ago; coming home was a formality, like signing a bill of sale. So little had changed, but it all seemed foreign. He knew he was afraid, and his perspective had been altered by his absence. But that couldn't explain everything. The buildings looked the same, the same dusty cars lined the streets, some of the houses didn't appear to have aged, or even to have gathered additional grime. But it wasn't the same place he'd left five years earlier. That was as certain as the fact that he wasn't the same person who had left it.

When he got to Halsey's, he sat on a bench out front, half afraid and half hoping that someone he knew would pass by. He looked over his shoulder through the dusty front window, but the gloom of the interior was impenetrable. He thought he recognized Halsey's bulk off in one corner, filling some shelves, but he wasn't sure. For all he knew, some other man, just as stocky, had taken the place over. He felt a growing unease and knew if he sat any longer he'd go back to Luke without even going in. He wasn't afraid he wouldn't be welcome. If anything, he believed Halsey was the one man besides Luke who wouldn't say a word against him. Getting to his feet, he suppressed a groan unconnected to physical discomfort. He walked stiffly toward the store's entrance and hesitated before pushing into the shadows.

Once inside, he shook off the afternoon glare. It had been Halsey stocking shelves. Peter walked slowly and quietly up behind the storekeeper, who was engrossed in his work, and cleared his throat. "You got any raspberry soda, mister?"

"Nope, sorry, that's the one soda I don't . . ." Halsey stopped in midsentence, jumped to his feet, and turned around. "Well, I'll be damned! Petey, is that you? How you doing, boy?"

"Course it's me, Mr. Halsey. How are you?"

"Damn, I knew it was you. Had to be. Or a complete stranger. Everybody knows I won't have that stuff in the store. I knew it was you, soon's you asked. I just didn't believe it for a minute."

"I'm not sure I believe it myself, yet."

"You really thirsty, or just pulling my tail a little."

"Both, I guess. Can I have a Coke?"

"Sure, sure you can. Sit down here while I get it." Halsey indicated a stack of unopened grocery cartons. "I'll be right back. You have to tell me all about yourself."

Halsey rushed over to the refrigerated case of beer and soda, reached in for a bottle, and stopped just long enough to pop the cap. He sat on a second stack of cartons beside Peter. He watched as Peter took a long pull on the cold soda. After wiping his lips on his sleeve, Peter placed the half-empty bottle on the floor between them.

"So, how about it, son? You back to stay, or what?"

"I guess. I don't have anyplace else to go. Besides, it's home."

"Well, that's great, great. I guess you must have got lonely and all, way up there with all them foreigners. Canadians, or what-all."

"Yeah, I did. I don't think I knew how much until just now."

"So, tell me, what was it like? What you been doing?"

"I can't now, Mr. Halsey. I just stopped by to say hello, and pick up a few things. Luke Darby is waiting for me. I got to get back to his office."

"You ain't in no trouble, are you?"

"No, no. Luke's giving me a ride home, that's all."

"All right, then. Just tell me what you need, and I'll round it up. You seen David yet? He's been home a while, now. Damn, but I bet he'll be glad to see you!"

"You ready, Luke?"

"Yup. You get what you needed over to Halsey's?"

"I think so. . . ."

"Then I guess we might as well hit the road."

Luke walked to the door after pausing to scribble a note for his secretary. He let the screen door bang behind him and pointed to his car. Peter picked up his luggage and the bag from Halsey's, hopped down the steps to the street, tossed both bags through the open rear window, then walked around to the passenger side. Luke got in from the curb side and slammed the door shut with a dull clunk, fishing for the keys in a pocket of his suit coat.

"I guess you want to go straight on home," Luke said.

Peter nodded, staring through the dusty windshield.

"The reason I ask," Luke explained, "is because I have the afternoon free."

"No. I think I ought to go home, before I lose my nerve."

"What in hell are you talking about?"

"I don't know. . . . I got a funny feeling, that's all. Maybe David's changed; maybe I have. I'm afraid it won't be like it used to."

111

"Most likely you both changed. Still and all, there ain't no reason for you to worry. You'd have changed even if neither one of you had gone anywhere. Folks change. That's all there is to it. And a good thing, too."

"Hell, Luke, I know that. But it's not that simple. I guess I'm afraid he'll blame me for what he went through. Like it's my fault, somehow."

"He doesn't believe that, Petey. You know he doesn't. He may not agree with what you did, but he knows it had nothing to do with what *he* did."

Peter didn't respond, and Luke stared out at the highway, humming to himself. It was hot, and with the sun beating down on the hood, he kept checking the temperature gauge on the dash. What little breeze there was seemed to lose itself in the tall grass before it ever got to the highway. Every now and then there was a little puff of sandy dust, when the air skipped across a bare spot in the fields.

Luke changed the subject. "Things look some different to you, I expect."

"Yes. Not as much as I thought they might, though. Besides, it's not things I'm worried about. It's people."

"Well, the main thing you got to keep in mind is not to rush. You boys got a lot of catching up to do. If you push it, it ain't gonna help. Lay back a little, and everything'll be all right."

As Luke concluded, the Hodges house came into view over the rise in front of them. He let up on the gas, as if he expected Peter to change his mind and ask to go back to town. But Peter said nothing, and Luke stepped on the gas again, clearing the rise and slowing to turn into the driveway. There were two cars already there, David's beat-up Valiant, its left rear fender starting to rust through, up toward the house, and, sitting behind it, Doc's Chevrolet Impala.

"Looks like you already got some company, son."

"Guess so. David's here, isn't he? I mean, one of those cars is his?"

"Yup, the old one. Other one belongs to somebody you don't know. Come on, I'll introduce you."

The two men got out of the car, Peter closing his door softly, as if to preserve, until the last possible moment, his ability to leave unnoticed, whereas Luke banged his closed as if celebrating the solidity of his old Buick. There was no sign anyone heard them arrive, and Luke led the way up the steps to the screen door. Inside, muffled voices could be heard. Luke pushed on in, shouting in his hearty baritone, "Anybody here?"

"Out here, Luke, on the porch," David answered.

Peter flinched at his brother's voice, then struggled to arrange his features in a smile. Luke knew it was going to surprise, perhaps even shock, David to see his brother after so long. Doc and David were playing chess when Peter came slowly through the door onto the porch, stepping ahead of Luke at the last moment. Both players looked up, ready to greet Luke. When he saw it was Peter, David froze. Doc knew right away who the stranger was, because the brothers looked so much alike, despite their different coloring. They were nearly identical in height, with Peter a bit softer around the edges, but still solidly built. David's hair was darker than Peter's, but it had grown since he'd been home, losing its military severity, and the Gulf sun had lightened it considerably. Both men had dark blue eyes, and the resemblance was altogether more striking than Luke remembered.

David was stunned. His animated manner of a moment

before became suddenly cold and reserved, if not openly hostile. Peter stood near the doorway looking confused, as if he'd come to the wrong house. Without a word, he turned and left.

"Petey, where you going, son?" Luke shouted, running after him.

Doc was puzzled by David's reaction. He watched the young man, waiting for him to say something, anything, but David just stared at the doorway. If Doc hadn't heard the front door close, he would have thought Peter was still there. When David maintained his silence, Doc asked what was going on, but got no answer. If he didn't push now, he might never get an explanation. "Did I miss something, David?"

"What do you mean, Doc?"

"Come on, son. That was your brother, wasn't it?"

"Yeah, it was."

"Well?"

"Well what, Doc?"

"For Christ's sake, boy! You haven't seen each other in . . . what? Five years?"

"Five years and two months tomorrow."

"And all you do is stare like you've never seen him before?"

"I guess."

"Look, David, I know it's none of my business, but I can't believe what just happened."

"Hell, I might as well tell you as anybody else around here. Maybe you can understand a little better than most of them."

Doc was surprised by the abrupt change, the vehemence that now replaced the zombielike demeanor of moments before. He had no idea what was coming, but somehow, once David began to speak, he seemed to know it all, word for word.

"You got a brother, Doc?"

"No. Why?"

"Well, I don't know. Me and Petey were about as close as any two people you ever saw. When he was little, I couldn't go anywhere without him showing up sooner or later."

As David talked, Doc could hear Luke and Peter talking, their voices audible but not intelligible. He wondered if Luke was getting Peter's version of the same memories. David looked dazed, drained of emotion. So much had happened, so many things had irreversibly changed. David looked at Doc for the first time since he had begun talking, and laughed.

"You don't want to hear about that stuff, anyway, do you? You want to know how come I didn't jump up and hug him, don't you? Well, I don't know, really. I'm glad to see him, I guess. I mean, I was worried about him, and I'm glad he's okay."

"You were in a lot greater danger than he was, son."

"I'm not talking about dying. Not physically, anyway. I'm not like him, Doc. I was always a loner, I guess. But Petey was different. He liked it here a lot more than I ever did, especially after Dad died. It must have been hell for him to do what he did, knowing how it would be received here. Oh, he pretended he didn't care what people thought, like when he quit playing football, but it mattered to him. I'm probably the only one who knows how much."

After a long pause, during which Doc strained, without success, to hear what Luke and Peter were saying, David laughed again, then continued in a dull monotone, as if trying to distill whatever emotional inflection his voice might have had.

"The funny thing is, I didn't want to go any more than he did. I just didn't know how *not* to go. Besides, Donny was going with me. All through boot camp, Donny and I used to cheer each other on, like it was us against everybody else."

His voice trailed off, and he glanced away from the empty doorway again. When he looked at Doc, his eyes were wet. For a moment, Doc thought he had finished, but David shrugged and resumed his subdued monolog.

"Anyway, I figured when his time came—and it sure as hell seemed like there was no way it *wouldn't*—it would be a lot easier for him if I went first, so . . . Boy, was I ever wrong, huh?" He laughed bitterly.

"Do you think Peter was wrong to do what he did?"

"What? Wrong? I don't know. What *is* wrong? I mean, if it's wrong to refuse to kill people, then it must be wrong *to* kill them, right? Hell, I don't even know if I know what I mean. Petey did what he had to do; that's all. Just like I did. Trouble is, everybody around here thinks he was wrong and I was right."

His face relaxed, and he smiled at Doc for the first time since Peter arrived. His voice took on more color, was more animated.

"Look, Doc, it's like this . . . or I guess this is as close as I can come, anyway. I don't know whether I thought I was wrong when I joined the Marines, but I guess I do now. What I can't decide is whether it was okay because I believed it was or whether, knowing what I know now, it was wrong no matter what I believed. But it was so long ago, and after what I saw . . . and . . ."

David's attention wavered and he was silent for a long time. He jumped once, suddenly, as if there had been a

116

loud noise, but Doc had heard nothing. Even the breeze, which had been slapping the screen door out front from time to time, had stilled. Then David spoke again.

"Hell, Doc," he whispered, "I just don't know. . . ."

When Luke stepped outside, he found Peter standing at the foot of the front porch, watching the sky. Peter turned to look at him, shook his head once, then walked in a small circle, as if he weren't sure where to go, but could no longer stand still.

"You sure left in a hurry, son," Luke said softly.

"Yeah, well . . . it seemed like the thing to do. I shouldn't have expected anything different. I should never have come back."

"Hold on, now. You got to give him a chance. He ain't seen you in a spell. He's got to get used to the idea you're back."

"I don't think it's that simple. He's sorry I came back, and I guess I don't blame him."

"Course he ain't sorry you came home."

"Then why did he act like that? He didn't even speak to me. Is that supposed to be welcome home, for Christ's sake?"

"He'll open up, when he's ready. Besides, maybe what you're telling me is more about you than it is about him. I didn't notice *you* saying anything, either. Maybe you feel guilty, and you think he blames you for something because you blame yourself."

"Oh, Luke, I don't know. . . . Maybe so. Maybe it's that simple."

"Hell, I didn't say it was simple. I said maybe that was part of it. Why not give it a chance? You ain't got much to lose, have you?"

"I guess not. I don't want to go back in yet, though. If

117

I give him time, you know, to get used to the idea that I'm back . . ."

"I got all day, son, if that's what it takes. You want to talk about it, or just think things over some?"

"No, I don't want to talk. Not now. Let me just sit here a bit, okay?"

"Fine. When you're ready, I'll go on in with you, if you want."

"Okay, thanks, Luke."

They walked over to Luke's car and leaned on the rear fenders, their backs to one another. After a while, Peter cleared his throat and said, "Luke, if you don't mind, I think I'd kind of like to postpone this a day or so. You mind running me back to town?"

"You sure that's what you want?"

"Yes."

"Okay, let's go."

As the car backed out into the highway, the front door of the house opened, and David stepped out into the bright sun. Neither man in the car saw him, and Luke pulled away, his tires slipping a bit on the sand before gaining traction. David felt a hand on his shoulder, and Doc Roth said, "Don't worry David. He'll be back. He's got to get used to a few things, too, just like you. It might even be tougher for him."

"I know, Doc. That's what scares me."

11

EVER since David had come home, Luke had wondered what it might be like when and if Peter followed. He knew how emotionally complex the situation was, but counted on blood to surmount it. Peter had been the missing half of an equation. Luke had been working in the dark, and reality caught him flatfooted. The evening of Peter's return, Doc met Luke at his office. Each of them felt compelled to help the younger men resolve their differences.

Peter wanted to be welcomed with open arms, and when he wasn't, he panicked. David was mired in ambivalence; he knew Peter had been disappointed by his reception, but he had his own problems to solve. Talking was what they needed, but getting them to it was going to be difficult. David, less rigid, would probably be easier to convince, and his uncertainty made him vulnerable to persuasion.

Doc felt he might be talked into a situation Peter would have to be tricked into. Luke would have to handle the less flexible Peter. They knew they had to work quickly, while things were still fluid.

"It ain't going to be easy, Doc," Luke said. "When you're as close as that, something like this is tough to get over."

"Can you think of anyone who might help?"

"Not too many folks care one way or another about Peter Hodges. Them that do ain't likely to help. Most of them would just as soon he never *did* come back, and they sure won't lift a finger to help make his stay anything but short. Petey was never one to let folks get too close. You just naturally had to get to know something about David, on account of his being so prominent. He was All-State in football."

"What's that got to do with Peter?"

"I guess folks expected him to take after his older brother in everything, you know. He was just as big, and just as good. Some said better. He could run faster. *Had* to, or he never would have kept up with David when they were kids. But he played only one year."

"Are you telling me people around here resent him because he didn't make All-State in football?"

"Not exactly. What I'm telling you is that folks resented him because he refused even to *play* football. Now I don't know about up north, Doc, but around here, football *matters*. Fact is, if David hadn't made All-State, I reckon most of Texas never would have heard of Witman. Then, when Petey quit playing, it was like he was thumbing his nose at the whole damn town."

"Sounds like you half resent him yourself, Luke."

"No, not really. But I can understand why folks were mad, but not surprised, when he went off to Canada. They figured if he wasn't American enough to play football, maybe he wasn't American at all. The boy might have had his reasons, and he didn't truly owe us anything, on the football field *or* off, but nobody cared about that. Fact is, sometimes I wonder which galled folks more, his leaving the team or the country."

"Well, what do we do, Luke? We don't want to get Kate involved. If it backfires, we don't want David getting angry with her, too."

"Hell, Doc, there ain't nothing short of a hurricane could keep those two apart. David can be stubborn, and so can Katie, but they've been together too long for anything to come between 'em. Our best bet is probably Maggie, though."

"Okay, I'll talk to Maggie."

"Doc, you mind me asking you something?"

"No, not at all."

"How come you even care about those boys not talking to one another? I mean, they ain't your kin or anything. Why's it matter?"

"I don't know, Luke. Maybe because I never had any kids of my own, or because I can't stand to see two people turning their backs on the only family each of them has."

"I ain't so sure you can help, and I ain't so sure, either, that you ought to try. It could get pretty ugly, if you were to get caught up in something that's a lot bigger than both boys put together."

"You mean Pat Riley, don't you?"

"Yup, I do. And those like him, of which there ain't a short supply."

"Well, I'll have to take my chances, Luke."

"You sure you want to?"

"Yes."

"Okay, then. Let's do it."

Doc drove to the waterfront, hoping to catch Maggie. He parked in a lot across from a row of piers jutting into the water like an open hand. Leaving his car, he walked out on the last dock, its once firm planking thudding dully, almost damply, under his feet, as if the lumber had lain too long, too close to the water. He had never been less certain of what he ought to do, while being more certain that he ought to do *something*.

With the *Setting Sun* in McIlhenny's yard for repairs, the pier was deserted. Doc sat on a coil of line near the end of the pier and watched the waves slapping against the barnacled shoring. Walls of the same planking were driven into the mucky sand, their weathered gray ends blunted or split by the pile driver.

Overhead, a gull shrieked. He found it in the bleached-out blue of the sky, where high clouds were barely discernible against the paleness. The bird shrieked again, and Doc watched it dive suddenly toward the surface. Tightly tucked, it plummeted, began, with a flurry of black-tipped white wings, to brake, changing its angle of descent into a flat arc, and plunged for an instant into the water. Then it climbed immediately, a silvery fish flopping in its bill.

Doc shook his head, as if to throw off the vision of the helpless fish and scanned the horizon for a trawler or a sailboat to take his mind off the unpleasant reminders of vulnerability crowding in around him. All of the other piers were as deserted as the one on which he sat, and the fish houses were quiet.

There was no smoke anywhere, and not a sail could be seen. He felt totally alone, not just on the pier, but also on the planet. Remembering David, he realized there was someone who felt as he did. He knew David was wrestling with the same barren isolation he felt, and had felt ever since Rose died. Although they had the same perception for different reasons, Doc knew the benumbing alienation that separated David from everyone, even from those who mattered most.

Instead of an idyllic drift into oblivion, he found himself alone on a Texas pier, more alienated from the future than he had ever imagined in New York. As if he didn't have enough trouble, he was now engineering a reconciliation between two people who were as pure examples of his new environment as he was a stranger to it. He couldn't deny he felt an affinity with David Hodges, and a sympathy for both brothers, but he wondered if his intentions were delusional, no matter how strong the temperamental kinship he felt. It probably couldn't matter less that he shared a view of the world with David.

But he swept aside the uncertainty. They were yoked together, and nothing, no difference or group of differences, was strong enough to separate them. They were alike in their bleak vision of the world, so in all things. Whatever reservations he had, he knew then that he could effect a reconciliation between the brothers, that he was the only one who could, and that he *had* to.

How was another matter. Without a plan, and with only Luke to help him, he would have to confront David directly, and hope for the best. He knew a complicated plan would collapse under its own weight. It would be more effective and honest to improvise. He still wanted to talk to Maggie, but it could wait. He got slowly to his feet and headed back along the pier, pausing once to search the darkening sky for the gull which had kept him intermittent company, but it was gone.

As he reached the end of the pier, he heard a rumble

rounding the corner and saw Maggie Riley's battered pickup pull into the lot next to his car. He skipped off the curb to cross the street and reached the truck as Maggie killed the engine. The door swung open with a squeal, and Maggie hopped onto the tarred gravel with the sprightliness he had come to expect of her.

"Doc," she said, breaking into a grin, "what in hell are *you* doing down here? You thinking of going out for shrimp?"

"Not likely."

"Then you gonna tell me why you *are* here?"

"I was looking for you, actually."

Alarm darkened her features momentarily before she asked, "Patrick ain't been hassling you again, has he?"

"No, no, nothing like that. . . . Can we sit someplace?"

"The dock suit you?"

"That'll be fine."

They crossed the street and walked out on the dock to sit on the same coil of line. Doc heard a gull again and looked up in time to see it wheel off toward the Gulf, its mournful cry trailing behind it like a train whistle receding into the distance.

"You ready to talk now, or do you need a drink? I got some whiskey in the shed over there."

"No, thanks. I'm fine."

"Well, get on with it, then. You're starting to get me worried."

"Luke and I need your help, Maggie," Doc said, unsure where to start.

"What kind of help? With what?"

"With David."

"What's the matter? Will you *please* tell me what's going on?"

"His brother, Peter, came home today."

"So, that's what this is about. . . . Why do you need my help?"

As she spoke, she stood and walked to the end of the pier, turning to look back at him as if farsighted, needing the distance to see him clearly.

"He and David are having some problems. Luke and I thought you might be able to help us."

"Why in hell would I care about that?"

"But, we thought . . ."

"I don't give a damn *what* you thought. If them boys ain't getting along, so what? Why should they?"

"They're brothers, and . . ."

"If it don't make no difference to them," Maggie interrupted, "why should it matter to *me*?"

"David is going to be your son-in-law! How can you not care?"

"David's old enough to take care of hisself. Old enough to know who he wants to talk to and who he don't. If he don't want to, brother or no, he's got a right. I sure as hell ain't going to interfere. Luke, at least, ought to know better'n that. It ain't nobody's business. Least, it ain't mine, *nor* yours."

She turned to look out over the water, seeming as unconcerned as if he hadn't spoken. Sliding her hands into the back pockets of her faded jeans, she rocked on the balls of her feet, then reached into her shirt for the omnipresent pack of Camels. Pulling matches from the cellophane, she lit a cigarette and tossed the match, trailing a thin strand of smoke, high into the air. After two quick, nervous drags, she faced him again. "Now, less you got something else on your mind, I got a few things I'd like to take care of."

"But I don't understand. Why won't you help?"

"No, you don't understand, or you wouldn't have to ask."

The next morning, as Doc drove to the Hodges house, he examined his motives one last time, knowing finally that his explanation to Luke was at best facile and at worst self-deceptive. He didn't know why, but he knew it mattered that two men he barely knew were prisoners of a misunderstanding of their own making.

He looked out at the grass sweeping away from the highway with the same sullen undulations he had seen in the waters of the Bay. Even the grass was more assertive, more arrogant, than the tame, downtrodden lawns of Central Park. The restless, self-assured green was not unlike the people. If only he could be like this fearless Texas greenery, he'd fit in among the people, too. Even the birds here were graceful, if not beautiful, stretching their wings in the endless freedom of open space, drifting in long, leisurely arcs, so different from the short, choppy hops of pigeons and starlings.

Wrapped in his meandering anatomy of the differences between his old and new homes, Doc nearly missed the turnoff to the Hodges house. He braked suddenly to navigate the sharp curve. As the tires crunched on the gravel drive, David appeared in the doorway. He waved in the noncommittal way Doc had initially taken for aloofness, and only later recognized as reticence. As he got out of his car, David smiled remotely and asked, "Doc, what brings you out this way?"

"Just thought I'd stop and see how you were doing, is all."

"You might as well come on in. I can tell you're uncomfortable with whatever's on your mind. Coffee?" he asked, leading the way.

"No, thanks. Something cold, though, would be nice."

David pointed to a well-worn armchair, "Make yourself to home, Doc. I'll be back in a second." He went into the kitchen, and Doc heard the clank of metal on metal as David opened two cans. He was back just as Doc got settled in the darkly receptive chair.

"You want a glass, Doc?"

"No, thanks, David. This will be fine. Thank you."

For a moment, Doc turned the rapidly dewing beer can absently in both hands. Then, regaining the resolve he had mustered at the pier the evening before, he began.

"Actually, the reason I'm here concerns your brother, as much as it does you. . . ."

David jerked visibly. "What's the matter, something happened to Petey?"

"No, why, no. I just . . ."

David sighed and sank back in the chair from which he had half risen.

Sensing an opening, Doc asked, "Some reason something might have happened to Peter?"

"Well, no . . . I mean, a doctor comes all the way out here without being called, you know"—he shrugged—"it's natural to think something might have. You said it concerned him as much as me. . . ."

"That's possible, I guess," Doc agreed tentatively.

"It's more than possible, Doc," David snapped. "It's so."

"No need to get your back up, David."

"Sorry, Doc. You're right. It's just . . . hell, I don't know. . . ."

"You sure there's nothing on your mind?"

"I never said that, did I?"

"No, you didn't. . . ."

David stared for a long time, Doc waiting patiently. His

earlier tenseness returned, hardening his face. Doc thought he could hear David's teeth grinding. Outside, it was quiet. Finally, gesturing with one hand, more to the air than to his interrogator, David spoke.

"Look, Doc," he began falteringly, "I don't know why you're asking all these questions. I don't know the answers, and I sure as hell know they're none of your damn business . . . but, I'm going to try to answer you."

He hesitated, as if realizing that once he started he would be unable to stop. Then, nodding almost imperceptibly, seemed to make up his mind that it didn't matter whether he stopped or not.

"You ever killed a man, Doc? Deliberately, I mean."

"In the army, yes. I was in the infantry in World War II, in Europe, forty-four and forty-five."

"But did you ever kill someone?" David asked with impatience. "Did you ever look right into a man's face and blow him away as if he were no more than a bug?"

"No. I mean, I shot at people, and I know I hit some of them. I was a pretty fair marksman, for a city boy. Not like some of the guys in my outfit, but I must have . . . killed someone. Our weapons weren't as sophisticated as they are now . . . but they were deadly enough."

"Do you ever ask yourself why?"

"Yes, often. I think . . ."

"Still, you have trouble believing you were right, don't you?"

"Well . . . yes. It's not an easy thing to excuse. Especially not for someone like me, who's spent his life trying to heal."

"Yet you had no doubts at the time? You knew that you had to fight, maybe kill someone, someone you didn't know and had no reason to *want* to kill?"

"No, I suppose I didn't have any doubts. Very few people did, after all. I mean, the war seemed necessary. But I guess they always do, don't they?"

"No, Doc, they don't. At least, not to me . . . not now . . ."

Again he fell silent. His eyes seemed to go out of focus, as if he were looking through Doc, seeing again something he couldn't *not* see, no matter how hard he tried to expunge it from his memory.

Afraid a long silence might become permanent, Doc asked quietly, "Then why did you enlist? Luke says he probably could have gotten you a deferment, and Peter, too, if you had wanted it. Why didn't you take it?"

"Doc, if I knew the real answer to that quesion, I'd be a different man. I keep asking myself, over and over, why I went, and none of the answers make any sense. See, the whole thing is, I never really asked myself why. I just *did* it. I don't know why I went. And I don't know why I came back, either."

"Do you mean why you and not Donald Riley?"

David peered intently at Doc, and simultaneously sank down in his chair, as if trying to shrink away from him, or from the question. "No! That's *not* what I mean, goddammit!" he shouted. "I mean just what I said. I'm not talking about fate, Doctor Roth, or natural selection either. I'm talking about reasons, explanations, justifications—not *chance*, damn it!"

His voice dropped to a whisper as he continued. "I mean I'm not sure why I went to Vietnam, and I'm even less sure why I came home, why I *chose* to come home. I spent a couple of years thinking about it before I finally made up my mind to come back. I even reenlisted twice because I didn't know whether I *could* come back."

David turned toward the window, pursing his lips as though he had a bad taste in his mouth.

"Damn it, I *had* no reason to go. That fucking war was

none of my damn business, and I shouldn't have gone. It was late enough that I should have known. I told myself it was something I had to do for my country. But that was just smoke, Doc. Smoke. Shit, it wasn't even good against evil, like it was for you. At least you had that excuse!"

He stopped abruptly, breathing in short, spasmodic gasps. His muscular forearms twitched, and his heavy tan was unable to conceal the whiteness of his knuckles as he squeezed the arms of his chair. He turned away with a deep sigh, to face the window again, this time keeping his eyes closed. When he turned back to Doc to resume speaking, David ignored the tears glistening on his cheeks.

"You want to know why I didn't welcome Petey with open arms? I'll tell you why. Because he thought about it, and I didn't. Because he knew, without going anywhere but Austin, what I had to travel ten thousand miles to find out. Because he was *right*, damn it, and he doesn't even know how right he was. He'll *never* know. And it's not fair, Doc; it's not fair that some of us have to see what I saw, and do what I did, to learn what somebody else already knows. I blame him for that, for being right. But most of all, I can't forgive myself for being wrong. And I *was* wrong, Doc. More wrong than anybody should be allowed to be and still live. The real question, Doc," he said, his voice sinking to a near whisper, "is why the fuck am I still alive?"

"Peter told Luke he feels the same way," Doc said.

David snorted disdainfully. "Why should he feel bad? He did everything right, didn't he? There aren't too many people in this country who don't wish there had never been a war in Vietnam. Peter, and those like him, are heroes now, or prophets at least. Shit, Doc, is it any wonder I'm fucked up? Usually people decide a war, once it's been fought and everybody who's gonna die is already dead, was a necessary evil. Only trouble is, this time everybody seems to have forgotten about the necessary. All they remember is the evil."

"Do you think they're wrong?"

"No, they're not wrong. It wasn't necessary, and it sure as hell was evil," David said, closing his eyes again and leaning back in his chair. "But what about me? And the others, like me—what about them? What about the guys who were blown into so many pieces we never found them all? And what about all the innocent people, the women, the children, the old men, the people who didn't know who we were or what the fight was about—what about *them*?"

"Aren't you as innocent as any of them?"

"No!" David shouted. "No, I'm not innocent. I was there, wasn't I? Maybe I didn't kill any women or children, but I was there. I *saw* it. How can I be innocent?" He was sobbing openly now. The faint glimmer of tears in the dim light filtering through the window was a steady stream, outlining his nose and mouth in bands of silver that shimmered fantastically.

His sobbing subsided, and he shook his head back and forth, as if to dislodge his pain like a physical thing, a thing with claws that tore at him, hurting him most at those times he fought most fiercely to throw it off.

"I tried to stop some of it, and when it got to be its worst, there was only one way to do it. And you don't walk away from *that* innocent, either, believe me. The only way not to have been guilty is not to have been there at all. That's the secret of the whole thing. Peter feels guilty for the wrong reason. Only, he's too damn naive, or self-righteous, to see it. Tell him that, why don't you, the next time he tells you *he* feels guilty?"

"Why don't you tell him yourself, David? The two of you might be surprised by how much you have in common.

The war left victims all over, you know. And some of the worst casualties never put on a uniform."

"Don't you think I know that? But you don't understand any better than he does. You can't. No one can who wasn't there."

"Isn't that just as true of Peter's kind of casualty? Can you understand that? Do you know what he's suffering? Do you even *care* that he's suffering?"

"Of course I care! What the hell do you think I am? He's my *brother*, for Christ's sake!"

"Then why don't you show it? Why don't you show *him*?"

"How?" It was not a question so much as a cry for help.

"Talk to him, David. Tell him how you feel; let him tell you how he feels. For God's sake, talk to him!"

12

AFTER they had left the house, Luke tried to convince Peter to stay with him for a few days. He was afraid he might bolt rather than face his brother again. Peter was reluctant, but left his luggage, saying he'd go for a walk to get his thoughts in order. He didn't return until well after midnight. Luke waited up to talk to him, but Peter adamantly refused to discuss the meeting with his brother.

The next morning, Luke looked for a chance to raise the subject again. He knew David was taciturn, Peter more volatile. Instead of trying, like Doc, to open a locked door, he'd be ventilating a burning building. If he was careless, he'd set off an explosion. One mistake was all he'd have the chance to make. When the opportunity finally came at eleven, he was ready. They were playing chess without really concentrating on the game when he asked, "You and David going to patch things up?"

"Hell, I don't know. David obviously doesn't want to talk to me, and I don't feel like I have anything to say to him, either."

Luke studied the board while considering his next conversational gambit. Heartened by the directness of Peter's response, he continued in the same vein.

"What was it like in Canada? Where'd you live up there?"

"It wasn't too bad, not at the start. I was full of myself when I went. I hit Montreal first, then Toronto. Some of the guys I met were more like refugees. You know? They'd been underground in the States, and were heroes to the rest of us. It seems silly, now, but at first it was an adventure. That didn't last long. . . ."

"What happened?"

"It just stopped being easy. The price was becoming real to me. I started missing home, the people I knew. It got to be a grown-up decision, with consequences I hadn't thought of. I was two thousand miles from home, and the only people I knew were as cut off from their homes as I was from mine. Then, when Mom died, and I couldn't come home . . . I didn't even know about it until two weeks later. Finally, I went to Boston, planning to turn myself in. I thought I'd do alternate service or something, but I didn't have to. They weren't interested in prosecuting people like me anymore. I was almost disappointed. I hung around for a while, then . . . well, here I am."

"It must have been pretty rough."

"Yeah. The worst was when I'd talk to Mom, you know. She . . . I couldn't . . ."

"I never knew," Luke said.

"You weren't supposed to. No one was. You know, there was a network, almost as good as AT&T. All of us were able to find out what was going on, usually late, but still . . . After a while, though, most of us stopped trying to find out. It hurt too much."

He paused thoughtfully, studying the board, then reached out to capture one of Luke's pawns. When he spoke again, it was more deliberately, the first rush of confession behind him.

"It's kind of funny. I figured this would be the conversation I would have with David. I thought we'd tell each other what our private hells had been like. Put all the mess behind us and get back to being the Hodges boy and his shadow, just like the old days. It doesn't look like that's possible, now." He shrugged. "Aah, what the hell!"

Peter paused again, this time to watch Luke slide a bishop out to take a pawn. Luke placed the captured piece silently by the edge of the board. Peter stared at the game as if it were a window.

"You know, Petey," Luke said, interrupting the reverie, "I'll bet if you try, you can have that conversation you were hoping for. David would welcome it as much as you would."

"I don't think so, Luke."

"Why don't you tell him what you just told me?" Luke asked.

"Look, Luke, you know how hard he is to reach. He might talk to you, but he doesn't resent you. You didn't desert him."

"How did you desert him?" Luke asked softly. "What could you have done that would have made any difference? Hell, son, he was already in the Marines before you had any decision to make."

"Yeah, he was," Peter whispered. "He was in, but I made it worse. I didn't carry my fair share of the load. Hell, Luke, I didn't even stay home to take my chances. My number wasn't that low. But I ran away from everything—

my responsibilities, my home, my *brother*. I should have been here to bury Mom. How are we ever going to be able to talk about that, to get over it? What could I possibly say to make it up to him?"

"You could tell him the truth," Luke suggested.

"What *is* the truth, Luke? I thought Canada was the truth. I thought resisting the war would end the war. Christ, how arrogant can somebody be? I was so damn naive. Jesus! . . . And then, when the war dragged on, and it started to cost me a little, I got bitter. People started to forget about it long before it was over. But I didn't forget. I couldn't, because my brother was still in it. All those people killed, every damn day for twenty years, and for everybody else it stopped when they shut the television off. For Christ's sake, if you were watching in black and white, people didn't even bleed."

He stopped abruptly, this time without the subterfuge of examining the chessboard. Luke reached into his pocket for a handkerchief, extending it without a word. Peter accepted it in silence and mopped his cheeks with quick, short stabs.

"You know, Luke," he snuffled, with a feeble attempt at a laugh, "I feel pretty stupid. Here I am, complaining about myself, about how little courage I have, and then I go right ahead and prove it by bawling my brains out."

"You don't have anything to apologize for, son," Luke assured him. "But you boys have an obligation to one another. You can't afford to waste energy on misunderstanding."

"Luke, believe me, I want to try, but I can't if he won't. You get him to talk and I'll make him listen, but he's got to meet me halfway."

"He will, if you go about it the right way. He wants to, but I think he wants to talk to the right person, and that ain't me; it's you." Luke held the phone out to Peter. "Call him. If he's there, I'll drive you out, and, by God, we'll get this thing ironed out today, even if we've got to lock you two in a room."

Peter reached out reluctantly, his hand shaking. He nearly lost his grip on the cold black plastic as he began to dial.

On the way out to the house, it was obvious Peter didn't want to talk, so Luke, too, kept quiet. Peter wanted reconciliation, but doubted it was as simple as Luke believed. Not knowing what else to do, he was prepared to try again.

When the car pulled into the driveway, the crunch of the tires on the gravel was the only sound until Luke opened his door and stepped out. David's Valiant was parked up near the house, where it always was when David was home, its slow drift into rust a monument to the irresistibility of natural processes. Doc's Impala was parked beside it. Luke got out and turned to look at Peter through the windshield. Peter was aware of his gaze, but was unwilling, just yet, to join him. Luke leaned in the open window.

"You want me to go on in and try to get something started?"

"No, Luke, thanks. I'll be all right. I just need a minute, okay?"

"Sure, take your time."

Seeing no point in postponing whatever might be coming, Peter yanked open the door, and bumped his head as he got out of the car. The sand and gravel felt odd beneath his feet, as if he were moon-walking. He was aware of physical sensations experienced countless times, but never under such circumstances, since, highly sensitized, every nerve was functioning at peak capacity. Looking toward the house, he was tempted to head off down the road, but knew if he did, he'd never come back. For an instant, he felt like a tourist in a country he had no desire to see.

"I guess we may as well get on with it, Luke," he said at last, looking over his shoulder and down the highway, considering flight one final time. Then, with a wave of his hand, he dismissed the thought. They made their way to the steps, Luke in the lead, and as they reached the front door, David came to greet them. Doc was right behind him.

"Luke, what brings *you* out this way?"

"Son, you know as well as I do. You and Petey got to sit down and settle this. Now's as good a time as any, so let's get going."

David stepped away from the door to let them in, without saying a word. While Luke was speaking, he had been looking past him, staring at Peter with a blankness in his eyes that betrayed nothing of what he might be thinking or feeling. Once they were all indoors, David walked back to the kitchen. The others followed him.

"Anybody want something to drink?"

"Nope," Luke said, his tone clearly signaling that no diversion was acceptable. "You and Petey are gonna work things out, and you're gonna do it now, today. That's it, plain and simple."

"What makes you think we have anything to work out, Luke, or that we can, even if there is something?"

"Damn it, son, you been back a while now, but you still ain't *home*. Ain't you nor Petey gonna be happy unless you can get some things behind you. If you can't do it alone, me and Doc will help. I ain't forgot I promised your mama I'd look after the two of you. Now, let's get to it, shall we? If you want, me and Doc'll wait outside, but we ain't leaving until this thing is settled, once and for all."

David glanced at Peter while saying, "Maybe you *should* leave us alone."

"Whatever you say, son. But Doc is gonna be out front, and I'll be out back. So don't either one of you think you can get away without giving this thing a try," Luke smiled, but no one in the room thought he was joking. "Let's go, Doc, unless you got something you want to say."

Doc shook his head, and the two older men headed toward the door. Once outside, Doc said, "You weren't kidding, were you?"

"No, I wasn't kidding. But they know it, so I don't have to wait out back. They know they better knuckle down and get this thing done, and done right. We can sit here in the shade and wait. They need help, we're here. But I don't think they need us now. All they needed was some-body to hold a gun to their heads and tell 'em to talk . . . and I just did that."

David had watched the men depart and the door close before turning to Peter, to say, "Well . . . here we are."

"Yeah, wherever that is." Peter nodded.

"I guess we both know the answer to that, don't we," David said. He walked to the table and sat down. "Pull up a chair, unless you want to see whether Luke was bluffing about surrounding the place."

"No. He's pissed at both of us. I don't think I'd want to tangle with him right now."

"I guess we better talk, then. . . ."

"I think we have to, don't you?" Peter asked.

"I guess."

"You've had a rough time adjusting to being home."

"I'll get used to it someday."

"Can I help?"

"How?"

"I can't answer that unless you're honest with me. What I can do depends on how you feel."

David got up. He paced nervously, then leaned on the

windowsill, his back to Peter. The dry grass rasped in a slight breeze, and the curtain wafted gently back and forth beside him. Framed by the glare, he was nearly motionless, except for the rise and fall of his chest, and Peter was, for a moment, uncertain whether he was seeing his brother or a memory of what he had been. The shadows partly obscuring David's face had erased many of the changes time and the war had engraved on it.

"I don't know if I know *how* to be honest anymore, Petey. I've changed so much, in ways I'm not even aware of. I didn't realize it until I came home, but when I'm with Kate, I know. I'm probably not somebody you'd want to know, if you had a choice."

"You don't think *I've* changed? How could either of us be what he was? But that's not what I want."

"What *do* you want, then?"

"I want us to understand what we've been through. It wasn't together, like it used to be. But that doesn't mean we can't still be close. It won't be shared history, this time, that binds us."

"What will?" David asked.

"Hell, I don't know . . . blood . . . love maybe."

"That *sounds* good, but what the hell does it mean?"

Peter reached for a cigarette and lit it before answering. "I'm not sure. Maybe it means we make allowances, understand our failures. At least, that's what I want it to mean."

"Failures? You want to make allowances for my whole life? That's *my* failure."

"Bullshit. That's self-pity. You never used to talk like that."

"I said I've changed. Maybe that's how. Maybe I just never knew how fucked up I was. Or maybe I wasn't, but I sure as shit am now."

"Why do you think that?" Peter asked, walking over to the window to confront David.

"Because I know what I am now. I never saw myself as clearly as I have since I came back. There's a lot about me I wouldn't like in somebody else. I don't like it any better in me, either. I can't make allowances, because I know what I am. And why . . ."

"Maybe you don't have to make allowances. Maybe I can do that for you. That's all I'm asking, really. You make them for me, and I'll make them for you. I feel guilty, too, but if somebody forgives you, it helps. I want you to forgive me. I *need* that. You remember that time we broke into Halsey's and stole a guitar, how terrible we felt? That's how I feel now. . . . But he forgave us, and we felt better. Not right away. It was months before I could look him in the eye again. The guilt went away, but it wouldn't have if he never knew we did it. *We* knew, and as long as it was our secret, there was no way we weren't going to feel guilty."

"Some things can't be forgiven, Peter. That's one thing I've learned in the past few years."

"What are you saying?"

"I think it's pretty plain."

"Are you telling me you can't forgive me?"

"You don't need any indulgence from me."

"Then what the hell do you mean?" Peter reached out and grabbed his brother by the arm, as if to shake loose whatever it was David was trying to tell him.

David pulled free and turned to the window again. "What I'm trying to say is that there are things *I've* done, things I can't forgive, and that no one else can forgive, either."

"*I* can, David."

"It doesn't matter. Not if I can't. Some things matter more to yourself than to anyone else. I know you think

141

I'm angry at you, but I'm not. I'm just angry. Not at people, just at things, at life. And that won't change, ever."

"How can you be sure if you don't try?"

"I can't be sure. But I can't try, either. No way."

"Please?" Peter begged. Stunned by the unexpected turn, he didn't know how to combat the self-loathing eating at David. Anxiety was replaced by concern. Feeling helpless, he returned to the table and sat down. "I swear, David, whatever it is, it doesn't matter. You're my brother, and I . . . I . . ."

David turned away from the window and walked over to place one hand on Peter's shoulder, squeezing it with the same reassurance Peter remembered all those nights in Canada, through endless permutations of the scene he now found himself acting. But the script was like nothing he'd imagined. He got to his feet and threw his arms around David. "If you can't talk about it now, you will. I'll wait, no matter how long it takes. I just want you to know that. Please."

David squeezed his eyes closed, nodding as he did so, then whispered hoarsely, "I guess you can tell the guards outside to go home. Everything's gonna be all right."

13

THOUGH reconciled with David, Peter was at loose ends. Coming home wasn't the same as being home. He needed something to occupy his mind, to order his life. He had to get his mind off the past. The sooner he did, the sooner it would truly recede.

One morning, Luke was driving back to Witman from Galveston at a leisurely pace. Not fond of air conditioning, he had all his windows open, letting the air move around him. As he approached the town limits, he spotted Peter walking along the road and pulled over to ask if he wanted a lift. Peter declined, saying he'd rather walk. But while Luke waited to pull back onto the highway after an oncoming van, he heard Peter holler for him to stop.

"Luke, hey, Luke, wait a minute. I changed my mind."

Luke leaned over to open the door, and Peter slipped in and pulled the door shut in the same motion.

"You going anyplace special, Luke?" he asked.

"Nope. You're up mighty early for a fella who ain't got anything to do with himself."

"Yeah . . . well, I don't sleep much these days."

"You given any thought to what you're going to do for a job?"

"Thinking about it, but don't have any prospects yet. I thought I might hire on to Maggie's crew, or one of the other trawlers, but David's trying to talk me out of it."

"Why?"

"He says some of the other guys wouldn't like it. Said they wouldn't be above taking me out one day and not bringing me back."

"Not likely," Luke said, though not quite sure. "But some of those old boys weren't too happy about your going to Canada, you know. They might not do you harm, but that don't mean they wouldn't like to."

"Hell, Luke, I don't give a damn what they think. If I was going to be scared of something like that, I wouldn't have come back."

"Look, son, I know you don't see eye to eye with David on some things. But he knows a lot of these people in a way you don't, and maybe can't. It's funny, but I think if *he* had gone to Canada instead of you, they'd have taken it better. They still wouldn't have liked it, but they might have understood. David worked with them, was one of 'em. At least *they* thought so, anyway."

"Thought so? Either he was or he wasn't."

"Now that's where you're wrong. See, it ain't always what it looks like to folks. Most of 'em see what they think they see. So, when you up and headed for Canada, they decided it was because you think you know better'n they do."

"But that's not what it was all about!" Peter snapped.

He was getting angry, but Luke didn't mind. Peter's frustration made him feel trapped, and he needed to let off steam.

"Wasn't it?" Luke asked. "I think that's exactly what it was about. You were telling folks a war some of 'em had fought in, and that others were gonna fight in, wasn't what they thought it was. Some boys from around here didn't come back, and you were telling their families they died for nothing. Now, how do you think that made 'em feel?"

"Luke, what I did was about *me*, nobody else. It was what I had to do, that's all."

"Petey, it just ain't that simple now, son. Everything you do means something to some folks. That can't be helped, and it don't mean we shouldn't do something we think is right. But we got to expect to be misunderstood."

"Maybe so, but we also have to accept the right of others to do what they have to do, don't we?"

"Within limits. But the question is, what *are* the limits? Maybe they don't go any farther than the limits of the narrowest mind in town. I've seen enough in my time I more'n half believe that. Ain't anybody freer'n the least free man around him, seems like."

"I don't believe that!"

"Well, son, I wish you'd think on it some, anyhow."

They lapsed into silence, Luke tapping the steering wheel thoughtfully as he drove. The tall grass on either side of the highway showed little green, its color bleached away by the sun.

Luke wanted to help Peter find himself, but his options were limited, and after discarding the unlikely and the impractical, he decided the best course was one that would allow him to keep an eye on Peter. After much deliberation, he settled on an idea without expecting it to succeed. He offered Peter a job in his office.

To Luke's surprise, he accepted enthusiastically. Peter was to help out with the general details of the office and some of the research Luke found so time-consuming. It would give Peter direction and broaden his exposure to the practice of law, something in which he had expressed an interest.

He was rather reserved around the office for the first few days, but by the end of the week was enjoying his work, and as he got involved in the routine, he seemed less tense. He still seemed wary, however, even with Luke, as if waiting for a remark that would require him to either fight or leave the office, and the job, for good. It hadn't happened, and Peter was beginning to believe that it didn't have to.

Mabel Dixon, Luke's secretary and office manager, made the transition easier than it might have been. An easygoing, older woman she had something of Alice Hodges in her manner. Peter kept his distance and was less than outgoing with visitors to the office and with Luke's clients, but everyone tried to leave him alone without being uncivil. They were neither hostile nor self-consciously garrulous, speaking to him only out of necessity or conventional courtesy. With Mabel, Peter was more at ease. Other than Luke, she was the only constant presence in the office, so it was an ideal transitional environment for him.

Peter had a good head on his shoulders, and Luke believed his interest in the law was more than polite conversation intended to flatter him. He was certain Peter would be well suited to a law career, and he tried to encourage him without burdening him with expectations. He was particularly impressed by Peter's incisive, logical approach to the law, so different from the passion with which

146

he approached his own situation. It seemed as if he sought, through immersion in the details of statute and regulation, to uproot his emotional side, or to ignore it as best he could.

One afternoon, toward the end of his third week on the job, Luke and Peter were seated on opposite sides of Luke's huge, battle-scarred desk, putting the finishing touches on a brief. It was the first complicated matter on which Peter had assisted, and he felt a certain satisfaction at having gotten through it. Considerable research had been involved, and he was pleased he'd been able to handle it. He'd spent many hours in the law library at the University of Houston, still more in the records office at the county seat.

Once the basic materials had been assembled, the structure of Luke's argument had been rearranged no fewer than four times. Then came the tedious refinement of language, striving for that forceful subtlety that Luke, for all his folksy conversation, preferred in his professional work. Peter was proud of his own contributions, adding a rewritten sentence here and a smoother turn of phrase there. The bulk of the written work was still Luke's, and, through it, Peter had seen a side of him, the perfectionist, that was carefully concealed behind an artfully cultivated public persona.

"Petey," Luke said, gently tamping the papers into an ordered spire in front of them, "I reckon we can call it a day."

"You mean we're finished? I thought we'd never see the end of this damn thing."

"Son, sometimes the best way to see the end of something is to make sure the beginning is done right. A little more polish on this bugger, and we'll be ready to file it."

"Then we're *not* done?" Peter asked wearily.

"We ain't, but you are. For today, anyhow."

"You never cease to amaze me, Luke."

"Son, the day I stop amazing folks is the day I start having less work'n I care to."

"I think I'll go over to the Header for a beer. Want to come?"

"Nope. I got to tinker with this thing a little more, and make it readable for Mabel to type, or she'll take my head off in the morning. You go on, but watch your step over there. There's some roughnecks ain't got nothing but time, these days. They get a few under their belts, they get mean. Maybe you should just go on home."

"I'll be fine." Peter got up and put some notes in a folder before heading toward the door. "See you tomorrow, Luke."

Outside, although it was nearly five o'clock, the heat was still oppressive. A beer seemed like just the thing to polish off his most satisfying afternoon since returning home. As he scuffed along, hands tucked casually in the back pockets of his jeans, he whistled tunelessly. Savoring his accomplishments, he nearly missed the sound of someone speaking to him as he made his way toward the bar.

"Where you going, boy? Ain't you got time to say hello to an old friend?" The voice sounded less friendly than the words suggested, and Peter stopped in his tracks. He turned warily to see who had spoken them, but saw no one on the sidewalk. Shrugging, he continued on. The person spoke again. This time he knew the confrontation he'd been dreading had arrived.

"You might at least look over my way, Petey," the voice drawled. It sounded vaguely familiar, but before he could place it, a bulky figure stepped out of a doorway down the block, stomach first, followed by thick wrists and a gun belt. Pat Riley loomed into full view, his dark moon of a face barely discernible in the shadow cast by the shingled *ramada* over the walk and deepened by the broad brim of his hat. "You been back for some time, now, ain't you, Petey?"

"Oh, it's you. I couldn't tell who it was," Peter mumbled.

"Couldn't tell, or couldn't care less?"

"I wouldn't say that, exactly," Peter responded, choosing his words carefully.

"No, I don't guess you would. Neither would I, if I was you. I bet you ain't gonna tell me what you think of me, even if I give you the chance."

"Fact is, Pat, I don't really think of you much . . . or much of you." He regretted the words immediately, but Pat's mood told him it didn't really matter. "Look, Pat, I have some things I want to take care of. I'll see you around, all right?"

"Not so fast, old son. I'm talking to you in a semiofficial capacity, so to speak. You better hear what I got to say."

"All right, but make it quick." Peter was rapidly losing his temper. He knew it wasn't wise to cross Pat, who seemed more ill-tempered than normal. Pat stepped ominously close before resuming the conversation.

"I ain't seen you around much. What you been doing?"

"What's it to you?"

"To me, it ain't no more than the sweat on a hog's ass. But the law—well now, that's a different story. The law likes to know where draft dodgers and dope fiends are, what they're doing, and such like."

"I'll see you around." Peter started to leave, but before he got halfway turned, he felt a grip on his arm, the fingers digging into his wrist. He pulled free and swung around to face Pat.

"You know, Pat, I think you just might be the hog whose ass you mentioned earlier, and if you grab my arm again,

I'll haul that hog's ass into court so fast, your head'll spin. Now get out of my way."

"Hodges," Pat hissed, stepping so close to Peter their belt buckles clinked, "I'm only telling you one time. You watch your step. Give me reason even to think you're out of line, I'll bust your head open. Then I'll see to it you go away again, and it won't be to no Canada this time around. And I'll tell you something else. Your brother ain't going to get in my way either. You understand me?"

"Hell yes, I understand you." He turned to leave for the third time, and again Riley grabbed his arm. Peter reached out with his left hand to break the grip, and Riley hissed in his ear. The smell of alcohol was unmistakable.

"You ain't as smart as I thought. That was assaulting an officer."

Peter felt a sharp thrust between his shoulder blades and sprawled forward on the pavement. Before he could get to his knees, Pat yanked him to his feet by the collar. As he spun around, a fist met him flush on the cheek. The blow sent him tumbling backward over an ornamental hitching post and into the gutter. His neck burning with anger, he got unsteadily to his feet as Pat closed in, this time with his hand on his gun butt. There was no one in the street, so he was at Pat's mercy. In court, it would have been his word against Pat's, and he had no doubt whose side the judge would take. Before he could decide whether to chance it, Pat spoke again.

"I know you been working for Lucas, but that don't cut any ice with me, motherfucker. I could shoot you through the head right now, and there ain't nobody'd do a thing about it. The next time I see you, I might feel like it. I might even *do* it. You might tell your brother that, too."

Pat turned unsteadily and swaggered up the block in the direction from which Peter had come. He never looked back, as if to say he didn't give a damn what Peter might think. He knew he wasn't going to *do* anything. Peter's first inclination, after discarding the idea of going after Pat with his bare hands, was to call Luke. But he knew the old lawyer would be outraged and call Randy McHale. He didn't want Luke involved, or McHale. Handling Pat by himself was best, and probably safest.

His jaw ached, and there was a dull throbbing in his left shoulder where it had been bruised by the fall. He straightened his clothes, dusted them off as best he could, and walked the rest of the way to the corner. Instead of continuing to the Double Header, he decided to go home and crossed the street to his ancient Volkswagen.

The crotchety engine turned over with a rasp, then broke into a wheezy rumble. Repressing the urge to make a U-turn, he chuffed down the block. At the next corner, he was careful to stop before making a right and heading back toward the main street, where the confrontation had taken place. He drove cautiously, ruefully aware that his run-in with Pat had instantly transformed him into a model driver. As he crossed the city line, he heard a car horn. Glancing into the mirror, he saw Pat's Stetson waving jauntily over the roof of his cruiser, as if to say, "Ya'll come back real soon, hear?"

As Witman fell away behind him, he grew bolder, merely watching the rear-view mirror closely. Considering his situation, he tallied debits and credits. He wondered whether he should leave town for good, and if not, why not. His only close family was in town, and he had a job he was growing fond of. On the other hand, David might not want to stay in Witman much longer. They could move to Austin and enroll in the University of Texas together. David wouldn't want to leave Kate behind, but there was no reason why she, too, wouldn't want to leave this Neanderthal backwater behind once and for all.

No reason, that is, except for Maggie, who probably couldn't, and surely wouldn't want to, give up the only life she'd ever known. Whether she'd be willing to let Kate go, and whether Kate would go without her mother's blessing, was something he couldn't guess.

Luke would understand. He'd probably even encourage him. He might be able to arrange a job for him in Austin. Luke wasn't political by nature, but he'd known virtually everyone in the county who was someone for the last thirty years or so, and that had to be worth something.

It might not be easy to persuade David, but he thought he could manage it, given a little time. As their suspicions ebbed away, their relationship had been improving. It still wasn't what it once had been, but there was every probability it soon would be. The house appeared on the horizon. Almost involuntarily, he speeded up, feeling both the adrenaline of his encounter with Pat and the excitement of possible change.

He cornered roughly into the driveway, skidding on the stones and sending several onto the front porch, and slipped out from behind the wheel. He shut the door, which made the spongy sound of a VW with windows closed. Recklessly, he bounced off the doorjamb as he sidestepped around the screen door and plunged into the living room.

"Jesus Christ, what happened to you?" David blurted out. He had been reading, and the book lay face up in his lap as he watched Peter blink into accommodation with the altered light.

Peter reached up to his cheek in embarrassment and rubbed the tender point of impact. "It's nothing." He laughed. "I just bumped into Pat Riley."

"Bumped into him? It looks more like he ran you over!

Or was it the other way around, I hope?" David smiled.

"Actually, no. It was more like your first guess."

"Well, what the hell *did* happen, then?"

"I suppose you might say Deputy Sheriff Riley took forceful issue with my right to be back home," Peter explained. "He chose to teach me the law-and-order point of view with about as much subtlety as you'd expect from so sensitive a man."

"He beat the crap out of you, is what you're saying, isn't it?"

"Well, yes. But it's a little more complicated than that."

"Complicated, hell. I should have kicked his ass when I had the chance. He's been looking for trouble since I got home. I ought to push his face in right now," David said darkly, getting to his feet.

"Come on, Dave, it's nothing. I can take care of myself; you know that. But it's not easy to figure how to punch out a lawman and get away with it. How the hell did *you* manage it, anyway?"

"Forget it. The question is, how do we make sure it doesn't happen again?"

"Well, we could get a restraining order," Peter suggested.

"Restraining order, my ass. They aren't worth the paper they're written on. If he got the chance, Pat could blow you or me away and probably get away with it. What good's your restraining order then?"

"Come on, David. There are limits, after all. Even for Pat."

"Limits? What good are limits? Are you satisfied if he can only push you around? Is that okay, as long as he doesn't shoot you?"

"Look, Dave, I don't like Pat, but I think I understand him. He'll let off some steam, and that'll be the end of it.

Besides, he was only doing what a lot of people around here want to, anyway."

Peter debated whether to mention the threat, but decided that if he wanted to persuade his brother to do it his way, he'd have to keep it to himself. "I don't think either of us has to worry about it anymore. He doesn't have anything against you. It was me went to Canada, not you. Christ's sake, you two even have Vietnam in common!"

"You ought to know better than that. We both had run-ins with Pat long before anybody ever heard of the war. He doesn't like me working for Maggie, and he doesn't like me seeing Kate."

"But you have to consider them, too. How would they feel about you taking him on?"

"They'd understand. They know what he's like these days."

"Well, it wasn't all that bad, and the worst is over. Why don't you just let it go? If you pick a fight with Pat, it'll just guarantee another one after that. If I whip him myself the next time he tries to push me around, that'll end it for sure. He'll find somebody else to pick on."

"Unh-unh! If he can't beat you himself, he'll get help. If he gets beat, he'll have to get even."

"So what good would it do for *you* to fight him? How can we put an end to this bullshit?"

"I wish to Christ I knew."

At the Double Header, Pat walked to the bar, pulling up a stool as he reached for his wallet. Rick Walker, the bartender, headed toward him as he put a ten on the bar. He stood in front of the deputy, drying his hands on the tail end of a moist apron. When Pat remained silent, he asked, "What'll you have, Pat?"

154

"Gimme a beer and a glass of ice, would you, Rick?"

"You having your beer on the rocks these days, Pat?"

"No jokes, Rick. Just get me the beer and the goddamn ice."

"Whatever you say, partner. Beer on the rocks, coming up. I mean beer and rocks on the side." Rick laughed, but Pat ignored him.

Pat gulped down half the drink, then took a few of the cubes, wrapped them in a napkin, and held the improvised compress to the back of his right hand.

The bartender watched him curiously for a moment. "Hurt your hand, Pat?"

"Now what makes you think that?"

"It ain't every day somebody wraps a few ice cubes around his knuckles, just to drink a beer. It's usually cold enough without that."

"Maybe today ain't every day, Rick."

"I guess. You don't have to talk about it if you don't want to," Walker said, sensing Pat's anger.

"That's right, and since I don't, why don't you just tend to your business and stay the fuck out of mine?"

"Fine by me . . ."

"Louise here?"

"Nope, but she'll be back in about an hour," Walker said, moving down the bar.

Pat turned around on his stool. He realized that no one he knew was in the bar, or somebody would have said something to him by now. Reaching behind him for the beer, he drained it off, walked toward the jukebox, pulled a quarter from his pocket, and punched E-9 three times. Over at the pool table, he reached up to turn on the lamp as the first notes of Merle Haggard's "Okie from Muskogee" sounded. By the end of the first verse, Pat had racked the balls and chalked his cue. Humming along with the tune, he cracked the cue ball down sharply, wincing as a sharp pain shot through the injured knuckles. He made a few tentative strokes to get the feel of the cue, then, with a thrust more violent than forceful, broke. As he did so, the front door of the bar opened, and Jimmy and Roger came in.

While Jimmy stopped at the bar to chat with Rick a moment and order a couple of beers, Roger moved back toward the pool table and pulled the nearest chair closer to watch Pat run three balls at random, then miss an easy bank shot in the corner.

"Playing with yourself again, eh, Pat? Louise know, or ain't she giving you enough to keep your mind off it?" Roger laughed.

"Go fuck yourself."

"Whoa, you in a *good* mood, ain't you?"

"Good's I oughta be."

"What's the matter?"

"My hand hurts, and I had a little chat with somebody I don't particularly like. That's all."

"Who?"

"Peter Hodges."

"What the hell you got to say to him?"

"I *said* my hand hurts, didn't I?"

"Oh, that kind of chat. He have anything to say to you?"

Pat laughed before answering. "He may be chickenshit, but he ain't a fool. Course not."

Jimmy came over with the beers and handed one to Roger before pulling up a chair of his own. Pat shot a few more balls while the newcomers watched. When he had run the table, he called over to the bar for another beer and sat down with the other two.

"Pat's been talking to our local hero," Roger informed Jimmy.

"Who?"

"Mister Hodges."

"Which one?"

"There ain't no difference between 'em, far as I'm concerned," Pat said.

"Hell, Pat," Jimmy said, "Davey's all right. A little stand-offish, maybe, but so what? I guess he's got a right."

"He ain't standing off far enough, if you ask me," Pat answered.

"That brother of his has balls, coming back here like he done. I got to give him credit for that," Roger said.

"If he had balls, he'da been with his brother—and mine—instead of in Canada."

"You right about that." Jimmy nodded. "I don't guess he'll be around long, though. Folks ain't as happy to see him as he is to be back. Shouldn't be too long before he ain't no happier'n we are."

"I'll make sure of that, don't you worry," Pat said. "That cocksucker'll wish he never heard of this town before I'm through."

14

LUKE struggled out of his old Buick and tossed some folders through the rear window. They landed in a heap. He never locked the car, and never raised the windows unless it threatened rain. Everybody in Witman knew everybody else's business, so there was no need for secrets. Theft wasn't a problem either. Ownership just meant headaches, and most people had more of those than they could use.

He walked to Halsey's for a few cigars. In the old days, he'd been partial to the Cuban variety, but those were hard to come by since Castro. He no longer cared what he smoked, as long as it was fat and, according to most of his friends, smelled bad. Lamenting the loss of his beloved smokes was as close as Luke ever came to a position on foreign policy.

Halsey's was empty on this hot afternoon, and John invited him to pull up a stool for a bull session, which the genial lawyer did, easing his bulk down with a groan.

"What you been up to, Luke?" Halsey asked. "Seems like I haven't seen you in weeks."

"Well, I been mostly breaking in my new assistant. It ain't easy to get a youngster used to my way of thinking. It'll pay off down the road, though, so I don't mind."

"How's he working out?"

"Pretty fair head on his shoulders, that boy has. Make a damn good lawyer, if he's a mind to."

"He want to?"

"I don't know. I try to talk him into it, every chance I get. He ain't made up his mind, but I got him leaning."

"You getting any flak on account of Petey . . . ?"

"Anybody knows me knows better'n to poke his nose in where it doesn't belong. Why? Anybody said anything to you?"

"Well, not exactly *to* me, but I have heard some folks talking about it lately." The storekeeper paused, nodding significantly.

"Let me tell you something, John, to pass along. I'll be damned if I'll sit by and let some idiots decide which mistakes ought to be forgiven and which not. John, I'm getting mighty tired of the big mouths around here trying to run everybody's business. Especially mine."

"Luke," Halsey said gently, "I hear all kinds of foolishness in this place. I can't avoid it. But that don't mean I pay any attention. All I'm saying is there're some folks around here who ain't too happy you give a job to Petey Hodges, that's all."

"It'll pass. Soon as folks shut up and start minding somebody's business besides mine."

Before Halsey could answer, the spastic tinkle of the doorbell interrupted. Luke reached into his pocket for a cigar while Halsey went to see who the new arrival was.

As Luke gnawed on the end of a big pseudo-corona, he tried to decide what, if anything, he ought to do about the talk John had mentioned.

Soon he became dimly aware of Halsey's raised voice, slower and louder than usual. Straining to hear, he realized that his friend was trying to make himself understood, probably by one of the Mexicans who lived in the area.

"I . . . DON'T . . . HAVE . . . THAT," Halsey was saying, pausing for each word to sink in as if it were a fluid. "NO . . . HAVE . . . THAT."

Strangely, Halsey wasn't using his peculiar pidgin Spanish. It sounded more like he was speaking to Charlie Chan than to a Chicano. Curious, Luke got to his feet and ambled toward the front, in time to see a small, dark-haired man dressed in faded denim leave, accompanied by another anemic tinkle. As the door closed, Halsey turned, and found Luke right behind him.

"Don't that beat all?" he mumbled.

"What was that all about, John? You had more than your usual difficulty making yourself understood."

"Damned if I know, Luke," Halsey muttered. "Damned if I know."

"How come you didn't try that fancy Spanglish of yours?"

"Cause the guy didn't speak Spanish, is why!"

"Well, what'd he want?"

"I don't know. I never got through to him, and he didn't make sense to me either. I didn't have a clue what he wanted. Strange little dude, too. Didn't look like no Mexican."

"It sounded like you were trying Chinese there for a minute." Luke laughed.

"I was, sort of, but that little feller don't really look all that Chinese, neither. I don't know *what* he was, but it don't matter, since he didn't buy nothing anyways." Halsey laughed, too. "How about a game of checkers, Luke? You and me ain't had a real set-to over the board in quite a spell."

"That'd be fine, John." Luke seemed distracted. "Whyn't you get the board and set 'er up while I take a leak?" He headed toward the bathroom. On his way, he considered an idea more unsettling than certain. Something about the recent customer reminded him of a news story he had seen. He turned before reaching the bathroom and went toward the front, intending to go back to his office to make a few calls. When he reached the counter, however, Halsey was clicking the last few checkers into place. He looked up as Luke approached.

"You ready to get whupped, Luke?"

"I'll take a rain check, John. I just remembered a couple things I have to do at the office. I'll be by later on, if you still want to play."

"I reckon you had time to think it over, eh?" Halsey chuckled. "I'll be ready for you. How about three o'clock?"

"Fine," Luke agreed. "I'll see you then. Maybe I'll even give . . ."

Before he could finish, the bell sounded again. The mysterious customer was back, this time with another man, who could have been his twin, and Father Alphonso Rodriguez.

"Afternoon, John," the priest greeted Halsey. "Lucas, how are you doing?"

The two men said their respective hellos, and Halsey turned to the two men with Rodriguez. "You know these fellers, Padre?"

"Yes, I do, John," the priest replied. "This is Ngao Dinh Tranh," he said, indicating the man who had been in the store earlier. "And this is Vinh Ho Bao." Both of the Orientals nodded, and Halsey stuck out a beefy hand, which

161

the smaller men shook hesitantly. Halsey turned back to the priest as Luke shook their hands.

"Tranh and Bao are Vietnamese refugees, John," Rodriguez explained. "They've just settled here in town."

"Why in hell they want to live around here, Padre?" Halsey stammered.

"Why not?" the priest responded gently.

"Well, hell, Padre . . . Sorry! What I mean is, whyn't they try to find a place more like where they come from? This here country ain't like what they're used to, is it?"

"No, not quite," Rodriguez replied, grinning at Halsey's discomfiture. "But there are a few things to recommend it."

"Like what?"

"Well, for one thing, they were fishermen back home. There's no reason they can't make a living here. It will be difficult enough to adjust to the new language and customs, without having to learn a new way to make a living."

"Well, I reckon so, Padre," Halsey agreed reluctantly. "But I don't imagine folks'll welcome the competition. Know what I mean?"

"I do, but most people will understand how difficult it has been for these men and their families. No one will begrudge them the chance to make a living," the priest said confidently. Turning to Luke, he asked, "How about you, Lucas? You agree with John, here?"

"I don't know, Al," Luke said. He looked around the store, as if its relatively unattractive appearance was an emblem of hard times just around the corner. Finally, he continued. "John may have a point. Seems like there's fewer shrimp out there every year. Folks might *not* take too kindly to more competition."

"Well, I still think there's such a thing as Christian charity, Lucas," Rodriguez insisted.

"Al," Luke said fondly, "you've always been more of a dreamer than most folks I know. I guess it comes with the collar. But you forget one thing. If there was enough charity to go around, either we wouldn't need it or it wouldn't be a virtue."

"Maybe so, Lucas, maybe so. Still, I *can* be realistic. I don't think I'm dreaming. Not this time."

"I sure hope not," Luke said. "But you know how folks are when they think somebody's trying to take something that's theirs. That's not to say they'd be right, but they *might* think it, Al. And if they *do*, it could get pretty ugly around here."

"I'll be surprised if anyone is less than helpful. And we're going to need quite a bit of help. These men are just the first of several who will be coming, with their families. In fact, I was going to come by later this week and see you, Lucas, to talk about legal assistance. I hope I can still do that."

"Come on, Al," Luke snapped. "You ought to know *me* better'n that. I just hope you don't need me as much as you might. Things have a way of getting legal right quick when folks' livelihood is involved. If that happens, you're going to need a lawyer and some help from upstairs, too. Sometimes the law ain't enough."

"Lucas, I'll tell you what: You take care of the Supreme Court, and I'll take care of the Supreme Being. Fair enough?"

"It's a deal, Al." Luke laughed. "I just hope you got more clout with him than I got with them. Now why don't you get on with your business here? Me and John got some checker playing to do, soon's you get through."

Halsey turned to the priest's companions, who hadn't said a word during the lengthy discussion. "I hope you have better luck talking to these here fellers than I did earlier, Padre."

"Well, John, I heard about your problem." The priest laughed. "If I'd known your French was rusty, I'd have come in with them."

"French? You mean that was French? Well, why didn't he say so? I get along in Spanish okay. French can't be all that different. Anyhow, what can I do for you . . . er, them? You *are* going to stay and give me a hand, ain't you, Padre?"

"John, I wouldn't miss this transaction for the world." Rodriguez grinned.

Two days later, Luke got a phone call from Rodriguez. He was anxious to talk, so Luke agreed to an afternoon appointment. He spent the rest of the morning halfheartedly trying to finish up a number of details cluttering his desk.

Around lunchtime, Peter returned from doing research in the law library in Houston. Dripping wet, he plopped down on a cane chair next to Luke's desk. He wiped his brow with an exaggerated groan, and Luke pushed the remaining papers on his desk into a heap before looking up.

"What're you moaning about?"

"The heat! Have you been outside?"

"Nope, but I got to get something to eat or I'll likely fall over long before sundown."

"I got a couple of sandwiches from Halsey's right here." Peter grunted, reaching toward the floor beside the chair.

Luke grabbed the bag and extracted one of the sandwiches. Peter took his own, placed it carefully on the corner of the big desk, and pushed his chair back to head for the rear, pausing to ask Luke what he wanted to drink.

"I feel like a beer."

Peter disappeared into the rear office. He returned with a beer and a Coke, sat down, and popped the two cans open. "This place has been pretty dull lately. We could use something interesting."

"Peter, my boy, a law office is *supposed* to be dull," Luke informed him. "Me, I like dull. I like it a lot. But I'm afraid we may have seen the last of it for a while."

He took a huge bite out of his sandwich and chewed with hardly a sound, watching his bewildered assistant with amusement. Peter looked at him quizzically a moment, shrugged, and turned to his own sandwich. Luke took a long pull on the beer and leaned back into his big leather chair, with its arms long since worn to suede. For a moment, he looked as if he were going to say something, but, as if he'd thought better of it, he took another sip of the beer and reached again for his sandwich, chewing with a thoughtful expression and a faraway look in his eyes.

When lunch was finished, Peter returned to his own desk, to sort through documents and photocopies, affixing the latter to the former with butterfly clips. As Peter worked, he couldn't get his mind off Luke's cryptic comment. Luke's foreboding contradicted his own recent sense of ease. He tried to recall whether any unusual business had come to his attention in the last few days, but drew a blank. Unable to concentrate, and ill disposed to study or browse through Luke's well-thumbed but extensive law library, he decided to take a walk. He preferred the stifling heat of the afternoon to the stuffy tranquillity of the office.

"Where the hell you going?" Luke growled, from behind his desk.

"I don't feel much like working."

"That sun is mean, son. It'll most likely cook your head, instead of clearing it." Luke laughed. Then he continued, more seriously. "That ain't it, is it? You feeling a little spooked by what I said earlier, ain't you?"

165

"Some, I guess."

"Well, I didn't mean to go and get you all upset, son," he said kindly. "But you know how I am, always fussing about something. I guess I was just shooting from the hip again, is all."

"No, you weren't, Luke. That's not your style. Something's going on, and you either know what it is or have a good idea."

The attorney looked thoughtful, not quite meeting Peter's gaze. He sighed and turned to the young man.

"Hell, I guess there's no point in keeping secret what, in all likelihood, is already yesterday's news around here. It might concern you more than most, so you might as well know as much as I do. Pull up a chair." Luke leaned back in his own, which creaked and squealed under his weight, and spun to face the open door.

"You know Al, Father Rodriguez?"

"The priest? Yeah, or, rather, I know who he is. I don't know him personally, if that's what you mean. Why?"

"I bumped into him a couple of days ago, in Halsey's," Luke said, pausing to let some significance, which totally escaped Peter, sink in. "He wasn't alone, either."

"So, who was with him?" Peter demanded.

"We have some new folks in town, some Vietnamese. I met two of 'em already, like I said. Not only are they planning to stay, but they're planning to shrimp. If somebody around here gets it into his head that he's got to do something about it, then I don't know what's likely to happen."

"Why should anything happen?" Peter asked.

"I don't think anything will. I'm just afraid it might. There's potential for ugly feelings here."

"I don't know, Luke," Peter argued. "It sounds to me like a self-fulfilling prophecy. I mean, just discussing what might happen is likely to give some people the idea that it ought to."

"Son, if there's one thing doesn't need encouragement, it's an ornery cuss with time on his hands. We got plenty of those around here now. You get a bunch of new fishermen in here, Vietnamese or no, and we're gonna have more than we know what to do with."

"So what you're saying is we sit on our hands and hope nothing happens."

"I'm not saying things can't be changed. I'm only saying *I* can't do it. Al Rodriguez maybe can, though, and I've got to try to convince him to do it. Al is not only in favor of the Vietnamese coming here, but he's behind it. He's a man with a mission, and won't see the danger, because he can't allow himself to see it. No missionary worth his salt ever got anything done thinking that way."

"Well, you can try to make him understand, can't you? Maybe he'll listen."

"Maybe. But if he won't, and I don't expect he will, then I don't know what the hell we'll do." Luke trailed off in sepulchral solemnity. He reached into his desk for a cigar and snipped it with the wire cutters he used as a paperweight. Puffing while the match flame rose and fell, he watched Peter out of the corner of his eye.

What concerned Luke most was the possibility that David might somehow be dragged into the situation. It was all but certain that one of the brothers would somehow become involved, and Luke preferred it to be Peter. It would be painful for him, but for David the implications were far more complex and potentially devastating.

David wasn't over the war, and he'd have to make the same painful decision again, this time complicated by the knowledge that no decision was the right one, but that inaction was worse than either choice. Before Luke had sorted through his options, Al Rodriguez, sans collar, burst through the glare in the doorway, momentarily throwing a shadow over Peter's face.

"So," the priest began jovially, "this is how you lawyers earn those fat fees you bleed out of everybody, eh? What a soft job!"

"How do, Al." Luke laughed. "You know Peter Hodges, don't you?"

"Never had the pleasure. How are you, Peter? Nice to meet you. When did you get back?"

"Father," Peter mumbled. "About six weeks ago, I guess. Wasn't it, Luke?" he asked, looking to the older man for confirmation.

"Lucas," the priest said, abruptly changing the subject, "you've known me a long time, and if there's anything I can't stand, it's wasting time."

He looked meaningfully at Peter, but Luke said, "You can talk in front of Peter, Al. If he plays his cards right, he just might inherit this practice in a few years. He ain't a lawyer yet, but if he's dumb enough to want to be one, he's smart enough to be a good one."

"Sorry, Peter. I just don't want to do too much talking in front of the wrong people."

"That's okay, Father. Luke was filling me in before you got here, but I don't think he finished."

"The fact is, I don't know all of it myself. I'm trying to make something happen that can happen in a lot of ways. What I want is for it to happen in the best way possible."

"I hope it *is* possible, Al," Luke said.

"Well, that's part of the problem, Lucas," Rodriguez confessed. "I have an idea, but that's about all I have. I guess I want you to tell me whether I have a chance of making it work."

"For a guy who doesn't like wasting time, you're sure

taking your sweet time getting to the point."

"Okay. I thought some of the Vietnamese refugees ought to resettle here. A lot of them are Catholic, and I figured there was no reason I shouldn't try to do something for them."

"Why you, Al?" Luke asked.

"Agencies can only do so much. I can't sit back and do nothing. As long as these people aren't going to be welfare cases, the government will help with their resettlement. But only if they have an invitation and a job."

"But why here, Al?" Luke insisted.

"Look, Lucas. The people you met are fishermen, as I told you. They know how to live off the sea, and that's about the only way *anybody* can live around here. This place is ideal for them. They know how to fish, fishing is *the* industry here, so what could be better?"

"But, like I told you, Al, there's only so much shrimp to go around."

"Lucas, Lucas," the priest said in exasperation, "we are talking about six or eight families, at best. That's all! Maybe twenty-five or thirty people. How can that hurt?"

"Come on, Al. You know damn well how it goes. Every damn nationality, yours and mine included, did the same damn thing. As soon as they got established, they sent for their families. What makes you think the Vietnamese are any different?"

"Lucas, this is *not* the same. These people didn't leave their homes looking for a better life; they were running for their lives. Even if we owe them nothing more than simple human charity, we do owe them that. And, by God, I'll make sure they get it!"

"You think the Irish weren't running for *their* lives? Or the Russian Jews? Don't you see? It's *exactly* the same thing. Al, you know I'm not questioning your motives—only your wisdom. Nobody ought to suffer any more'n they have to, and these folks have had more'n their share, but you have to be realistic. Otherwise, we'll have another Vietnam War, right here in our own backyard. And I don't have to tell you who'll win, do I?"

They were raising their voices with each exchange, and Peter recognized in them the halves of himself. More than once, he was tempted to join in, now on the priest's side, now on the lawyer's, but the idiocy of the conflict paralyzed him. This time, in confronting the insoluble, he was capable of nothing, not even flight.

"Al," Luke said softly, after a brief lull in the dispute, "as God is my witness, I hope you know what you're doing. I'll help you every way I can, but I don't believe you stand a snowball's chance in hell. I hope I'm wrong, and, if I can summon the gall, I'll even *pray* I am. But I'm *not* wrong, I just hope the worst that can happen doesn't."

"Lucas," the priest said, smiling, "do you honestly think you've raised a single objection I haven't raised a thousand times? I've walked the floor. I've prayed all night more nights than I care to remember. I still don't see that I have a choice."

"But were you prepared to *be* convinced otherwise?"

"Yes, I was. The only reason I didn't discuss it with *you* sooner is that, deep down inside, where it really counts, you believe that I'm doing the right thing. And I believe that, in my shoes, you would do exactly as I have done. There is no other moral choice to be made, Lucas."

"You son of a gun, Al." Luke chuckled. He shook his head and turned to Peter, a half-smile on his face, and said, "You know, Petey, I suspect the padre here should have been a Jesuit, instead of some backwater parish priest. He knows every trick in the book, and when none of 'em works, he flatters hell out of you. But he sure gets his own way, doesn't he?"

Peter smiled wanly, strangely less resilient than the two older men. He excused himself and walked out into the late-afternoon heat, the wind ruffling his hair. He sat on the bench in front of Luke's office, trying to shut out the murmur of the two men inside. He knew that, for the moment, everyone concerned would concentrate on the petty formalities of property acquisition, citizenship applications, and so on, and that the real threat, having been acknowledged, however grudgingly by the priest and with whatever foreboding by the lawyer, would be pushed aside in the hope it would never be more than a groundless fear. As the men continued talking, their voices drifting through the window behind him, Peter didn't notice the slight breeze kicking up around him, or the clouds drifting between himself and the sun, dampening the sharp light in the deserted street.

15

LUKE knew the biggest obstacle to Al Rodriguez's plan was the priest's own reckless enthusiasm. To persuade him to be cautious, he'd have to lead him without seeming to. After their initial discussion, Luke spent most of the night considering alternatives. After innumerable false starts and incalculable cups of coffee, he decided to use Peter as his emissary to the priest. He wasn't comfortable with the idea, but justified it by the legal experience it would give him. Although he trusted Peter's capacity to think on his feet, he wrestled with the fear that he might get him into something uncontrollable. It was one thing to ask Peter to monitor the niggling legal details of immigration and small-business enterprise, another to send him, blindly, into a potential maelstrom.

Rather than content himself with an hour of restless

sleep, Luke put on another pot of coffee and wandered out back to watch the sun rise. The sky was graying rapidly as he sat in his swing. The single visible star disappeared before he could prop his feet on the porch railing. When younger, this had been his favorite time of day. It had been a long time since he had permitted himself the simple joy of watching the sun come up.

To quiet the tingling nerves at the back of his neck, he made his plans. He knew he could appeal to the priest's sense of community, the strength of which was precipitating the current crisis. Because of his own minority membership, Rodriguez placed social obligation high on his priority list. It would be difficult to muzzle him, but the situation called, above all else, for restraint. As with many of the best intentioned, Rodriguez seemed to lose sight of small inhumanities under his nose when absorbed in grander tragedies. Not that he would sacrifice his parishioners for the sake of immigrants, but he might not even recognize it *was* a sacrifice.

Rodriguez had a dangerous blind spot: the economic condition of the fishermen who constituted the bulk of his parish. Those who were not directly involved in catching the small fish were engaged in either its packaging or its transportation. While the last two groups would not necessarily suffer because of the influx of Vietnamese, they had an allegiance to those who might. Fiercely loyal, most of them wouldn't even see a choice to be made. Exceptions fell into two categories: those who, like the Hodges brothers, had experience of the war and its consequences in human terms, and those who, like Halsey and Kevin McIlhenny, were more thoughtful than most but, by nature or inclination, unlikely to get involved.

The coffee, which had given up calling attention to itself

by sound, now assaulted Luke's nose. Getting up reluctantly, he shut it off and left it to cool without pouring another cup.

He realized there was another exception: Doc Roth, who was probably unique. An outsider himself, even more skeptical than Luke, Doc was an interesting unknown in the current equation. If he sided with the Vietnamese, he'd have no influence on most of the town, even those who accepted him, like Halsey, or felt they needed him, like some of the minority fishermen.

He belonged to Witman by choice, and could leave as easily as he'd come. He would be less an antagonist than an irrelevance. Luke wasn't even certain Doc would have an opinion. He'd been trying to seem as natural to Witman as the torrid summers. Taking sides was something he might prefer not to do. Luke decided to feel him out, hoping in some quiet and as yet unforeseeable way he might play an influential role in the days ahead.

Luke stepped off the porch into the yellowish grass behind the house. He walked heavily, almost in a daze, toward where the sun would be coming up. As he drew away from the house, his step became more determined. He believed the worst miscalculation was preferable to the paralysis of passivity.

As he headed down toward the Bay, the immensity of the rising sun, twice its size at high noon, appeared to be growing, gorging on the edge of the sea, inexorably gnawing its way toward him. In the face of so huge a thing, Luke was incapable of crediting humanity with much more than marginal value. The daily cycle had gone on for billions of years. There was no reason to believe man could disturb it, let alone destroy it. If someone or something had created all of this, the human race wasn't much more than an afterthought, an expendable grace note in a symphony so overpowering its absence would be missed by no one but the composer, who couldn't care less.

Luke found himself thinking of Maggie Riley. He'd always admired her single-minded insistence on dealing with life on its own terms. She never whined and never wavered. He had met her once years ago on one of his morning rambles. She had been alone on a high dune, so much of a piece with the surrounding sweep that it occurred to him the dune might have been designed for her, that it had been intended from the onset of creation that she one day sit there. It was as if the entire cosmos turned on this jewel of a woman, like the workings of a gargantuan watch pivoting on a single ruby.

He had watched her for a few moments, debating whether or not to interrupt her and, having decided not to, was turning to leave when she said, "Luke, are you going to sit, or not?"

He hadn't known she was aware of him, didn't know how she could have been, yet he wasn't startled by her voice, which seemed at that moment a part of the natural order. Without turning, she patted the sand to her right, and Luke struggled up the interminable side of her pinnacle to sit beside her.

For a long time neither spoke, Maggie intent on whatever had been absorbing her before his arrival, and Luke in awe of the woman and the setting and, especially, the imposing silence of the water that shimmered in the bright red glare as far as he could see. When, finally, Maggie broke her silence, and the spell it had woven, she said only, "Luke, it's been a pleasure."

That was all, yet Luke came away feeling she had poured out her heart to him. Somehow, in that simple exchange, he had learned more about her than he could have from weeks of conversation.

Thinking back on that moment, Luke now realized that, if anyone could help him avert catastrophe, it was Maggie. The more he thought about it, the more natural it seemed. He couldn't imagine how he had overlooked it until now. Despite making her way in what was generally regarded as the province of rugged men, or perhaps because of it, Maggie had considerable clout with the other shrimpers. It was as if they admired her because she had overcome not only the sea but also their own reluctance to accept her. There was nothing deferential or condescending in their respect. It was simply that, in their view, she had done as well as anyone, and far better than many, against vastly greater odds. In a way, they took guidance from her in some mutually unacknowledged pact.

On the other hand, their problem and hers were the same, and Maggie might feel as threatened by the Vietnamese, and as anxious to see them fail or leave, as any of the more volatile fishermen. If he kept the shrimpers off balance and persuaded her to remain noncommittal, he'd have a chance. If she'd join him, he could win. Whether he could do either remained to be seen, but the possibility gave him hope. Luke had faith that Maggie's essential humanity wouldn't throw her into the opposing camp, at least not immediately. It would give him time. He made a note to see her that afternoon, if possible, and looked up from his contemplation just in time to see the sun emerge, a brilliant, oblate red egg, smearing a broad swath to the edge of the sand—bright as a cardinal's wing, he thought . . . or blood.

Luke also realized it was important to involve Peter as soon as possible. He needed the younger man's emotional perspective and to establish him as someone the Vietnamese could trust. One man couldn't be everywhere at once, and he doubted that even two would be enough. But, for the moment, two was all he had. Al Rodriguez would help where and when he could, but the priest's time was seldom his own.

He'd take Peter over to the rectory that afternoon. Then, if all went well, they'd see the two men he'd met in Halsey's store. He worried that it might be difficult to control Peter's impulsiveness, and they couldn't afford a single mistake. The smallest gap in their logic could cause exactly the kind of trouble he most feared.

And involving Peter might cause another run-in between Pat and David. Pat had obviously been trying to provoke one when he attacked Peter. The last thing Luke wanted was for the affair to turn into a grudge match between them. His first concern had to be for the Vietnamese. Thousands of miles from a culture they could lean on, they would be helpless without a guide through the intricacies ahead.

Sitting there now, alone on the sand, which had never really cooled down from the previous day's heat, he felt as though he were stranded in an alien country. The loneliness gave him a peculiar empathy with his new clients. It was hard to imagine such turmoil revolving around a small fish that would, in any but an economy that depended on it, be either ignored or deemed pestilentially prolific.

Glancing at his watch, Luke saw that he had just enough time to change and get over to Peter's, on the pretext of driving him to work. If he was lucky, he'd also catch David at home. He hurried back through the saw grass, smacking at sandflies beginning to buzz in the tall weeds. Nailing one on the back of his neck, he swore to himself, and ground it into dust. Once inside, he took a perfunctory shower and dressed hurriedly.

He drove without his customary caution. When he reached the turnoff to the Hodges place, the car lurched as it nosed into the narrower road. He didn't blink as the speedometer fluttered near seventy. Braking as he drew near the house, he tore into the gravel driveway with a shower of stones. Out of the car before the engine stopped turning over, he was on the porch before the tick of the cooling engine had begun.

David met Luke at the door and gave him an odd look as he stepped aside to let him in.

"If I didn't know better, Luke, I'd swear you were practicing to chase ambulances," David said. "Something wrong, or you planning to try the NASCAR circuit?"

Luke laughed weakly before responding. "No, nothing's wrong. I just figured I'd drop by and give Petey a lift. I had to hurry so's not to miss him. I didn't, did I?"

As David was about to answer, Peter stepped out of the kitchen, fixing his employer with the same stare of curiosity with which David had greeted him. "Something wrong?"

"No, no, nothing's wrong. Just wanted to make sure I didn't miss you, that's all."

"Luke's getting on, Petey," David said. "He forgot you have your own car."

"Well, then, pull up a seat," Peter said.

"All right," Luke agreed. Turning to David, he asked, "You going to join us, David, or do you have to leave?"

"I'm off for a couple of days. Something tells me there's more on your mind than giving a ride to a man who owns a car."

Luke ignored the implicit question and pulled a chair up to the table. David and Peter sat across from him.

"So," Peter asked, "what's *really* on your mind?"

Before responding, Luke reached for the spoon in a half-empty cup of coffee in front of him, staring into the dark swirl for a few moments as he considered how to begin. This was the start of what could be a long, difficult project.

It had to be broached with care, making certain the brothers fully realized the intricacies of the situation into which they were about to be drawn.

When Luke looked up, the brothers were watching him intently, as if they knew *what* he was going to say, but not how. They seemed as anxious as he to get it into the open, as if naming their trouble was the most difficult step to its solution. But, before he could begin, David broke the silence.

"It wouldn't happen to be about the new folks in town, by any chance, would it?"

"New folks?" Luke asked, taken off his guard.

"Yeah," David continued. "The new folks. The Vietnamese."

"Well, uh . . . actually . . ." Luke stammered, "it does sort of concern them. At least indirectly . . ."

"Indirectly, huh?" David smiled. "Luke, I've known you for a long time. Don't you think I can tell what's on your mind?"

"I suppose I might as well get right to it."

"Might as well," David agreed. "But just because I have an idea what you're up to, don't think I'll have anything to do with any scheme. I've had enough of Vietnam to last a lifetime."

"I know that." Luke nodded. "I know you have. Yet and still, you might not have much to say about it. . . ."

The sky was low enough to touch, and thick air clung to the skin like jelly. David never got used to the claustrophobic humidity so much a part of the climate here. When it threatened to squeeze the air out of his lungs, he liked to go down to the edge of the sea. Vietnam had been that way, too, but there was more than moisture in the air to worry about. Oddly, at the shore, where the sand and the tall dry grass spoke of aridity, the sea excused the excessive moisture. The beach air seemed dry compared to the spray from the modest rollers. It was so different from the astounding crash at Wildwood. Visiting one of his Camp Lejeune barracks mates before shipping out, he couldn't get enough of the solitary thunder. While Ralph crawled the raucous shore town every night, David had walked alone on the desolate beach, away from the dives and screaming boardwalk. *It's party time, baby. Let's do it!* Ralph was gone now, and he couldn't look at the sea without thinking of him.

A touch of the sweet melancholia that colored that week swept over him at the memory. He never heard pounding waves without recalling it and the serenity it fostered, despite the countless beaches and numberless kinds of thunder he had known since. Ralph—well, that was something else. He didn't want to think about that at all. Tonight the feeling was different, more precise, as if he were feeling it for the first time. It was immediate, strange yet strangely familiar, like some primeval disposition, waiting for the right combination of emotion and experience to revive it. On his feet, reaching for his cigarettes and lighter, he was heading for the sea before he knew he was going anywhere.

Once on the porch, the overwhelming darkness came as a shock. The sky had been gray, pasted with thick clouds that seemed more threatening than they were, as if a different kind of breaker were cresting miles above him. It probably would rain, rain like hell for a while, but nothing would change when the rain had spent itself.

David was undeterred by the prospect of getting wet, even drenched. Some of his happiest moments had been spent in a teeming downpour, soaked to the skin and chilled by insistent winds. There was something restorative about such storms. He knew he was hoping it *would* rain, partly to reduce the oppressive humidity, but mostly because he needed the elusive feeling of forgiveness.

Luke had upset him. Not Luke, and not the substance of his news, but the inevitable, logical extension of that news. He knew, had always known, that the war wasn't over for him. He wasn't sure it ever would be. It had followed him home, always there at the ends of his nerves, waiting for something to rekindle the terror. A flash of light, even a sudden firefly, might be enough.

As often as he had considered that past, like a child examining the first butterfly he ever caught, he never failed to discover some previously unseen nuance of color, an unexplored pocket of brilliance or darkness, which cast the whole in an entirely new light. Then he'd have to start again, to see how different the new perception was, and what it did to his earlier assessment. And always he felt that just one more piece was all he needed to fit the puzzle of his conduct together so he could nod and say, "Yes, *that's* it. . . ." Then he could close his mind's eye for the night, knowing that when he woke the next morning, and every morning thereafter, the pieces would still fit.

More than once, he'd achieved what he thought to be the final explanation, only to shatter it himself as he drifted off, seeing a bright flash that demolished the neat arrangement so painstakingly assembled. It was again nothing more than a jumble of discrete parts, components that defied formal assembly. He would lie, cold sweat on his forehead, his mouth agape, as if expelling a silent, agonizing vacuum that sucked everything out of him. It roared away in the dark as quickly as it came, leaving him drained in the soaking sheets, to toss the rest of the night.

He envied others their certainty. It couldn't be contradicted, couldn't be killed, except in the real world. But they carried everything inside self-sustaining enclosures.

181

Like every self-contained system, David knew, these were vulnerable, could be ruptured by the unforeseen. But he wished he could be as indifferent, as willing to risk that vulnerability for the peace that came with the sense of imperviousness, no matter how fragile.

He didn't notice the first rain. Startled back to the present by a particularly bright flash of lightning, and a clap of thunder, he thought his eardrums had ruptured. The lightning had struck nearby, because the thunder had been nearly simultaneous. The acrid smell of ozone bit at his nostrils and constricted his chest. Very near the beach, he thought about turning back. But, soaked through, he decided it was pointless. The rapid scud of the clouds told him the worst of the storm would soon be over. The rain was already slackening, and though it would continue for a while, the lightning had probably spent itself, sky and sand having restored their precarious electrical equilibrium. The diffuse flashes behind the clouds posed no threat, and the distant rumble of the thunder was subdued and vague.

Continuing toward the beach, he nearly stumbled at the foot of the first of several dunes that gradually lowered toward the shoreline. Climbing was easier than usual. The rain-thickened sand was covered by a dark crust that gave beneath his feet with a barely audible crunch, leaving gaping, doughy holes in staggered, straggling strings behind him. On its top, a few tufts of stiff grass clung in defiance of the brisk winds. David paused to catch his breath. Out over the Bay, the trailing edge of the storm was marked by patches of naked sky darker than the grayish clouds, so thick just minutes before. He heard the water slapping at the sand more vigorously than usual, but it was still hidden behind tiers of sand.

The heaving in his chest subsided quickly, and David

pushed down the front of the last dune, his feet slipping forward in his haste, as if the sea were pulling him, as forceful and unseen as gravity. He could see the gray green foam of the waves and hear their hiss as they ebbed away, leaving a jumble of seaweed and flotsam in broad arcs of clearly discernible darker sand slowly paling as the water leached through and seeped back to the sea.

Here and there, in the darker sand, he could see nearly dissolved lumps tossed up by the feet of someone who had passed by within minutes. Each print was now little more than a low mound and gentle depression, indicating the direction of travel. The prints were small, and closely spaced, indicating a leisurely pace. Curious, David set off in the same direction, wondering who else was out walking on such a night. He had no need to hurry, since his stride was nearly double that of his quarry, who could not be too far ahead of him. The now feeble lightning afforded no opportunity to see who it might be. He considered calling out, but if the person was as jealous of solitude as he, a call would only spur him to preserve it.

For a second, he thought it might be Kate. They had often walked on the beach late at night before he went overseas, but she was always uneasy at the overwhelming quiet, and the darkness drove her to endless chatter, trying to ward off whatever it was that gave her the feeling she could only describe as "spooky." It wasn't likely Kate would be out alone when she'd not been at ease even with him along.

With a shattering explosion, a flash of lightning struck somewhere behind him, so close that light and thunder were indeed simultaneous. He realized he was prostrate on the sand. There was a roaring in his ears and silence all around him. His eyes wouldn't focus. As the roar faded to a distant hiss, he heard, "David?"

There was a second, more distant, explosion, but he was half buried in the sand even before its echo had died. Hands clasped over the back of his head, he ground one cheek into the gritty beach. He felt a dull ache, which he knew must be from a small shell digging into his flesh. There was a burst of rain, and he heard moaning. He strained to recognize the voice before the rasping of his throat told him it was his own. Then he heard the first voice again, this time closer. "David, is that you?"

It was a familiar voice, one he knew but couldn't place. It didn't belong on a rainy beach in Texas. As he started to raise his head, to pull himself away from the sand, he felt hands on his shoulders, tugging at him, as if trying to save him from slipping beneath the surface of the beach. And then, almost as if he recognized the hands, he knew the voice, somehow defying time and geography to find him at this moment. He struggled to his knees, still reeling from the shock of his collapse.

It had finally happened to him, just as they had warned him it would, and despite his conviction that it would not, because he knew it was coming and it could not surprise him, and, mostly, because he would not let it. He had been thrown back into the jungles of Vietnam. Time and circumstance had conspired to remind him of the hundreds of times he had thrown himself on the mercy of the earth, clawing at the soil and the grass, or burrowing in the mud, to escape the bizarre, beautiful light slavering around him, followed by hot metal and an unearthly roar, so awful he knew he'd never hear again.

He screamed, staring at the sky that had played so cruel a joke on him, and rose against the pressure of the hands. He tore himself free and turned to see who sought to restrain him and, with a gasp, saw that he had been right.

"Nancy, you!... What are you doing... here? How

did you get here? What . . ." His surprise wrenched question after question from him, pushing him on from one to the next before the woman could answer the first. She watched him, then, with a swift, graceful gesture, placed a finger over his lips.

"Ssshh, David. Sssshh," she cooed, as if to a child. She brushed the sand from his cheeks and pushed sand-clotted hair from his eyes. Standing back, she waited for him to calm down before answering.

"What are you *doing* here?" he asked again, this time more in wonder than surprise. "I didn't know you were . . ." He paused, unsure what it was he didn't know, and fell back to his knees, his shoulders sagging under a sudden weight.

"I live here," she said, watching his face to see whether he understood her and if so, what it meant to him.

He stared at her as if she had spoken in a foreign language. She repeated it, this time more slowly. As she spoke, there was a series of dull flashes, barely noticeable after the blazing thunder that had thrown him to the beach. Her face and slender figure were periodically outlined against the sky, and there was no room for doubt, no matter how slight, how lingeringly suspicious, that it was she.

"I live here now, in Texas, with my mother and my brothers."

"When . . . how long have you been here?"

"About two weeks, I think." She paused uncertainly. "I have not been able to tell time very well for a long time now. Not since . . ."

"Why didn't you let me know?" David demanded, sitting up abruptly, brushing away the hands fluttering about his face.

"I . . . I didn't know you were here. I . . ."

"You didn't know I was here? I *live* here. Where did

185

you think I'd be?" David said harshly. "This is my *home!*"

The woman didn't answer. Instead, she got to her feet and stared out over the waves, which were beginning to diminish in their savagery despite the continuing rain and the distant, ominous rumble that followed every subtle flash of illumination. She wheeled toward him, but before she could speak, he cut her off.

"You didn't want me to know you were here, did you? Why?"

"No, it's not that. It's . . ." She trailed off, as if she couldn't decide quite how to say something, or whether she wanted to say it at all. "I . . ." she began again, only to shake her head violently and turn back to the sea.

"Nancy," David said, his voice now softer. "Tell me, please. I won't be angry. Just tell me, please?"

"How do you know you won't be angry unless you know what I want to say?" she whispered. It sounded more sorrowful than bitter.

"How could I be angry if you were telling me the truth?"

"You haven't changed, have you, David? You still think the truth is more important than people, don't you? More important than their feelings. Yours. Mine . . . You think the truth is more important than anything else in the world, don't you?" She turned to face him, her lips trembling, warring with the tightness of her jaw. "Don't you?"

"Nancy . . . the truth is all there is. You *know* that!"

"Do I, David? Then why do I have so much trouble believing it? Why is it so much harder for me to accept than it is for you?"

She started walking, slowly scuffing her bare feet in the sand, moving down the beach. She turned back to him, as if suddenly finding the will or the words she had been looking for, but said nothing. He got slowly to his feet, and as he bent to brush the wet sand from his jeans, she turned away again, this time to run down the beach, her long hair too heavy with rain to fly behind her as he had seen it so many times before, on another beach.

Stunned by her flight, and his understanding of what it meant, he stared after her for the time it took her to disappear in the night, more slowly but no less mysteriously than she had appeared before him minutes earlier. When his straining eyes could no longer pick her out of the darkness, he sank back to his knees with a groan and buried his face in his hands, not feeling the harsh grit of the damp sand still clinging to his palms. He heard only the distant thunder, and the wind in the tall grass behind him. There was another, greater, difference between this time and all those other times, one he knew instinctively, before he took his first step in pursuit. This time, he knew, she did not want him to catch her.

16

PETER spent more energy on his work with the Vietnamese than Luke could have hoped. After meeting with Rodriguez, they had agreed their first priority should be helping the immigrants become self-supporting. Peter introduced himself to the newcomers with some misgivings. He was frightened by the enormity of their problems. Some were simple fishermen and farmers, others white-collar workers who hadn't a prayer of getting similar employment until they learned English, if then.

Focusing on the language issue, Peter convinced Luke that an English class was essential. Rodriguez volunteered the church basement, but persuading the people to attend was more difficult. For many, English was the language of nightmares. Most couldn't hear it spoken without being displaced in time, and ten thousand miles, to a place where English had to be shouted to be heard at all, and bellowed into the ear to be understood. Even for those who were fluent, it was a tongue of fire and smoke that taught them to run for cover. They instinctively did so now, and shrank from the notion of learning it.

Peter did find allies among the Vietnamese, who saw things differently. No less scarred by their experiences, they yet knew English was their key to survival. Fishing might put food on the table, but it would take more than that to buy the table. Van Ngo Dong, an accountant in Saigon, was Peter's most vocal advocate. Of the thirty-five Vietnamese now living in Witman, Dong was one of the few who had more than a rudimentary command of English. He would be coteacher.

Within weeks, the school held its first class. Attendance was sparse, mostly children, and Peter was disappointed. It was essential, of course, that the children learn, but the adults were the key. It was they who had the most immediate need, and if they turned their backs on the school, the children wouldn't attend for very long.

In the hastily improvised classroom, Peter sat in one corner while Dong explained to the small turnout why the classes were important. He urged everyone not only to work hard, but also to convince others to attend. The students sat on folding chairs, flimsy notebooks spread out on long cafeteria tables normally used for bazaars and church suppers. While a green chalkboard teetered on three chairs behind him, in impassioned Vietnamese Dong pleaded with the students to apply themselves.

Peter was pessimistic about the school's possibilities. For most of the kids, it was their first formal education, makeshift though it was. The experience was alien, its purpose a murky shadow hastily sketched by relatives and now zealously, if somewhat mystically, intoned by Dong. In what Peter took to be a formal introduction of himself as the English teacher, Dong concluded and nodded in his direction. Peter stood and walked over to the chalkboard. He looked at the blank faces before him, turned to the board, and stopped, seeing there was no chalk on the ledge. He looked about helplessly. Dong looked quizzically back at him.

"There's no chalk."

"Behind the board, Mr. Hodges. There should be a box. I bought it myself this morning."

Peter pulled the board forward, withdrew the box, and, his back still to the class, removed two pieces. The students watched expectantly, as if he were about to begin a magic act. Thinking it would be that at least, and more likely a miracle, if he pulled it off, he cleared his throat and introduced himself.

"I am Peter Hodges. I mean . . . my name is Peter Hodges. I . . . I want . . . This is going to be a very important class for you all, and I want it to be . . ." He stopped, realizing he didn't know whether anyone other than Dong understood him. He looked again at the accountant.

"Do . . . do any of them speak any English at all?"

"Ask them, Mr. Hodges."

Peter cleared his throat again and turned back to the class, to ask, "Do any of you speak English?" Three or four heads—he wasn't sure—nodded, which he took for assent and felt emboldened. Ready to plunge forward, he stopped as the door opened. A young woman stepped through, pulled it closed behind her, and said, "Excuse me. I'm sorry I'm late." She walked toward the front of the room, appearing to glide on tiptoe, and sat in a vacant chair toward one side.

With his fragile momentum dissipated, Peter looked at the young woman. She appeared to be about twenty-five, with the longest, blackest hair he had ever seen. Her face, a delicate oval, had the pale cast of a Chinese painting. It was, he thought, the most perfect face he had ever seen.

"You haven't missed anything," he said. "I was just about to start. I mean, I guess I was about to start. I'm not sure."

"I'm sorry for interrupting you."

His composure now completely deserted him. Not knowing what else to do, he turned to the chalkboard and wrote his name in shaky block letters that seemed barely discernible against the pale green of the board. Regaining his balance, he turned back to the class.

"As I was saying, do any of you speak English?"

The same heads bobbed, joined this time by that of the newcomer, confirming his first impression. "In that case, I want you to understand what we're trying to do here. The work will be easier for you, but you will have to help those who don't understand, until it becomes easier for them. Mr. Dong is going to help me, of course, and . . . and, well, this is the most important class you will have. I hope, eventually . . . later, you will move on to the local school, and maybe college. But those schools won't help unless you can understand what is being said in the classroom. That's why we're here. And with any luck, we won't be here long. That will be up to you, all of you, but especially those of you who understand some English already."

Over his nerves, at least for the moment, Peter spent the rest of the evening learning the names of the students and, with the help of Dong as translator, outlining the rudiments of English grammar. As the class drew to a close, he gave each student a grammar book. Al Rodriguez had hustled three dozen copies of an introductory textbook from a friend who was principal at a Catholic elementary school in Houston.

When he had completed distributing the books, Peter announced, "I know that these books are useless to many

191

of you now, but please take care of them. They will be very important in the next few weeks. I'll see you again on Wednesday at the same time. Please tell your friends about the class, and thank you for coming."

Dong repeated the announcement. Then, with a scrape of shoes and squeak of sneakers, they were gone, leaving only Peter, Dong, and the woman who had arrived late. They folded the chairs and stacked them, upended the tables, collapsed their legs, and carried everything into the boiler room. They worked silently, Peter stealing an occasional glance at the young woman. She had introduced herself as Nguyen Thi Hoa during the class, and said that everyone called her Nancy.

When they had finished, Peter was anxious for their impressions of the class. "It didn't go too well, did it?" he asked.

"It will get better," Dong assured him.

"I don't know. I'm not a teacher—as if you couldn't tell."

"I was always told," Dong said, "that the most important quality in a teacher is the desire to give learning to others. You have that, certainly. You mustn't be too hard on yourself. The confidence will come in time."

"That's the problem. I don't *have* time. If I lose these people, they'll never come back. I have to make them want to be here so they'll get others to come, even if only out of curiosity."

"Don't worry. They know how important it is. Even those who did not come tonight know, especially those who were educated already. They know they need English to make something of this opportunity. They are frightened, and many of them see this as their last chance. Perhaps it is, but all the more reason for them to learn."

During this exchange, the woman said nothing. She

192

seemed to ignore the conversation, as if it were one she shouldn't overhear. Peter turned to her, and asked, "What do you think, Nancy?"

"I think Dong is right. I think everyone wants this to work. But you have to be patient. If they see you are taking them seriously, they will be here. You have to understand how difficult it has been for them. There have been too many false hopes, too many unfulfilled promises. They want to be certain this is not another, before they allow themselves to hope. Do you understand?"

"Yes. I think so."

"You must not think so. You must understand. I know you want to, but that isn't enough. You must *do* it."

"You make it sound so desperate," Peter said.

"It is."

Dong nodded in agreement. "We will help you all we can, Mr. Hodges. But it is up to you. If you don't believe in what you are doing, they will know. *We* will know. It would be better to stop now, if that is the case, before too much is expected."

"There's no way I'm going to quit!"

"I hope you understand yourself better than some Americans I have known," Nancy said. "Good night."

David was still shaken by his meeting with Nancy, and his relations with Kate, already strained, deteriorated. Since the encounter on the beach, he and Kate had been fighting more or less constantly. He wondered whether they had any future, whether they still had anything in common, if they ever had. Dinner with Kate and Maggie was supposed to be a chance to relax, clear the air a bit, and be just plain folks for a change.

He still loved Kate. Of that, he had no doubt. But did he love her enough? Enough for what? How much was enough? And did he love Nancy, too? Could that be possible? He had once thought so, and if he did, how long could his emotions be torn between them? Questions, too damn many questions.

As he pulled into Maggie's driveway, he hoped the quiet sense of family Maggie always fostered would put many of those questions to rest once and for all. Turning off the engine, he sat in the car trying to regain a little of the joy with which he had first anticipated the evening. If only he didn't think so much. Kate peeked through the curtains, and he got out of the car, walking slowly to the porch. Kate stepped aside to let him in, and he pecked her on the top of the head as he passed.

"Sorry if I'm late."

"You're not late." Kate smiled. "You know Mother— nothing ever suits her anyway, so we're still deciding how to fold the napkins."

"Can I help?"

"Sure. Let's go to the kitchen."

Kate led the way toward the back of the house, where Maggie was puttering with silverware. She looked up as they entered.

"David," she greeted him, "maybe you know . . . how come they give you so damn many spoons and forks? Why can't folks eat salad with the same damn fork they use on meat and potatoes?"

"You got me, Maggie."

"Well, I'm giving us one fork each. You want another, you know where they are. Sit on down there. I'm about finished."

David sat at the large round table, only partly set, and fiddled with his spoon, while Kate folded paper napkins. Maggie bustled back and forth between stove and table, bringing mashed potatoes, peas, and a huge roast in quick

194

succession. Kate set glasses out. After putting a large pitcher of iced tea on a cork-topped tray in the center of the table, Maggie sat down.

"There, that ought to hold us, don't you think, kids?"

"I don't know, Mother. There's only enough here for twelve."

"Maggie, there's plenty, please, just relax," David said.

"You're a fine one to preach about relaxing," Kate reminded him.

"Just because *I* don't do it, doesn't mean it shouldn't be done."

"If you two are gonna argue, I think I'll eat on the back porch. Anybody'd think you were already married," Maggie said.

"You're right, Maggie," David answered her, looking at Kate. "Why don't we all just have a good meal? I'm leaving for a couple of weeks tomorrow morning. I don't want to be out there thinking about a fight the whole time I'm gone."

"Then shut up and carve the roast," Maggie said, smiling.

David picked up the old, antler-handled carving knife, its blade honed so often it was now a thin sliver of matte-finished steel. With unwarranted concentration, David bent over the meat, carefully cutting thin, still-bloody slices, stacking them on one side of the platter. Maggie took another knife to cut thick slabs of fresh bread, thickly buttered one, then loaded her plate with meat and vegetables. The others followed her lead, although with more restraint, while Maggie poured the iced tea. The only noise was the clink of the ice cubes rearranging themselves in the tumblers.

"How you feel about them Vietnamese coming into town?" Maggie asked, breaking the silence.

"I don't care one way or another, Maggie," David said.

"A lot of folks ain't too happy about it, I can tell you."

"I thought you told me skill made a good shrimper, Maggie. If that's true, we don't have much to worry about. By the time they get the hang of it, they'll seem like they've always been here. Or else they won't figure it out, and they'll move on."

"Maybe so, but I still don't think it's a good idea. And some folks're doing their best to see they do get the hang of it."

"Mother," Kate cut in, "you can't blame David for what Peter does."

"I'm not *blaming* anybody. Peter has a right to do what he wants. I'm just saying it might not be as simple as David thinks, is all."

"Well, *I'm* blaming Peter," Kate said. "He had the gall to ask me to help find them an English teacher. Can you imagine?"

"What did you tell him?" David asked quietly.

"I told him there was no way in hell I would help him. If he cared so much about those people, he could teach them himself. That's what I told him."

"And he is, too," Maggie said. "I kind of admire him for that. But I don't want those people interfering with me making a living. Some of the other shrimpers want to make them leave. I don't hold with that, though. I wish Kevin hadn't rented them that pier, but there's nothing to be done about it. I think we got to make them understand that there ain't enough for everybody. If we can do that, they'll leave by themselves, for sure."

"I don't think so, Maggie," David said.

"Why not? They got to make a living, too, don't they? They'll see how hard it is."

"They've been through rougher things than scrabbling

for some shrimp. I don't think it'll be easy to convince them to give up."

"Well, then, somebody *should* make them leave," Kate snapped.

David looked at her hard, wondering if she meant more than she was saying. Deciding he was overly sensitive, he shrugged it off. "I think we should leave them alone. Let them make up their own minds," he said.

"Since when are you so friendly with Vietnamese, David?" Kate asked.

"I'm not friendly. I'm just not unfriendly," he said sharply.

"Actually, I was hoping you'd be on the committee," Maggie said.

"What committee?"

"Some of the owners are getting together to ask them to leave."

"Are you one of them, Maggie?" David asked.

"Sure am."

"You sound proud of it."

"Not proud. Just determined's all."

"Well, you can count me out," David said. "I had enough of Vietnam and Vietnamese to last a lifetime."

Before Maggie could reply, they heard the front door open. "That'll be Pat," Maggie said.

As he came into the kitchen, Pat tossed his Stetson back into the living room, aiming for, and missing, a hatrack on the wall.

"Evening, folks. You, too, Davey," Pat said. "Looks like I'm in time for supper."

He drew up an empty chair, taking a seat between David and his mother. "I hear you folks talking about the Vietnamese?"

"Yup," Maggie said. "But we're just finished with that, so let's move on to another subject."

"Davey, here, knows a lot about them people. Don't you?" he asked, ignoring Maggie. "Fact is, I hear he's helping his brother with that damn school they got going. That right, Davey?"

"No," David said. "I'm not. I'm just not interfering."

"Same thing," Pat said. "You know, I think . . . Hand me some of that meat, there, would you, Katie. I think you better give that boy a good talking to, before somebody else does."

"What's that supposed to mean," David demanded.

"It means he's gonna get his nose broke, or his neck, if he don't leave well enough alone." Pat smiled. "Believe me, I know what I'm talking about. Some folks is mighty upset about what he's doing."

"That's his affair!"

"It is that," Pat said, nodding agreement. "Course, if somebody decided it was theirs, I guess that'd be okay, too. Wouldn't it?"

"Now hold on, you two," Maggie interrupted. "The dinner table ain't no place for that kind of talk. You boys can argue all you want, but not here, and not now."

"I wasn't arguing, Ma," Pat said. "Just discussing, civilized like. Just like that doctor friend of Davey's would like. Civilized as all get-out, that's me."

David was surprised, and disappointed, that Kate had remained silent during the exchange. She did not agree with Peter's actions, and made it perfectly clear, but that was different. It wasn't his brother being attacked; it was he, and Kate didn't say a word. Suddenly he wasn't hungry. He pushed back from the table and got to his feet.

"I don't think I ought to stay, Maggie," he said. "I'm sorry, but I've lost my appetite."

"David, that's silly," Maggie scolded. "Sit down. Pat will

behave himself, like the gentleman I always wished he could be. Finish your supper."

"I don't think I can, Maggie, really." He looked at Kate, expecting her to try to persuade him to stay, but she stayed silent. Pushing his chair back in, he said, "Don't get up. I'll find my way out." Kate avoided his gaze, but, reluctantly, got to her feet.

Leading the way to the door, she maintained her silence. Out on the porch, she looked at him for a moment, then turned away to look off down the road. "I don't understand you," she said.

"I guess that makes two of us."

"Why do you take Peter's side? Because he's your brother?"

"Nope. A brother can be wrong, like anybody else. Believe me. But maybe Petey's right. Maybe what he's doing is the right thing. Maybe I'm wrong for not helping him."

"That's ridiculous," Kate said. "Is it right to help perfect strangers take food out of the mouths of people you've known all your life? Your friends, your family, *my* family?"

"My family? Petey's all the family I've got. Maybe I ought to help him do what he thinks he has to. Just because I don't have a clue is no excuse for sitting on my hands."

"You know, David, sometimes I don't think I know you at all anymore. Sometimes I wonder if I ever did."

"I wonder, too, Katie." He put his arms around her, feeling her stiffen at his touch. "I wonder, too. I love you. Good night."

He descended the steps and walked over to his car before turning to wave, fearful that she might not be there when he did. She wasn't.

The next day he quit his job.

17

OUT in the Bay, the swells rocked a battered boat that showed signs of having been worked on, but not finished. As the small craft rose and fell, it was apparent the hull had been scraped and refinished up to the water line. There was a sharp contrast between the gleaming paint below and roughly primed upper hull. Its owner obviously felt it was more important to use it than to wait for complete refitting. At its rear, an outboard that had seen better days struggled against the unpredictable surge of the sea.

Three men were patiently working the Bay, tossing nets overboard and peering into the water, as if for something lost, while a fourth sat at the engine, fighting to hold a steady course. Attempting to minimize confusion, one man would haul in his net as another cast his, steeling himself against the drag. The third was untangling his net, preparing to take his place in the cycle of netting and hauling, sorting the trash fish, pulling out an occasional shrimp and snapping off its head before tossing it into a basket of crushed ice. The catch was meager, but every shrimp brought a smile, while a particularly large one invited admiring comment in rapid Vietnamese. Most vocal was the man at the engine. Having little to do with the actual catch, he participated in the excitement as best he could.

Dong, unused to such hard labor, was breathing heavily, sometimes stopping to look at his hands, the soft palms of which were red and raw. This wasn't what he had in mind when he left Vietnam, but it would have to do until something in accounting came along. He was already organizing the finances of his fellow immigrants, and hoped it would eventually lead to enough work to keep him ashore. He was willing to work as hard as anyone else, but knew he'd make his best contribution by doing something he did well. Looking into the one basket with any shrimp, he had his doubts there would ever be enough to warrant a full-time accountant for the Vietnamese community. His hands were soft, but he was tougher, and they would follow, if only he had time to learn this new trade.

The man at the tiller watched Dong examine his hands. He said something that made the others laugh. Dong, embarrassed, left his seat and made his way to the rear of the boat, steadying himself with one hand on the gunwale. When he reached the stern, the man at the engine slid to one side, still holding the rudder while they traded places. Dong wore an apologetic smile, and the other man patted him on the shoulder, as if to say, "Never mind; you'll get the hang of it."

Grateful for the chance to rest his hands and aching shoulders, Dong watched the other man work his way forward to the net he had just relinquished. Glad for the relief, it still stung him to realize that his lack of stamina was obvious to the others. They were all in this together, but he was the only man in the boat who hadn't known at least one of the others before coming to the United States. There was a camaraderie among them that made him feel like an outsider. They were tolerant, but he was still the most frequent butt of their jokes.

Sitting at the stern now, watching net after net being hauled in, their paltry loads headed and iced, while unwanted fish flapped in the bottom of the boat and crabs scuttled from side to side, claws scraping the wood as they tried to climb back into the water, it struck him how little thought he had given to what he would do once he reached the States. What he had wanted was to get here. His focus had been on escape. At the time, that had seemed enough. Now he knew it wasn't, and probably never would be. He was alive, and for that he was grateful, but he wasn't used to this. His life had been far better ordered, each day predictable, safe, even as the war raged to its conclusion. Like many of his class, he'd been insulated from the worst of it. He'd even known how it would end long before it did, but there was so much to do then. Consideration of the aftermath was a luxury.

Suddenly, the boat slowed dramatically, and tipped to one side, its gunwale dangerously close to the water line. The other men chattered excitedly, and he knew that one of the nets had caught something heavy. If they were lucky, for a change, it might be a school of shrimp. If it was the usual, false excitement, it would be some waterlogged piece of driftwood, suspended between surface and bottom. All three men grabbed the line and began hauling, hand over hand. The net slowly, painfully, came to the surface. One of the fishermen turned to holler over his shoulder, telling

Dong to slack off on the engine, which labored heavily. He could smell its hot oil as the strain of the net pushed it beyond its limit.

Placing his hand on the overheated housing, he regarded it with a mixture of contempt and envy. It was old, nearly worn out, but at least it was doing what it was made to do. If only he could feel that he was wearing out in pursuit of the usual. Looking over the side, he could see the water begin to boil as the net, full of thrashing, resistant life, neared the surface. The men struggled to haul the net, a few of its rotted brown strands already burst, others white with the strain, over the side, where it landed with a rush of water and an immediate scramble of the frenzied catch.

Pulling open the mouth of the net, they stepped back to pour its contents onto the bottom of the boat, then bent to toss overboard everything that wasn't a shrimp. Delighted by their first real netful of the day, the men laughed and joked, despite the heat. Dong was thankful the sun was only dimly visible through the heavy overcast. While the others scrambled to sort the catch, he grabbed a second net and tossed it as far as he could. Then he started the engine again and cruised slowly in a circle over the approximate area where they had struck the shrimp. He hoped to hit again, to make up for the nearly fruitless effort of the morning, and to atone for the sins of inexperience. A sudden drag on the new net warned him not to kill the engine. He pulled on the line of the second net, but it was already taut, and beyond his strength to pull in any farther.

His companions were down to little more than shrimp and a few evasive crabs. He bent to help, apprising Tranh for the first time that he had caught a second haul.

Tranh looked over the side at the taut line and smiled. "You really do feel bad, don't you?" he asked.

Dong nodded, grabbed a crab in each hand, and flung them far astern.

"Oh, oh. It looks like we have visitors," he said, standing up in the unsteady boat and shielding his eyes from the dull glare off the water. "Look!"

Tranh and the others turned to follow his outstretched arm and spotted a larger boat, more suited to the catching of shrimp than their oversized dinghy, bearing down on them. It was a small trawler, and its crew was gathered at the bow. They were yelling at the Vietnamese, but from too great a distance to be understood. The small trawler's engine roared, further drowning out the words.

"I think we better get that second net on board," Tranh said, reaching for the line. They all grabbed the line and began tugging. It seemed heavier than the previous net, and they realized that if it was full of shrimp, they'd have all they could handle for the day. They strained, but the net resisted. The boat listed dangerously, taking on water as a couple of the larger swells broke over the side.

The trawler was now nearly on them, and seemed as if it didn't intend to slow up. The men were still hollering, but now they could be understood. The captain shushed the others, and his solitary voice boomed over the rapidly narrowing gap between the two boats.

"What the hell are you doing?"

"Catching shrimp," Dong yelled back through cupped hands.

"Like hell, you are," the captain yelled back. "You caught my fucking net, is what you caught."

"No, we catch shrimp," Dong repeated. "Look." He indicated the full baskets.

"I don't give a shit what you got in them bushels. I'm telling you, you got my net. Cut your line."

"What?"

"Cut your damn line. You got to untangle us. There ain't no other way to do it."

"How do you know it's your line?" Dong demanded.

"Look, Buster, you and them other slanty-eyed bastards either cut your fucking line, right now, or I'm gonna cut it for you. If you think you got a net full of shrimp, you're crazy. And if you think I'm gonna lose a brand-new net, you're *fucking* crazy. Now *cut that line!*"

The two boats were no more than twenty yards apart. The trawler's engines had throttled down, but the slow rumble was no more reassuring than the full-throated roar of moments before. The boat was so much larger than the Vietnamese craft, the immigrants were at a real disadvantage.

"We can't give up our net. We need it," Dong said.

The captain turned to one of his crew, who quickly disappeared. When he returned a moment later, to stand beside the captain, he had a shotgun cradled in one arm.

"Either cut it or I'll cut it for you," the captain hollered.

The Vietnamese huddled for a moment. Aware they had no choice, Tranh reached for his knife. He jumped as the shotgun went off, twelve-gauge pellets splashing a few feet astern.

"Hold it," the captain of the trawler said. "What's he doing?"

"Getting a knife to cut the line, that's all."

"All right, slow . . ."

Tranh reached again for the knife, slowly this time, and bent to saw through the heavy line. No sooner had it parted than the trawler's drag winch started up, and its steel cable whipped through the water, hurling a fine sheet of spray. After about thirty-five fathoms had been hauled in, the captain hollered for the winch to go more slowly. Suddenly, a net appeared, tangled around the trawler's cable.

It was full of shrimp and other thrashing fish. The trawler's two headers grabbed the line and swung the net inboard. As the line went slack, it collapsed to the deck. Both men sank out of sight as the Vietnamese watched.

"What are they doing?" Dong asked.

"I think they are cutting our net off their line."

After a few minutes, the headers reappeared at the rail of the trawler, carrying pieces of the Vietnamese net, flung them overboard, and went back for more. After three trips, they went back to the helm and conferred with the captain, who turned to the Vietnamese.

"You're lucky you didn't damage my line," he said.

"We didn't mean any harm," Dong replied.

"I don't give a damn what you meant. You nearly screwed me up good. You assholes ought to learn how to fish before you go jerking around out here. If you don't know the rules, somebody's gotta teach you. This here's your first lesson. Throw them baskets overboard."

"But that's our shrimp. We worked all day for that. Besides, it's already been headed. Why throw it back?" Dong asked.

"Oren, show him who's boss here." The man with the shotgun raised it to his hip and fired another barrelful of pellets. This time a few of them rattled around the stern of the smaller boat. "Now throw them baskets overboard, I said."

This time, Dong and Tranh bent to pick up a bushel each. One of the other two men, neither of whom understood any English, grabbed each basket by the rim. Sensing what was about to happen, he grappled with his companions for a moment, until Tranh said something sharply in Vietnamese. The other stopped, looked over at the captain of the trawler, then shrugged. Dong and Tranh threw the baskets into the water, where they quickly sank. As the ice turned transparent, the headless shrimp began to drift off in the current. Crabs and other fish suddenly surfaced to pick at the free meal.

"All the baskets, gentlemen," the captain said, as Oren chambered another shell.

The remaining baskets were tossed overboard and just as quickly disappeared below the surface. The trawler's engines kicked in again, and the crew huddled together, mouths open in shared laughter hidden under the roar, as the Vietnamese watched the fruits of their day's work torn apart and devoured. The trawler pulled away, made a quick turn, righted itself, and headed off in its original direction while the crew stood at the stern watching the huge wave thrown up by its turn break over the small, now strangely barren, Vietnamese boat.

As soon as they made land, Dong called Luke's office. Peter answered, and when he learned what had happened, he rushed to the dock. There, he found Dong and the others still shaken by their experience. He tried to get the details, waiting impatiently as Dong translated his questions into Vietnamese, and the answers into English. The men weren't sure of the name of the trawler, but thought it might have been *Miss Suzy*, or something very like it. When he learned as much as the men could tell him, Peter got on the phone to Luke. Not sure what he ought to do, he filled Luke in on the details and listened while the old lawyer counseled him to remain patient.

"I don't want you doing anything you'll be sorry for later on," Luke told him. "If we wanna kill this thing before it gets going, we can't play into their hands. We can win if we wait it out, but if we start a fight, we'll get whipped so bad those people will be gone before the smoke clears. That won't help them, now will it?"

Peter knew Luke was right, but his anger demanded he do something. He hadn't discussed calling the sheriff, and he wasn't sure what Luke would think of the idea, but he didn't want to waste time finding out. He grabbed another dime from his pocket and got on the phone to Randy McHale's office. McHale wasn't there, so Peter left a message and the number of the pay phone he was using.

Hanging up, he told Dong and the others to go on home, suggesting they travel in a group, just in case. After they left, Peter passed the time by examining the battered boat the men had been using. They'd greatly improved its seaworthiness since acquiring it at McIlhenny's Boatyard, but it was still less than ideal. Its shortcomings were more than cosmetic. The paint was only half restored, and the interior of the boat gave every sign of dry rot. Parts of the hull looked as if they would yield to a careless foot. There was little except paint between Bay and fishermen.

Even the pier the Vietnamese were using—"forced to use" might be a better way to describe it—bespoke the poverty and tenuousness of their situation. Kevin McIlhenny, who had agreed to rent the pier at a nominal charge, wasn't making much of a sacrifice. Peter doubted anyone else would have been tempted to use it. Its timbers were little more substantial than the questionable craft tethered there. Not that there was any reason to find fault with McIlhenny's gesture. His old pier had been the last resort, certainly, but it had been courageous of him to rent it at all. He had reservations, but his basic decency had finally persuaded him, and at a price that was not unreasonable, at least when compared to what others had asked.

"I ain't real glad to do this, Petey," he had said. "You got to understand that. But I sure as hell don't like what some folks are saying about them people. They been through hell enough already. It ain't right to add to their troubles."

The Vietnamese had been grateful, but McIlhenny wasn't sure it was deserved. He thought it might just postpone the inevitable.

"Take my advice, Petey," he had said. "You tell them people, the first sign of trouble, they ought to move on. There ain't enough shrimp out there worth getting killed over."

Peter had doubted it would come to that, but that had been in the first flush of optimism. Now, he wasn't so sure. There had been some squabbling on the docks. Some fish processers even refused to buy Vietnamese shrimp, while others offered insultingly low prices. To compensate, the Vietnamese had been teaching themselves the full scope of the business, from netting to selling processed shrimp. There was more than a little resentment among the fish handlers.

The fact that shots had now been fired, and without any apparent concern as to whether or not they hit anyone, was alarming. Sitting on the quiet pier, he felt a chill unrelated to weather. The dock was in a nearly abandoned section of the small harbor, separated from the main working area by a stretch of flotsam-littered beach and tall weeds. He looked across the water at the more active piers, where a few trawlers were unloading catches that would have made the eyes of the Vietnamese bulge with disbelief. Hearing a sound behind him, he turned to see Dong and Tranh, both carrying rifles.

"What are you doing?" Peter asked.

"Maybe we need to show that we have guns, too," Dong said, smiling grimly.

"That won't solve anything, Dong. You know that."

"It might not, but it might make some people think twice before they shoot at us again."

"Dong, forget it. You're dealing with people who play

with pistols in their cribs. You don't realize what you're getting into."

"Peter, we are tired of being pushed around. Look at this pier! Is this how a man should have to make a living? We are willing to pay a fair price, and *this* is all we are able to rent, this wreck."

"Guns won't get you a better deal. Not in this town. Your best hope is to fit in as well as you can, make as few waves as possible."

"We have been hearing that, but others are not backward about making waves. Turnabout is fair play—is that not the saying?"

"Dong, in this case, turnabout can be suicide. Why don't you go home. We have class in a couple of hours, and I'll see you there."

"No. We want to talk to the men who humiliated us this afternoon."

"Why?"

"To tell them it should not happen again."

"You're asking for trouble. . . ."

"So be it."

Dong and Tranh brushed past him and, after one last desperate effort to dissuade them, Peter gave up. The men went into the work shed and came out with a pair of chains, nodded to Peter, and walked back the way they had come. It was beginning to get dark, and Peter was annoyed that McHale hadn't returned his call. He fished another dime from his pocket and dialed the sheriff again. After a few rings, the same deputy answered. He told Peter the sheriff hadn't returned yet, but he would be given the message as soon as he did. Sighing in exasperation, Peter hung up. He walked to the end of the dock to look out over the water, which seemed to share in the general decrepitude of his immediate surroundings. It had a thick, oily sheen, but there wasn't enough light for the rainbow glaze a slick generally imparts.

As he watched the viscous water rise and fall, he heard shouts, quickly followed by the roar of an inboard and several gunshots. His first inclination was to run toward the sound of the commotion, but he needed McHale more than ever. Reaching into his pocket again, he realized he was out of change. Without a coin, he couldn't raise the operator, and if he left the dock, he might miss the sheriff. He ran back to the end of the pier and strained to see what was happening, but it was too dark. He paced back and forth for several minutes, until he heard the crunch of tires on the shelly gravel at the landward end of the dock. He ran out to meet the sheriff, and encountered Pat Riley with several armed and angry shrimpers instead.

"Might of known *you'd* be here," Pat snarled.

"What's going on?" Peter asked. "I heard shots."

"You ain't heard the last of them, neither," Pat said. "Where were you about twenty minutes ago?"

"Right here. Why?"

"What the hell are you standing there jawing with him for, Pat?" one of the shrimpers demanded. "Why don't we do what we come for?"

"What are you talking about?" Peter said.

"Hodges, you can make this easy or you can make it hard. What's it gonna be? Personally, I hope you make it hard."

"What happened over there?"

Another of the shrimpers spoke up. "A couple of them gook friends of yours stole Gus D'Andrea's boat. Pulled away from the dock while it was still tied up, and ripped the fucking thing in half. You wouldn't know anything about that now, would you?"

"No, I wouldn't," Peter answered nervously. He was

about to continue when one of the shrimpers caught him a glancing blow on the temple with the stock of his shotgun. Stunned, Peter went to his knees, and a second blow put him out completely.

He didn't know how long he lay unconscious, but when he came to, the dock was in flames. The work shed was little more than embrous stubs and glowing sheet metal. Ashes rained into the water, hissing and sputtering, and, as he watched, the end of the pier collapsed into the water with a roar. In the eerie flicker of the flames, he could see the remains of the Vietnamese boat, its hull smashed and gunwales stove in, drifting sluggishly away, barely above water and slipping deeper even as he watched. His head ached, and sharp pains shot through his chest with every breath. Trying to rise to his feet, another pain shot up along his leg. He lay back to number his bones, finding the most severe damage to be a couple of tender ribs, probably cracked, and his leg, which was not broken, but felt as if it should have been. He groaned and tried again to get to his feet.

Before he could manage it, he heard another car on the gravel, and dragged himself into the weeds. He didn't know if the car was coming or going, but he couldn't wait on the pier to find out. Flames were licking along its length, devouring it at an alarming rate. Safe, he hoped, in the tangled undergrowth, he dragged himself to a sitting position and parted the weeds, to see Randy McHale standing in the infernal flicker.

"Peter?" he called "Petey, are you here?"

Suppressing the urge to call out, Peter decided to wait. For all he knew, McHale was part of all this. Though he and Pat didn't get along, McHale played his cards close to his vest. Even if he'd normally side with the law, these were not normal circumstances, and Peter was in no shape

212

to defend himself from another attack. While he watched, McHale walked gingerly out along the remains of the dock, going as close to the blazing timbers as he dared. He spied the boat and muttered a curse. "I'm going to put somebody away for this mess," he mumbled. "Petey, are you here?"

Reassured, Peter called softly to the sheriff, who turned to see where the owner of the barely audible voice might be. "Peter?" he called again. "Is that you? Where the hell are you?"

"Over here, Sheriff."

This time McHale placed him and rushed over to the weeds. Pushing them aside, he knelt beside Peter, reaching for a flashlight as he did so. Clicking it on, he played it quickly over Peter, exclaiming, "Jesus Christ, what *happened* to you?"

"I got run over by the fire brigade," Peter said, smiling as best he could through cracked and swollen lips.

18

THE violence seemed to be a safety valve for both the shrimpers and the Vietnamese, but Peter wondered how long it would remain quiet. Recuperating in the days following the attack, he heard little more than rumbles of resentment. There were no further incidents, and life was returning to normal. He organized a meeting of the Vietnamese, and, unlike attendance at the school, there was a good turnout. Most of the immigrants now realized that their future was far shakier than they had wanted to believe.

After explaining the purpose of gathering, Peter introduced Luke to the audience. Presenting the shrimpers' view, Luke emphasized the need for order. He told them that, although he understood what motivated it, he deplored the violence committed by both sides. There was a murmur of dissatisfaction, so Luke invited Dong to act as spokesman for the Vietnamese position. Dong was reluctant and conferred with some of the others before getting to his feet.

"Mr. Darby," Dong said, after rising, "we appreciate what you and Mr. Hodges have done for us."

"I'm not here for thanks, Dong," Luke said.

"I understand, but *you* must understand that what I say does not mean that we do not appreciate the efforts you have made on our behalf. But . . ." Dong paused and looked uncertainly at the assembly. Someone said something in Vietnamese in a stage whisper, and Dong shook his head in the affirmative. Then he resumed. "We are not here to cause trouble for anyone. All we want is to be left alone to lead our own lives. It was also what we understood to be the right of an American citizen."

"It's not that simple. You can't live without regard to what goes on around you. You have to recognize that."

"I do. We all do. But we don't understand why it should matter to anyone that we are fishing here. Surely there is enough for everyone."

"I'm not so sure of that. But what I think doesn't matter. What *you* think doesn't matter, either. What matters is other folks, and they think you're taking food out of their mouths."

"Perhaps if we met with them, and explained things . . . ?"

"You have to realize these people spend half their time these days fighting somebody or other, just to keep on doing something they been doing for a hundred years. It's all they know. They're scared."

"There was no reason for them to attack us."

"I know that, but *they* don't. There's a town meeting on Tuesday. It might be good if some of you showed up. Not *all* of you. That'll only get their backs up. But if a few of you came, it might help. They'd see you're fishermen, just

215

like they are. And they'd see you're people, just like they are. Right now, I think the first one's more important, but they'll both make a difference in the long run."

"How many should go?"

"Four or five ought to do it, I think. What do you say, Petey?"

Peter nodded. He was going to the meeting as well and, like Luke, thought a Vietnamese presence would be helpful, as long as it wasn't a threatening one. Too many would focus the wrong kind of attention.

"Mr. Darby," Dong said, turning to Luke, "we would like to consider the matter among ourselves. Before we decide, though, I would like your opinion on something, if you don't mind."

"Go ahead," Luke said.

"Will those who attend the meeting be in any danger?"

"No, I don't think so. Most troublemakers don't have the nerve to start anything in front of other folks. And if you show you're not going to cut and run, some people who'd like to see you move on will respect that. Win their respect, and you got a better chance of changing their minds."

"I see. Thank you. I will call you tomorrow to let you know."

Luke grunted, then he and Peter left the church basement. The sun had just set, and it was a beautiful evening. Luke paused to look at the sky out over the Gulf, and observed, "It doesn't seem right, somehow, that folks should have troubles on a night like this. It ain't natural."

On the way home, Peter couldn't match Luke's optimism. No matter how he looked at it, he came up with the same answer: leverage. Somehow, they had to get some leverage, a way to get the fishermen to back off from their angry, confrontational stance. They couldn't be forced; they

216

had to be persuaded. Someone they respected had to make the case for the Vietnamese. There were only two candidates: Randy McHale and David. Luke wouldn't do. He was too close to the Vietnamese. Doc Roth was still an outsider to the more vocal shrimpers. Maggie was aligned with the fishermen, although more susceptible to reason than some. It was too political for the mayor, and too bad for Halsey's business. McIlhenny had stuck his neck out far enough already. That left McHale and David.

McHale couldn't afford to appear partial at this early stage. It would compromise his ability to keep the peace later, if things got out of hand. That left David. But would he do it? Peter didn't think so, but he had no choice. He'd have to ask.

David was reading on the porch when he got home. He went to the kitchen and came back with a beer for each of them.

"The meeting didn't go well, I gather?"

"It was all right," Peter said. "It's a bitch, though."

"I guess so," David said. "What are you going to do?"

"The real question is what *you're* going to do."

David took a pull on the beer before answering. "Me? I'm not going to do anything. I'm not involved, and that's the way it's going to stay. As it is, Maggie and Kate aren't speaking to me. I don't even have a job."

"You're the only one who can make people understand what's going on here."

"What *is* going on?" David sipped his beer, watching Peter around the upturned bottle. "Seems like what's going on is groups of people disagreeing with one another. I've had enough of that, thank you."

"There's more to it than that, David."

"Sure. Always is. But I'll be damned if I want to get in the middle of it. Besides, there's nothing I can do about it. All I want to do is make a living and be left alone. Not as alone as I am now, maybe, but reasonably alone, anyhow."

"Katie will come around," Peter said.

"Maybe." David cracked the bottle down on the floor beside his chair. "But not if I get involved in this mess. I'll be lucky if Maggie ever talks to me again as it is."

"Look. Maggie feels threatened. That's natural. But when she sees what's really at stake, she'll see it our way."

"What do you mean, *our* way? I don't *have* a way, here. I'm out of it, and I'm going to stay out."

"Would you at least talk to Doc Roth with me?"

"What the hell for?"

"Just talk to him, that's all. You trust him. So do I. We're too close to this thing. A different slant on it might help."

"Look. I like Doc. He's a good man. But he doesn't have a stake in this. If things go sour, he can just walk away. Where does Maggie go? Or Eric Swenson? Do you think they can just move on to the next town and start over?"

"No, of course not. But Doc isn't going anywhere. He's here to stay, like the rest of us. Not so much that he wants to be here, but he *has* to. Like me. And you."

"I'll tell you what. I'm not making any promises, but if you'll feel better, I'll talk to him. Nothing else. Okay?"

Peter nodded and stood up. "I'll call him. Maybe he can come by this evening." He went inside, and David heard him on the phone, although he couldn't make out the conversation. He leaned toward the window and, hearing the phone replaced, yelled, "Bring a couple more beers out, would you, Petey?"

Peter returned a moment later, carrying a trio of Lone Stars. "He'll be here in a little while," he said, taking his seat again. The brothers chatted while they waited for Roth, who arrived fifteen minutes later.

"All right," he said, taking a seat. "What's so important you had to drag me over here at this time of night. And where's my beer?"

"Right here," David said, handing him the third bottle, slippery with condensation. Peter and David took turns explaining, sometimes agreeing, sometimes arguing. Doc let them, and after about twenty minutes, he nodded and leaned back in his chair.

"I still don't see why I'm here," he said.

"Because," Peter began, "David won't listen to me. But I convinced him to listen to you."

"That so, David?"

"Not exactly. I agreed to hear what you had to say. I didn't say I'd do anything."

"Well, I don't have any business saying anything about what's going on. I'm not at risk, no matter what happens."

"That's precisely why I wanted to hear what you had to say," Peter interrupted. "There's nobody else in town who doesn't have something tied up in this mess. You're the only one who can be dispassionate about it."

"I don't think dispassionate is the right word, Petey. I have my passions, too, you know."

"Well, what do you think should happen, then?" Peter demanded. "At least tell us that."

"I think it's an explosive situation. I agree the real issues are getting lost in the shuffle. I even agree people might listen to you, David," he said, nodding toward him. "But nobody has the right to tell you to speak up, any more than he has the right to tell the fishermen to shut up. What maybe *can* be done, though, is to get people to step back from their personal interests. There's certainly room for compromise."

219

"I don't deny that," David said. "But it's not my business. I don't have the right to tell these people what they should do. I don't know what they should do."

"No, you don't have that right, David. But you have the right to say what you think. And you *are* involved. You're a fisherman."

"So what?"

"So, if you ask them to think about it, maybe they will. It can't hurt, can it?"

"I don't know. . . . I'll have to think about it."

"That's all I'm asking," Peter said. "Just think about it. If you were to speak at the town meeting on Tuesday, maybe . . ."

"I said I'd think about it," David cut in. "Just let it be, a while. I said I'd think about it, and I will."

Peter stayed silent.

David got to his feet and stretched. "I think I'm going to take a walk," he said. "See you later, Doc. Thanks for coming by."

"I'll be heading home," Doc said, standing. "Thanks for the beer."

Peter remained seated after the others left. He had no idea whether he had accomplished anything, but knew it was his last shot.

The high-school gymnasium buzzed as if full of angry bees. As people filed in, the undercurrent grew. The noise could be heard from the parking lot, even over the roar of arriving cars and trucks. No one knew what to expect, but everyone knew the meeting was essential. Even the more independent shrimpers, who seldom did anything in concert with their fellows, wanted to be present, to help shape the town position, or at least to know what it was.

Peter got there early, as did Dong, Tranh, and three

other Vietnamese. They gathered in a rear corner of the gym, sitting in a tight circle and talking among themselves. At other such meetings, Peter had been interrupted by a new arrival stopping to exchange greetings or good-natured banter. It had been a long time since that sort of thing had happened. Tonight, he knew, would in no way remind him of that past.

Although the meeting was scheduled for eight, the hall was full long before. Frank Willard would chair the meeting, and he wasn't looking forward to it. He recognized the potential for trouble, and hoped Randy McHale wouldn't be needed officially. The sheriff sat against the wall with two deputies. Willard was pleased neither of them was Pat Riley. Everyone knew about Pat's run-in with the Vietnamese, and more than a few of those present were hoping for a rematch.

At seven-thirty, a full half hour early, Willard sat down at the table from which he would preside and turned on the public-address system. There was a brief blare of feedback, and a burst of static, as he adjusted the volume.

"I know," he said, "we're supposed to start at eight, but I guess everybody's here who's coming, so we might as well go ahead."

There was a scrape of chairs as the attendees took their seats, and a slowly dying hum as people closed interrupted conversations.

"I guess we all know why we're here, but in case any-body's been away longer than I think, I'm going to sum-marize the agenda for tonight, and then we can get started. Any objections?"

When no one stated any opposition, Willard continued. "There's only one piece of business tonight, and I don't rightly know whether it's old or new. We've been talking about this sort of thing, one way or another, for as long

221

as I can remember, so I guess it's old business, although the present circumstances are new."

"Why don't you get to it, Frank?" Ed Breslin, one of the more vocal shrimpers, yelled from the back of the hall.

"Now hold on there a minute, Ed," Willard answered with some annoyance. "I want to make one thing perfectly clear right from the word go tonight. I am going to let everybody speak, and I know most of you have some pretty strong feelings, but I ain't letting this meeting turn into a barroom brawl, not at the beginning, and not at no time. Now, is that understood?"

The fishermen rumbled their understanding of, if not their agreement with, the mayor's point.

"Ed," Willard barked into the microphone, his sharp words bouncing off the folded bleachers at both sides of the gym, "did I make myself clear on that?"

"Yeah, Frank, you did. I reckon I'll remember it, too, come Election Day next."

Willard stood up, raising the mike to be heard over the murmur of agreement with Breslin's comment. "Now look, Ed. I'm not running for anything tonight. Nobody is. We have a problem, and we ought to deal with it like grown men. If you have anything to say about my re-election, keep it until next fall. If you don't want to participate tonight, that's fine, but hold your water so those of us who have something to say get a chance to say it."

The audience nodded its agreement with Willard's point, although the endorsement was less than enthusiastic. They seemed to be saying he was right, but that they didn't particularly like it.

"Now, let's get on with it. Randy wants to say something first, and I expect you all ought to pay attention. Then, anybody got anything in particular they want to say, get up there in line, over to the other microphone. And let's try not to take too much time. There's no point in fifty people saying the same thing fifty ways. Okay, you ready, Randy?"

McHale got up and walked toward the table, stopping to speak to one or two of the fishermen on his way through the crowd. Behind the table, Willard stepped aside and offered McHale his chair, but the sheriff disdained it, choosing instead to pick up the heavy microphone and hold it against his chest.

"All right, I'm going to say this once, loud, and everybody better listen up." He paused to sweep the crowd with his eyes while waiting for the murmur caused by his remark to die down. "I don't guess there's anybody here who don't know what happened last week. Now, far as I'm concerned, it's over. There's two busted-up boats, a burnt pier, and a bunch of hurt feelings. That's all there's gonna be. And you all should know, I ain't the only one watching. We had calls from all over, and there's people here from TV and a bunch of newspapers. Some of them are gonna be around for a while. I want this shit to stop right now, before anybody gets hurt bad. Anybody got anything he wants to say to me say it now. After tonight, I'm not gonna be in any mood to forget anything that happens."

He put the mike down on the table, its amplified clunk echoing from the bare cinder-block walls of the gym. There was some grumbling among the men, but no one seemed inclined to argue with the sheriff, so he thanked Willard and went back to his seat, where he sat watching the podium with his arms folded across his chest.

Eric Swenson was first in line, and he mumbled into the mike uncertainly for a moment before clearing his throat and looking around at the crowd.

"I reckon we all know why we're here, but I'll put it on the table, plain and simple, anyway. I ain't got anything particular against anybody. We got some new folks here, and we all know who they are. I guess them people had it pretty rough, and I'm sorry about that." He looked meaningfully at the Vietnamese and shook his head, as if in sympathy for their recent troubles. "The thing of it is, though, I got to make a living."

Several in the crowd shouted approval, and Swenson waited for the noise to abate before continuing. "Everybody knows there's less shrimp every year. This year ain't as bad as some, but it's a lot worse than most. I got four kids. Most of the rest of you got families. Like I say, I got to make a living. I can't sit here while some stranger takes food off my table, and money out of my pocket. I don't want to see nobody starve, God knows, but I got to look out for myself first. That's all I got to say, I guess."

One by one, a half-dozen fishermen followed Swenson to the mike, reiterating his concern. As each man stepped up to speak his piece, the approval of the crowd got louder and more insistent. It seemed to Peter that each man was feeding on the words of his predecessor, and each proclamation got more intense and harder edged. The Vietnamese, sensing the bitterness of the crowd, began to fidget.

Dong leaned in to whisper in Peter's ear. The latter was so surprised to see David leaning against the wall in the back of the hall, he had to ask Dong to repeat himself.

"I don't think anything we can say will change anyone's mind, Peter," Dong whispered.

"We have to try, Dong. If we speak up, they'll at least have to listen."

"If you say so."

At the microphone on the stage, Willard was calling to Peter to get his attention.

"I guess most of you people know Petey Hodges," Willard said, when he had caught Peter's eye. "I think he's got a few things he wants to say on behalf of our newest community members."

"Who in the hell wants to listen to *him?*" Swenson hollered.

"Eric, you had your say. Why don't you shut up and listen to somebody else, now?" Willard said with some heat.

"Now hold on, Frank," Breslin said. "You got no call to talk to Eric that way. Hodges ain't got nothing to say anybody wants to hear, if you ask me."

"I *didn't* ask you, Ed. And what's more, I'm not gonna. Now, this here's a town meeting. Anybody in this town has a right to be heard. That includes you, Peter Hodges, and Mr. Dong, there, for that matter. If you can't be quiet, now, I'll ask Randy to show you the door."

"I know where the damn door is, Frank. And I think certain folks would do well to use it while they still can." Breslin stared at Peter as he spoke. "I see such a person's brother in the back, there. Maybe he ought to talk sense to him, before the rest of us have to. I reckon he might be a little easier on him than we will."

"Ed, no more of that, I'm warning you. Randy, if he so much as raises his voice, escort Mr. Breslin outside," Willard said.

Peter made his way to the floor mike during the exchange, worming his way through the crowd. No one made it easier than he had to for him to pass. A few whispered insults during the passage, but Peter did his best to ignore them. Once, he cast an eye over his shoulder to where David was standing, but the latter had not moved so much as a muscle. He seemed almost to be sleeping. Once at the mike, Peter waited for the uproar to fade. He was getting uncomfortable. Willard called for quiet once more, and the hubbub died down to a dull hiss.

Unsure what to say, Peter decided to make an appeal to the sense of fairness he still, though less certainly, attributed to his fellow townspeople. No sooner had he begun, however, than an argument broke out in the audience. At least one person was in favor of giving the Vietnamese a hearing, and was willing to give or take a punch to back up that willingness.

"Look," he finally began, "I know most of you are having it rough lately. But that doesn't mean it's always going to be that way."

"You're damn right," Swenson broke in. "We get them damn slopes out of here, we can go back to making a living, like we used to."

"You're not trying to blame your poor catch on the Vietnamese, are you, Eric?" Peter challenged. "Maybe you're using the wrong net. I heard you had that kind of trouble more than once."

A few in the audience tittered, and it seemed to enrage Swenson. "Maybe I can grind up your damn face, and use it for bait, Hodges," he snarled. "I'll bet whatever I catch, it'll be yellow."

"Hold on, Eric," Kevin McIlhenny said. "You had your say. Let him finish."

"He is finished, as far as I'm concerned," Swenson shouted. "His friends ought to get out of here, and take him, too. And it'd be a whole lot easier to run 'em off if you hadn't give 'em that pier."

He made a move in McIlhenny's direction, but two or three men grabbed him by the shoulders and held him back. One of them walked toward the microphone and leaned in past Peter to say, "Frank, you got to make allowances for how folks feel. I notice David Hodges back there, and I wonder what he has to say. Maybe he wants to come on up here and tell us whether he agrees with his brother. How about it, David?" he asked, turning to the back of the hall. Everyone, including Peter, turned to follow his gaze, but David made no move. He waved his hand, as if to say he didn't wish to speak, then turned and walked out of the gym before anyone could stop him.

Outside, David walked over to his car and sat on the trunk, watching the front door of the gymnasium. He debated whether to go back inside, but knew he wouldn't. As much as he agreed with Peter's intention, he was unable to take a position. Determined to stay out of the argument, he wouldn't even say he had nothing to say.

Appalled by the ugly feeling jumping from man to man like an electric spark, he was reminded of too many things he'd rather forget. He'd had his fill of rage. He doubted anyone in the hall understood its explosive potential, and knew none of them would be willing to confront it once it took effect. They'd take refuge in anonymity, or explain that they couldn't help themselves, that they were sorry, that they had never meant for any of it to happen. He'd heard all of it before, seen its effects, smelled the blood it had spilled. He'd had enough of that, too. He wanted to help Peter, but knew he couldn't.

What Peter was battling was beyond the ability of one man, or one man's reason, to control. The violence that danced from man to man would soon take charge, despite the fact that there hadn't been a man there who, if asked, would have said that was what he wanted. Even Pat Riley would disavow any malice in his angry belligerence, choosing to see it, instead, as the logical extension of a situation he hadn't wanted but couldn't turn away from. It was that helplessness, which he once would have dismissed as capitulation, that terrified David. "Enough," he whispered. "I've had enough. No more."

He jumped off the car and made his way back to the

gym. As he mounted the steps, the doors burst open, and an angry mob spilled down the steps, like lava flowing over the lip of a volcano. The men were arguing among themselves, and David knew it was already too late for reason. The worst wasn't coming. It was already here.

19

NANCY and her family lived in a cottage along the beach. It had seen better days, but freshly planted flowers beside the porch and recent carpentry gave evidence of renovation in progress. Her brothers worked on the house when they had time, and it was now solid, if in need of a paint job. The porch had several new boards, whose acrid smell bit into David's nose as he rang the bell. A voice deep in the house answered, and soon the door swung open. Nancy's mother pushed open the screen, her face briefly betraying her recognition before she said, "Yes?"

David asked for Nancy, and the old woman disappeared. A moment later, Nancy was at the door. David hadn't expected to be greeted effusively, but the cold, tight smile was a shock.

"What do you want, David?" she asked.

"I wanted to talk to you," he answered. "But I guess

maybe I shouldn't. I'm sorry." He turned to leave, pausing at the first step and, when she said nothing, descended. It had been a long time, but hadn't seemed as long as that hesitation at the top step. Back on the gravel, he turned, not expecting to see her. But she was still there.

"What did you want to tell me, David?" she said, stepping onto the porch.

"I don't know. I . . . Nothing special. I just wanted to talk. We haven't talked in a long time."

"You didn't have anything to say the last time, on the beach."

"No, I didn't, did I?" His face struggled with a smile. "But I . . . I never thought I'd see you again. It was a shock, that's all."

"Would you stay for dinner?"

"Yes, I'd like that. Thank you."

"Come in."

Barely aware of what he was doing, David reclimbed the steps, holding the door as Nancy stepped through. She led him to the parlor, asking him to sit while she told her mother he'd be staying. When she returned, she sat across the room. Her lips moved momentarily. He thought she was deciding whether to smile.

"Why did you come here, David?"

"I don't know. I . . . wanted . . ."

"To tell me that you don't love me? I already know. You don't have to say anything." She laughed, and the harshness of it stung him more than a slap would have. "The truth is, you don't really have anything to say to me. I know that, even if you don't."

"Look, I know that I haven't been fair to you, but . . ."

"You haven't lost your gift for understatement. I guess some things never change."

"More things than you could ever know," he said.

230

"Katherine, Kate, is very pretty. You are fortunate she waited for you. I'm sure she needn't have."

"No, I guess not."

"Have you told her you were less faithful than she?"

"No."

"She knows, though. Women always know. It is probably the worst thing about being a woman."

"I suppose she suspects. We haven't really been getting along lately. It's not only that we . . . that is, you and I . . . ."

"So that's why you're here."

"No, Nancy, no, that's not it! I'm here because, because . . . I wanted to come, to see you, to talk to you. I miss you, that's all."

"That is the same thing, isn't it? You aren't getting along with Katherine, so you come to see me. It's why we got together in the first place, wasn't it? Because she was here, and you were there. I was convenient. But now you have a problem, since we are together, all three of us. Don't you?"

"My problems have nothing to do with you or with Kate. My problems are my problems, that's all. They're not why I'm here."

Nancy's mother appeared in the doorway. She said something softly, in Vietnamese, and Nancy rose, saying, "It's time for dinner." She walked into the kitchen, leaving David to follow on his own. When he entered, she was already seated. She looked surprised, as if seeing him for the first time. She pointed to an empty chair, and he sat.

"My brothers aren't home yet. We will have to eat without them. I don't have much time, because I have to get over to the school, for the English class."

"My brother is teaching that class," David said.

"I know. I've met him."

"Does he . . ."

231

"No, he doesn't know I know you. The subject hasn't come up, nor, I expect, will it. There is no reason. He has been very helpful to all of us. He reminds me of you, a long time ago, in some other country."

"In another life, it seems like."

"Perhaps it was."

"I don't want to believe that."

"Why not?"

"Because the best part of my life is in the past. If it's as distant as it sometimes seems, well . . ."

"You're not as smooth a talker as I remember, David."

He felt the barb, but ignored it. "You always gave me more credit than I deserved."

"So I have learned."

"Nancy . . . Nancy, why don't we stop sparring with one another. We were friends, still can be. There's no need for hostility."

"You don't think so? Your brother knows just how essential hostility is at the moment. Ask him. Dinner is ready."

Nancy took a large bowl of rice from her mother and placed it in the center of the table. The old woman returned to the stove for vegetables and shrimp. Another trip, this time to the refrigerator, and she was back with iced tea and a bottle of beer. "You still drink beer?" she asked, setting the bottle in front of David.

"Yes, thank you, Mrs. Diem."

"So formal. You used to call me Mama, David. Don't you remember?"

"That was a long time ago," he said, looking at his plate to avoid her gaze.

"Not so long. Not so long. Things change, but they change back. Nothing is here forever or gone for all time. You will see."

"Mother, David has no patience for eastern mumbo jumbo. Don't you remember?"

"That is not eastern. It's just human. Isn't it, David?"

The dinner with Nancy upset him. Something in her tone wasn't in her words, as if she were speaking on two levels at once. Her manner, so reserved and cool at first, had gradually thawed, but her words remained brittle and hard.

He knew he was still attracted to her. He had felt it on the beach, but tried to dismiss it. Now, his relations with Kate exponentially deteriorating, he was forced to consider the implications more seriously. He didn't know whether Nancy was attractive because Kate was increasingly distant, or if cause and effect were reversed. He didn't even want to know.

Once he had quit Maggie's crew, his days were as shapeless a mosaic of blank tiles as they had been when he first returned. Prospects for another job were slim. He was well liked by many of the fishermen, but they had their own problems. They would give him work if they had it, but most of them had barely enough for themselves, and couldn't afford charity. He wouldn't accept it in any case.

Maggie had called to try to persuade him to come back to work, and said that he and Kate were just edgy, that they'd been together too long for a squabble to disrupt their lives. He countered that the only way to save their relationship was for him to be less a part of things for a while. It ended in an argument. He had to put some distance between himself and the volatile situation before it blew up in his face.

It was late August, and school would be opening in another two weeks. Once Kate settled into the routine of the school year, their lives might be better ordered. Leaving Maggie's after dinner the night before he quit, he had wanted to run to Nancy. Now, leaving Nancy's, he wanted to run to Kate.

Stepping off the porch, he hesitated before starting his car, then pulled onto the road without knowing where he was going. Peter would be at his school, and he didn't feel like talking to anyone else. At the first intersection, he had three choices, two more than he was capable of handling.

Edging into the intersection to go home, he swerved on impulse. Before he knew it, he was heading toward Maggie's. He felt like an automaton. Off to the side of the road, red sunlight shimmered on the stiff grass as it would on water, the shiny sides of its blades twisting in the wind. As he neared the Riley place, he slowed down.

He parked the car and took a deep breath, glad Pat's car wasn't there. He didn't need another argument. Kate heard the car and came to the screen door. For a moment, they stared at one another. Finally, realizing the burden was on him, he opened the car door and walked to the house. As he reached the steps, Kate stepped onto the porch.

"I hoped it was you," she said.

"How are you?"

"Not good."

"Me either. Want to go for a walk?"

"All right."

She walked down the steps and linked her arm in his, taking control of the direction in which they would walk. Off in the distance, David could see the lights of a trawler, heading out toward the Gulf. It hooted twice as they walked toward the Bay. Mosquitoes were mercifully absent as they moved through the tall grass. Kate twisted to drape his arm across her shoulders. She hadn't said a word since they left the house, choosing instead to lean her head on his shoulder. As they walked, from time to time she squeezed his arm, and he stroked her hair in absent response.

At the edge of the water, they sat down, and David lay back on the beach to look at the sky. Kate made circles in the sand with one finger, and wrote his name in block letters.

"It's over, isn't it?" she said.

"What's over?"

"You and me. Us."

"Why do you say that? We're having a rough time, that's all."

"No, it's over. You know it is."

"If it is, it's because you want it to be."

"Don't put the blame on me. I've heard things. I know what's going on."

"What are you talking about, Katie? What things?"

"You and that woman."

"What woman?"

"That Vietnamese woman. Nancy, isn't it?"

David sat up abruptly. He grabbed her shoulders, and she turned to face him. "I don't know what you're talking about, Kate. . . ."

"Don't you? How long have you been seeing her?"

"I'm not *seeing* her."

"Then you do know her?"

"Yes. I know her. For God's sake what does that have to do with anything?"

"You can *ask* that? David, how stupid do you think I am?"

"But it's not like that. I . . . I've known her for a long time. Over there. I . . . ."

"Known her? Just how well do you *know* her, David. How well?"

"Look, Kate, I . . . Damn! All right! All right!" He punched the sand and got to his feet. Out on the Bay, the lights of the trawler were tiny points. He watched them until they vanished, then sat down with his back to the water, to face Kate. "It was a long time ago. There's no excuse, I guess."

"You guess? You guess? You damn well better believe there's no excuse. I sit here for four years waiting for you, and you guess there's no excuse." She laughed. Raising her hand as if to caress his cheek, she slapped him as hard as she could. She began to strike at him wildly, most of the blows missing, an occasional one glancing off his shoulders, screaming, "You . . . guess . . . you . . . guess . . . you . . . guess . . ."

David grabbed her wrists, trying to restrain her without hurting her. She twisted in his grasp, her skin chafing under his grip. He squeezed tightly and shook her, her head wobbling with the violent motion.

"Stop! Damn it, Kate. Stop it! Listen to me!"

Her fury drained, Kate was sobbing. David got to his feet and reached down for her, but she ignored his hand. He sat again, this time beside her, and put his arm around her. He rocked her gently, as if she was a frightened child, and stroked her hair.

"Look, I'm . . . I don't know what to say. I'm sorry, but it's not what you think."

He paused, hoping, waiting, for her to ask what it was, but she said nothing. He looked out over the water. The trawler was long gone. "Oh, God," he whispered.

As he began to talk, pent-up emotion spilled out in a torrent. For the first time in his life, nothing seemed too private to reveal to her. All he had seen and done, felt and been moved by, that repelled, fascinated, and tormented him, flooded into the open. From time to time, he would

236

stop, as if he feared he was poisoning the air. He caressed her soundlessly, stroking her hair, occasionally kissing the top of her head.

Kate listened quietly as he told of meeting Nancy while on R and R. Her shoulders grew taut, but he pushed on. He was determined to wipe it all away, to purge himself of the accumulated complexities, the emotional contradictions that were a by-product of the war.

As he spoke, he realized that he still loved Kate. It might be too late to salvage what they had, but if they were to have any chance, he'd have to be completely honest, let sunlight into the darkest corners of himself, sweep away everything that haunted him. Or almost everything.

"Did you love her?" Kate asked, so softly that for a moment he wasn't sure she had spoken.

"I thought so at the time. Now I don't know."

"Don't know whether you did, or do?"

"Did."

"You're not telling me something. I can feel it."

"I'm . . ." He paused. She was right. He wasn't telling her everything. And he didn't know if he could. But he had to try. If there was to be a second chance for them, he would have to tell it all. Purgation, rebirth would be meaningless if he didn't. A partial confession was no confession at all. He knew it, and he knew, too, that if he told her everything, they might not have a future together. But if he didn't tell her, they surely wouldn't.

"You're right. I'm not telling you everything."

"Will you?"

"Yes."

"Now?"

"Yes . . ."

He stood again to face the water, stretching to relieve the stiffness in his legs. He could feel Kate's eyes on his back. The moment he had feared for so long was finally here. He had known it would come, that it had to. And he knew nothing would change when he finished speaking. The past would remain as it had been, but his relationship to it would be transformed. And so, still looking past Kate out toward the Gulf, he began. As he considered how to frame it, it grew in vivid flashes, bursts of flame so bright he could feel their heat on his cheeks. His brow felt as if it had been seared, the skin about to peel.

"It was a routine patrol, a search and destroy in Quang Tri province, near a little village. So ordinary, so pretty. We'd seen a thousand just like it. It was tiny, no more than a dozen or fifteen hooches. Actually, there were fourteen. It's so clear, I can count them in my head."

beehives, I could hear buzzing, she won't understand

"We weren't even interested in the village. It was just a place we had to go through to get from here to there. People sitting outside, some kids playing, chickens, cattle, the usual. We passed through, paddies on one side, jungle on the other. We'd been walking for two hours, so we stopped for a break before going back into the jungle. We were watching the trees, for snipers."

were they chickens or something out of Bosch by way of Hanoi, nothing was as it seemed, a cow could be a Buick on a good night

"Donny and I squatted against a tree to have a cigarette. We were talking to another guy in the unit, a guy from New Jersey. Ralph Ordway, his name was. The three of us had been together for months."

Kate listened quietly, watching him intently. It was the first time he'd mentioned Donald since he'd been home.

"Everything was green, such a bright green. There were birds, bright red and blue, green parrots and some yellow things I'd never seen."

238

were they birds, or not, who could tell

"The colors were unbelievable. The sun was out for the first time in days, and the jungle looked like it was on fire."

ropes of color to climb like Tarzan, swinging from the fire, beating my chest

"The leaves were all wet; the light splashed all over, burning. It was beautiful. If you didn't look at anybody else, forgot you had a gun, it was beautiful. Ralph stood up and lit a cigarette. There was an explosion, and he was gone. Wham, just like that, vanished. A grenade . . . I don't know . . .

"I looked at Donny, and there was blood all over. Ralph never knew what hit him. For a minute, it was quiet. Then Donny started to moan. It was the most horrible thing I ever heard in my life. It wasn't human. I thought he'd been hit. I thought he was going to die if he stopped, and I wanted him to stop. I couldn't stand the sound."

it was a sound with teeth, ripping, tearing, I was red meat, food for this beast from someplace out of science fiction

"I crawled over to him, on my belly. There was something in his lap, but I couldn't see it clearly, until I got close. It was Ralph . . . his head. In Donny's lap. The jaw was twisted, the skin blown away. It was a death's-head. Oh, sweet fucking Jesus it . . . I . . ."

Suddenly David ran to the water. Bent over, turning away from Kate, he retched, his shoulders quaking with the violence. Three times he started to turn back, only to stop again. His stomach was empty, but his body wouldn't accept it, trying again and again to purge itself as completely as his memory was doing. Finally, he regained his composure, stooped to rinse his mouth with the salty water lapping at his feet, and walked back to Kate, who had neither moved nor spoken. So motionless was her quiet, she could have been an idol before which he was making his confession. When he continued, his voice quavered.

"Donny couldn't take his eyes off the head and he couldn't stop moaning. Then he howled. His voice was raw, hoarse, an animal growl. The eyes were staring straight at me, and I knew why Donny was screaming. I started screaming myself. Then I had to stop to throw up. Some of the other guys ran over, and Lieutenant Parker saw what had happened. They started running in every direction."

ants, boiling water

"Everybody knew it had to be the ville. You can't throw a grenade too far. It came from the ville. It had to have. Maybe. I don't know . . ."

David turned for the first time since he had resumed speaking, and Kate saw that he was crying. He sat in front of her and continued.

"Parker started running toward the ville, a bunch of guys right behind him. Firing into the air, like great white hunters trying to scare the natives. At least at first. There was so much noise. You couldn't tell what was going on. One guy got hit. For all I know, it was one of our own bullets. Parker was out of control. The guys didn't know what to do. All we knew was we had to do something."

there's a barrel, there's fish, you shoot

"When Parker got closer, he started shooting into the huts. He'd empty a clip and jam a new one in; other guys were with him. We couldn't see a soul. I don't know whether one of the villagers had done it, or whether they just saw it happen, and knew what was coming. Parker started with grenades, and the hooches were going up, one by one, big puffs of smoke."

black magic mushrooms, they grew and were gone

"Then, as quick as it started, it was over. They were all gone. Every hooch leveled. And still we couldn't see a single human being. Then Dick Faber saw something move, behind what was left of the hooches. He started firing again, and ran toward the trees. He went down, and two other guys started firing, too. I looked for Donny, but couldn't find him."

a great whirr red and gold flurry a pillar of fire, parting the jungle

"Suddenly, parrots, hundreds, thousands of them rose up in clouds. I stayed where I was. There was something funny about it. Nobody was shooting back. Nobody had. The parrots were gone. It was absolutely quiet in the trees. When Dick got up, nobody saw him but me. He had just slipped in the mud and fallen. I hollered to wait, but one guy kept on firing. I yelled, and he didn't listen to me . . . nobody listened, dammit . . . nobody.

"On one side of the clearing was a bunch of kids. I yelled again to stop shooting, that it was kids. But the guy didn't hear me. I don't know, maybe . . . I yelled again to stop, but he just kept walking toward the kids, firing his weapon. I screamed at him to stop, but he wouldn't. I couldn't hear myself, and everything was moving real slow. I thought I was underwater, that I was drowning. I raised my rifle, and it took an hour. I fired into the air, but he kept going."

see the ball, watch the rotation, the seams

"I swear, everything in the world slowed down. It was like I could see the bullet moving real slow, spinning, and all I could think of was Ted Williams, how he used to say you should see the ball, watch its spin.

"I ran after him, but my legs wouldn't work. I fell down, and I watched him. He was going to butcher those kids. I could see dead bodies on the ground among the trees. Nobody else was moving. I yelled to stop. They were kids, little kids, three, four years old. He was pointing his rifle at them. I hollered for him to stop, but he didn't hear me, didn't understand me . . . I don't know. I could hear myself, and my voice was different, hoarse from all the yelling. I couldn't stand it. I yelled again to stop, and he pulled the trigger. I shot him, and he fell. I ran over to him, and knelt down. And all during this time, the kids hadn't moved. They hadn't made a sound. They just stood there. And stared. Huge, empty eyes."

moon craters

"They were terrified, but they didn't cry. It was like they couldn't, maybe didn't know how . . . I don't know. And I remember thinking, this is not happening. Guys I knew didn't shoot kids. I got to the guy I had shot and turned him over. It . . . "

David broke down and buried his face in his hands. The tears in the moonlight streamed like silver fire through his fingers.

"It was Donald, wasn't it?" Kate asked.

David nodded.

"And you killed him, didn't you?"

"Yes. God, I . . . I didn't know. I didn't mean to. But . . . I couldn't . . . It was awful. Those kids . . . I yelled, and he just . . . he . . . I couldn't let him kill those kids. I couldn't. He was too far away. I didn't know who it was. I fired a warning shot, but he ignored it. There was only one way to stop him. I didn't know. I just wanted to stop him somehow, but . . ."

Kate stood up and turned her back to him. "And you slept with that woman. You killed my brother, and you slept with her. No wonder you and your fucking brother want them here."

"Kate, I . . ."

"Go to hell!"

She turned abruptly and started walking back toward the house.

David watched her go, and knew she wouldn't come back. He wanted to call her, but knew it was pointless. He fell prostrate to the sand. All he could hear was the sound of waves.

20

DAVID seldom visited the Double Header. Its atmosphere was a little too depressed, a little too desperate. He didn't feel much like being sociable, and the few times he did stop in, the forced conviviality grated on his nerves. Drinking there was something one did because one had nothing else to do. And he was afraid of drinking too much. Now, though, times were changing. Jobless, time on his hands, and little interest in anything, he joined the club. The booze didn't make him feel any better, but if he didn't look too closely in the mirror he could pretend he was enjoying himself.

The worst thing about the place was the absence of women. There were too many men too much like himself for him to be comfortable. Louise and the other waitress brightened things a little, but when she was there, Pat was usually there, too. David knew he'd have to deal with Pat sooner or later, but didn't care enough either to avoid it or to force the issue and get it done with. In a way, it was exciting, sitting there with a beer and waiting. One day, Pat would come in and it would start. Then it would be over. Whether anything would be settled was doubtful. On the other hand, he and Pat understood one another better than either of them knew or would admit. Each of them needed the fight. They complemented one another. Cathode and anode, they were opposites who meant nothing alone.

His relationship with his brother had deteriorated again. Peter had been giving him a hard time about his drinking, and about not working. It was so easy for Peter. He had fallen into a job. Peter had the school to occupy him in the evenings. Peter had a future. All he had was a past, and it had just blown up in his face.

The worst aspect of Kate's reaction had been her eerie calm. It would have been so much better, probably for both of them, if she had exploded, lost herself in her anger. But she hadn't. It was as if she had known what he was going to tell her. Perhaps she had. The way she had asked him was so reserved, so . . . so damned *knowing*. "It was Donald, wasn't it?" she had said. Just like that. "It was Donald, wasn't it?" Damn her, how could she be so calm about it?

Oh, she had hit him, screamed at him, but it wasn't about Donald; it was about Nancy. She was angrier about that than anything else he'd said. Maybe, overwhelmed by the enormity of it, she'd needed something ordinary to be angry about. Maybe she couldn't deal with it any other way. Maybe.

Working on his sixth or seventh beer of the afternoon, he wasn't sure. His image in the mirror was getting a bit smoky. He saw himself wavering in the glass, and wondered whether he was losing his balance or if it wasn't a mirror at all, but a projection of some other David Hodges. The features were blurred but familiar, the sneering smile less so. God knew, he had nothing to smile about. The mirror seemed far away, the space behind the bar an impassable gulf. He couldn't reach that picture of himself. Maybe it *was* someone else. Or some part of him that knew better, that knew *him* better. There was a smugness in the scrutiny; the figure in the glass looked as if it knew something he didn't.

Louise sat on the stool to his right. She had been friendly of late, but David was so suspicious of people, he suspected she had something specific in mind. He couldn't imagine what it might be, but there was no other reason for her to be so attentive.

"How are you, David honey?"

" 'Kay, Louise, you?"

"All right. School starts next week."

"So?"

"You won't be seeing as much of Kate."

"I'm not seeing much now, to tell the truth."

"Oh, something wrong?"

"Louise, look. I know you're trying to be friendly, but I'm not in a real good mood. Besides, if Pat comes in, he wouldn't be too happy to see you and me sitting here talking. Would he?"

"No."

"Fine. Then how about you get me something to eat and another beer? I'll be fine. Don't you worry about it." He patted her hand.

"If that's what you want."

"What I want doesn't matter. It's the way it has to be. How about a burger, medium, and some home fries?"

She nodded and went off to the kitchen. He wondered

if he'd been too suspicious. There was no law somebody couldn't be friendly. But everything seemed so out of control. His temper was bad, and getting worse. It didn't take much to set him off. Events seemed to spring up full blown, the way a tornado howls out of the sky and disappears before you're quite sure what it was.

Rick Walker got off his stool and slid along the bar with a wet rag, sopping up the puddle in front of David.

Shit, there was no reason to be where he was. David knew that. But where the hell was he supposed to be? That was tougher to answer. Without Kate, there was no place to turn, no place to go. No one to talk to, the way he could talk only to her. It hadn't always been like that. At one time, he could talk to Nancy as freely as he could to Kate, but that was long ago. She had no use for him anymore. Or did she?

Why was it so damned hard to read people? Why couldn't they just say what was on their minds, without games, without parables, sometimes speaking in tongues absent even at Babel? On the other hand, he was no master of plain speaking. Not until the other night. And what good had it done? Instead of relief, he felt empty. It seemed as if, surrendering his secret, he had nothing left, as if the secret, like a cancer, had fed on him voraciously, leaving room for nothing else. Or maybe there had never been anything else.

Louise came back with the food, then stepped behind the bar to open a bottle of Dos Equis. She waited, but when David said nothing, she sighed and went off to the kitchen again. He picked at the burger with a fork, tossing the bun to one side of the plate. There was no catsup, and he didn't want to talk to Louise anymore, so he doused his fries in the mustard reserved for pretzels, chewing without interest. When he finished, he downed the rest of his beer, threw a ten and some singles on the bar, and waved to Rick as he got up to leave. He slipped once, righted himself, then pushed into the street, wondering whether he might not be drunk, a little.

Here he was, on the loose, with no place to go. He thought of Kate, of how much he wanted to talk to her. It was that, even more than the sex, that he was going to miss. On the other hand, he'd shown little interest in sex since he got home. Not that Kate had complained; she hadn't. But it worried her, he knew, partly because she wanted it, and mostly because it wasn't like him not to be interested. Futilely, he tried to picture Kate, preferably naked. He wondered if he'd ever seen her naked, or whether he'd recognize her body if he saw it. It frightened him not to be sure.

Angry now, he struggled to visualize her skin, the shape of a breast, a thigh, but couldn't do it. The images hovered behind a gauzy veil, tantalizingly out of reach. But when he shifted his focus to zero in, they'd slip away as if they'd never been. He wasn't even sure it was Kate he was seeing. The skin seemed darker, a bit, the hair much more so. Almost like . . .

But he resisted the thought. He shouldn't be thinking of Nancy. He was trying to recapture, however fleetingly, the image of Kate. Katie. Katherine Riley. But then, she wanted nothing more to do with him. Perhaps it was only natural that her image would reject him as well. Maybe some people had that much control. He knew he didn't have it. He had control, total control over some things, but not over that. He loved Kate and he wanted her, but he couldn't have her. Not now, and maybe not ever.

He tripped getting into his car and realized with some satisfaction that he *was* drunk. There was no need to pretend he wasn't. No one would be offended, the way Kate would have been. She didn't want him? Very well then, he would be his own boss. He could get drunk if he felt like it, and when he felt like it. He could drink, or not drink. He was mumbling as he started the car, and belched once as the engine turned over.

Damn Kate anyway. She was being pigheaded. As bad as Pat. She didn't, or wouldn't, see that Pat was heading toward the same mindless violence that cost Donald his life, and for the same reason. Blind hatred that had little to do with the facts, such as they were. And as a final irony it was directed against the very people he and Donald had fought to protect, and Pat, too, for that matter, though he suspected Pat fought more for pleasure than anything else. So, now the war had come home, and promised to be just as bloody. It might not be a real war, but it would be the closest thing anybody had seen on Texas soil in a hundred years.

Fuck Pat, he thought, as his car wove from side to side through Witman's empty afternoon streets. Fuck Pat, and Eric Swenson, and Ed Breslin. Fuck Dong and Tranh, too. Fuck 'em all. He had no stake in their argument. If they wanted to kill one another over a bunch of goddamned fish, let them. As he drove he was getting angry, punching the steering wheel again and again. By the time he left town behind, he was crying, flailing against anything he could reach with fists and elbows, words and curses. Damnation worthy of a fundamentalist preacher he wished for one and all, himself included.

The worst thing was the impotence. He couldn't influence events. His own life was beyond the reach of controls he or anyone else could exert. And Maggie. She was a surprise, and a disappointment. If there was one person in all of Witman he thought might have seen through all the smoke, seen the simple human truths involved, it was she.

249

But she hadn't. She might have been less vitriolic than Pat, but she was no less adamant. Reason, it seemed, had no place in this dispute. It was guns and fists and Katie bar the door. Katie. Like hell, she would. She was as bad as any of them. And all those helpless Vietnamese—not helpless, really, but bewildered, confused. They were in deep shit and didn't know it. Maybe the truth of American behavior in Vietnam had been as lost on them, as it had on most Americans. Maybe they deserved no better, applauding the use of napalm and Agent Orange, air power and plows the size of Staten Island tearing up the earth as far as the eye could see.

That earth had been so green, so lush. The rain, soft at times, at times violent, seemed to wash it to a bright green glow. And now, crater lakes and moonscapes, twisted wrecks and rusted trucks were all that was left of American aspirations. That and thousands of barren lives, sundered families, vanished limbs, sightless eyes, and for what? So a bunch of Vietnamese and Texans could play cowboys and Indians in San Antonio Bay.

What he ought to do is take Kate and get the fuck out of here altogether. But she wouldn't go, and he didn't want to go alone. Maybe Nancy would go? Why not? What did she have to lose? No more than he, certainly; probably less. Excited by the idea, he headed for Nancy's house, blushing in his excitement. He had loved her once, maybe, why not again? Maybe not again, maybe still. Maybe that was why he and Kate had been such strangers. But that didn't matter, or wouldn't, not if Nancy would go with him, stop at the Louisiana border to shake off the Texas dust and never look back.

No one was home, and he debated whether to wait or to give up the stupid notion as unrealistic and unworkable. He wasn't even sure he remembered why he was there.

Or maybe she knew he was coming and didn't have the heart to refuse him. At that thought, he laughed aloud. He was more than drunk; he was beginning to feel positively deranged. Everything was coming unglued. The thing to do was go home and sober up, then try to pick his way through the jungle of options as carefully as he would a minefield. At the moment, he was his own worst enemy.

He didn't remember leaving the driveway, when he awoke several hours later. He remembered being there, and why, but that was all. That and the insistent notion that he was going to go back with the same purpose. Witman had never been much of a rose to begin with, but now the bloom had definitely vanished. He was confident Nancy wouldn't turn him away or, worse, laugh at him. And he was going to go. He had known all along that Kate would never be able to forgive him, as much as he wanted to believe she'd understand. She would never forget—he knew that—but then, neither would he. If she understood, truly understood, she'd see that circumstances had left him no choice. He even thought that, in his shoes, she would have done the same thing. But now it didn't matter. She didn't understand. He'd been wrong and he had to live with it.

He showered to rid himself of the barroom stink and his head of lingering cobwebs, dressed hurriedly, and ran to his car. He was moving like a man determined to get out of town before sundown. As he started the car, it dawned on him that that's exactly what he was, a fugitive. He wasn't sure what he was running from, but it was right there in Witman. It might even have been Witman itself. He drove hurriedly but not recklessly. He wanted to be at the house before Nancy got home from the English class.

Once parked, he sat in the car. Lights were on, and he knew that Mrs. Diem was home, probably getting dinner ready for Nancy and her brothers, all of whom attended the class. While he waited, he tried not to think about what he would do if she said no. He wouldn't allow it. He couldn't. After twenty minutes of insistent, self-induced semicoma, he heard another car on the gravel.

He left his car and walked to the rear, to sit on one fender. Nancy and her brothers were just getting out of their jeep. The men looked at him curiously, but went on into the house. Nancy walked to him, saying nothing. Her face was impassive.

"Want to go for a walk?" David asked.

"All right."

He took her hand, and they went out of the drive onto the shoulder of the highway, where they walked for a few minutes in silence. They came to a sandy road little more than two ruts in the grass, leading to the beach. He had swum here as a child, and the ruts seemed so familiar he was tempted to look for the prints of his own bare feet in the sand. The moon was rising, the sandy path clearly visible. After a quarter of a mile, they were at the beach. There was no surf to speak of, just dunes capped with stiff grass, clear sand for fifty feet, and water, the waves far less aggressive than the last time he had seen her on this beach. They walked on, David not knowing what to say, Nancy not knowing why he had come or why she was with him.

Breaking the silence, he asked if she wanted to wade in the waves. She didn't answer, but kicked off her sneakers and bent to roll up her jeans. He did the same, and they walked to the edge of the water. It was cooler than he thought, and she shivered at its first contact. They walked farther away from the house, toward a more desolate stretch of beach, still silent, though more comfortable than at first. It all seemed so familiar that he kept waiting for the sound of a chopper, or the distant rumble of mortars. It was ironic that he was home, where he had once dreamed of being on such walks, yet no more at peace than he had been then.

Nancy's hair shone in the moonlight. More relaxed than he would have expected, she let go of his hand to unfasten her hair, then shook her head to let it fall over her shoulders. With a sudden maneuver, she turned and started walking backward, kicking the water to try to splash him. She giggled and turned to run, as she had the last time. But unlike that night, this time David knew she wanted to be caught.

Laughing, he began the chase, running on the packed sand where footing was more secure. He closed the gap quickly, reached out, and grabbed her arm. They stopped, as suddenly as they had started. It hadn't been a long sprint, but they were breathless. His shoulders were wet from the water she had splashed on him. They stopped laughing, and he held onto her hand. Uncertainty on her face, her lips quivered, flashing dimly in the moonlight.

"You know why I'm here, don't you?" he asked.

"No, David, why *are* you here?"

He didn't answer. Instead, he reached out with his free hand, and she grasped it, closing the circle. For the moment, they controlled all that was between them. She watched expectantly, moving closer and tilting her head to look up at him. With a movement so measured it might have been slow-motion, he drew her close, wrapping her in his arms so carefully and deliberately he thought he could feel each nerve respond as her body pressed, cell by cell, against him. Her breasts flattened against him as he slid his hands along her back, down to her hips, drawing her closer still.

"Why *are* you here?" she repeated, smiling.

She sank to the sand, drawing him with her. He kissed her and thought he would never breathe again. The sensations of a lifetime ago were still there, the same urgency, the same fears that this time would be the last, all combined into one burst of emotion, and suddenly he was crying. Nancy kissed each cheek, her tongue darting out to catch the tears, and David noticed that she, too, was crying. She drew back, and he was certain she was going to leave again, this time forever.

Instead, she undid two buttons on her shirt, slipped it over her head, and lay back in the sand. David bent over her to stare into those eyes, so dark he once told her they could hide the sun. Her cheeks glistened, and her breath was shallow and spasmodic, echoing his own. He kissed her again, then reached for the zipper on her jeans, pausing to caress her stomach while he traced the line of her throat with his lips, ending with a nipple softly clenched between them. He lost himself for a moment in the childhood sensation of suckling.

He knew they would make love again, and that she would agree to go. But, for the moment, nothing mattered but the insistent rhythms that surrounded them, engulfed them: the sea, her heart and his. They were together, and he reveled in the mindless joy of it. The heat, the sweat of their bodies, the sounds they made, all testified that here, with her, or anywhere with Nancy, was where he had to be.

Lying side by side on the sand, the rising tide now threatening to drench them, they watched the moon slip toward the horizon. Neither of them had spoken, and neither seemed to want to speak. As inevitable as each knew speech to be, it wasn't yet time for it. There was still a quiet joy to be savored. Talk was for later. She would come with him. Saying so hadn't needed words.

21

THE following day David awoke late. He showered quickly and put a pot of coffee on. After slipping bread into the toaster, he sat down to wait for the coffee. When the toast was done, he buttered it haphazardly and ate standing by the stove. Finally, the coffee was ready, and he poured a cup. He was just sitting down again when the doorbell rang.

He couldn't imagine who would be visiting in the middle of the day. For a moment he thought it might be Nancy, but remembered she was going to be out on the Bay with her brothers and Peter. The shrimp had been running well, and they wanted to grab it while they had the chance. When he opened the door, he was shocked to see Maggie Riley.

"I guess you're surprised to see me." She smiled, somewhat nervously. Her voice was tentative, and lacked her normal confidence.

"Yes, I guess I am, Maggie. Come in. Want some coffee?"

"Wouldn't mind."

David led the way back to the kitchen, and went to the cabinet for a cup and saucer while Maggie sat down. He poured a cup, returned the pot to the stove, and sat down across from her. He wondered why she was here. It had to be something extraordinary for her to come unannounced. Her manner was restrained, her hands restless. She played with the cup, turning it this way and that in the saucer. Finally, she took a sip and replaced the cup with a crack.

"I don't quite know why I come all the way out here. I mean, I know why, but I'm not sure I'm thinking clearly. David, you've got to come back to work."

"Why?"

"You *should* be working, and for me. It was dumb to quit, and dumber of me to let you. I don't know what I was thinking."

"You know I can't, Maggie. Too much has happened."

"Nothing that can't be fixed."

"I wish that was true. . . ."

"Look, I don't know what happened between you and Katie, but whatever it was, you can bet it ain't the first time somebody argued about it. It happens all the time. Matt and I used to fight something fierce. Two strong people can't help it. But it don't mean they shouldn't be together."

"Maggie . . . I . . . I'm not sure you'd feel that way if you knew what this fight was about. Besides, what you and I say doesn't make any difference. It's up to Kate. As far as she's concerned, we're finished. There's no going back."

"You're wrong, son. She hasn't been herself since you two had that spat. She's been moping around, spending

256

most of the time in her room. You have to talk to her. She wants you to, but she's too damn pigheaded to make the first move. She's just like me."

"No, she's not. You're here. Kate isn't. And I know she didn't send you. You wouldn't let her do that."

Maggie shifted uncomfortably in her chair.

"Would you?" David asked.

"No. You're right. But that's not the only reason I'm here. I'm worried about Patrick."

"He can take care of himself," David said, repressing the urge to be sarcastic.

"I don't mean what you think. He's getting pretty mean over this Vietnamese thing. I'm afraid he's going to hurt somebody. He's out to all hours, hanging around with those worthless friends of his. They're looking for trouble, or an excuse to cause some."

"You didn't exactly drive the welcome wagon, Maggie."

"I know that, and I was wrong. I can see that now. But I don't know what to do about it."

"There's nothing you *can* do. Whatever's gonna happen is gonna happen. It probably wouldn't have made any difference what you did."

"You can stop it."

"No, I can't. And if I could, I don't know if I'd want to. All I want is to get out of this town. The sooner the better."

"It's not that simple. I don't want you to go, but I can understand why you'd want to. We haven't exactly been fair to you since you come home. But, damn it, David, it ain't right. It's not like you to cut and run, and I can't sit here and watch you go. I already lost Donald, Kate's miserable, and . . . and if you go, she'll stay miserable. Unless you were planning to take her along?" She looked at him, hoping, but not expecting, he'd confirm it.

"I don't think so, Maggie. I doubt if she'd go even if I

was, but I wasn't planning on that, no. Too much has happened. We don't have a future, because we have too much of a past."

"But the whole pack of you have seen enough trouble. Why look for more? You and Katie belong together. I know that, and you do, too. Nothing's changed enough for that not to be true. And if you two was to get married, I think Patrick would change some, for the better. He loves Katie, too, you know. Wants her to be happy."

Maggie got up from the table and walked to the window. David remained seated and watched her. She had aged markedly since his return. Things were taking a greater toll on her than he would have thought. She had always been tough, in her own way maybe tougher than anyone he knew. But lately her toughness seemed to have deserted her. Events left her reeling, uncomprehendingly, from one piece of bad news to the next. She no longer seemed able to take charge of things. Instead of shaping things to her will, she was shaped by them, worn away like a rock that can no longer withstand the flow of time and weather.

As he watched her, and thought over what she had said, he knew that Kate had not told her the full truth about Donald, and for that he was grateful. He could not have told her what he had done without telling her why. And he would die before letting the bloody shadow of that split second fall over the rest of Maggie's days. There were times when silence was better than the truth.

Suddenly, Maggie whirled back to the table. She stood behind her chair and challenged him. "Are you going to talk to Patrick, or not?"

"To say what?"

"To clear the air, to say, look, let's put this horseshit behind us. I don't know. Whatever it takes to talk sense into him. He's not a bad man, just confused. You know that. You've known him all your life."

"Maggie," David said gently, "Maggie, Maggie. Patrick was never what you thought. I know that can't be easy to accept, but he's not just confused. He's dangerous, and he's mean. It won't make any difference what I say to him. He's like a locomotive out of control, and he'll keep on rolling until he runs out of steam . . . or until he runs into something. I don't want any trouble with Pat. I don't like him, but I don't hate him, either. I feel about him the way I do about a rattler. I'm not afraid of him, but I'll go out of my way to avoid him if I can. The only difference is, you kind of respect a rattler. It is what it is. Pat's what he wants to be. I can't change him, and don't particularly want to try."

Maggie's face fell, and she pulled the chair out and sat down. David knew what she was feeling, and would have spared her if he could, but there was no way to do it without causing her even more pain. She had been a second mother to him, and he respected her more than anyone he knew. She was the supreme pragmatist and had a remarkable ability to change, to grow, to accept things she didn't like and make the best of them. He envied her flexibility. But it had deserted her now, when she needed it most.

"Can I have another cup of coffee, David?" Her voice was barely audible, and David got the coffee without answering. Conversation was inappropriate, would only be disruptive. It was better to sit quietly, their thoughts circling the problem they shared like buzzards scouting a corpse. And, like buzzards, sooner or later they would swoop down for a closer look.

While Maggie sipped her coffee, David went to the refrigerator and got a beer. He twisted the cap off and tossed it on the counter by the sink, where it spun like a coin, rattling slowly into silence. In the quiet, a car pulled onto the gravel driveway, and David looked curiously toward the front door. He wasn't expecting anyone, but then, he hadn't been expecting Maggie, either. It struck him as odd that, in trying to withdraw from society, he had more visitors than he was used to, as if it wouldn't let him go without a fight. He excused himself and went to answer the door before the bell could ring.

He opened the door in time to see Doc Roth get out of his Chevy and look up at the sun. Doc turned and walked slowly toward the front porch and mounted the stairs deliberately, seeming to stop between steps. He was watching his feet and gave a start when David addressed him.

"Doc, what the hell brings you out here at this time of day?"

Doc didn't answer, merely nodded hello and continued his slow ascent. David stepped through the screen door with his hand extended, and Doc took it in silence. He turned to look out over the fields across from the house, still not having said a word.

"Doc?" David said. "Is there something wrong?"

He turned to face the younger man, and David realized he was crying. The tears were bright smears in the afternoon sun, and his cheeks glowed with reflected fire.

"For God's sake, Doc. What's wrong?"

"Let's go inside, David."

"Will you tell me what's going on?"

"Inside, son."

Doc pulled the screen door open and pushed David through before him. He shooed him on with a brisk movement of his hand, and David complied, looking over his shoulder as he walked toward the kitchen.

Maggie heard their voices and came to see what was

happening. Doc nodded to her, and she smiled. "It must be bad news," she joked, "because I've never known a doctor to . . ." Something in Doc's face stopped her. She turned to enter the kitchen ahead of the men. Once through the door, she wheeled about to confront them, half supplicatory and half defiant. "Something's wrong. What is it? What's happened?"

"Both of you, sit down . . . please," Doc said, his voice hoarse.

They did as they were told.

"I . . . David, I . . ."

"Doc," David snapped, "what the hell is going on?"

"I . . . it's Peter, David. I . . ."

"What happened? Is he hurt?"

"He's dead, David. I . . . I'm sorry."

David buried his face in his hands, and Maggie groaned. "What happened? How . . ." she asked.

Doc looked at David, who raised his head to hear the answer, although Doc guessed he already knew what it would be.

"He was shot. A couple of hours ago. He and three other people."

David knew where Peter was going, and with whom. "Who else, damn it? Who else?"

"Three Vietnamese, two brothers and a sister. They . . ."

"What about them?" David demanded. "What about them? Are they . . . ?"

"One of the brothers was also killed. The other is in critical condition. He'll be laid up for a long time, but he'll probably pull through."

"The woman, Doc, what about the woman?"

"Dead."

Maggie and Doc looked helplessly at one another. David looked bewildered. He stood up, then sat again. "What . . . ?"

He didn't finish the question. Instead, he stood again, watching Doc. Suddenly, he picked up his chair and hurled it through the kitchen window. Glass and splintered wood went flying in every direction. He left the kitchen before Doc could stop him, through the back door, ripping the knob from its handle as he did.

Doc stood in the kitchen, helplessly watching the empty doorway. He felt a hand on his shoulder and turned to Maggie.

"What happened?"

"You can guess, I think, Maggie."

"I want to know. Tell me what happened!"

"The four of them were out in a small boat, shrimping. They were attacked by a bunch of thugs in another boat. There was an argument, and the thugs opened fire. Peter and the woman were killed instantly, the other two men were left for dead. A second Vietnamese boat heard the commotion and saw what happened, although from some distance away. They caught the Vietnamese boat, which was left adrift, and brought the victims in. They radioed ahead to the sheriff, and he called me. I was there when they got in, or there might have been four dead, instead of three."

"Doc, I'm afraid there still might be."

"This is so unimaginably stupid, Maggie. What the hell is wrong with the people around here?" Doc punched the refrigerator door. "I don't understand."

"We got to get David, Doc. I don't know what he's liable to do. See if you can get ahold of him, would you? I'm gonna call Randy McHale." She started for the phone in the living room but stopped and turned back to Doc. "Does anybody know who did it?" she asked.

"I don't think so, Maggie. Why?"

She didn't answer. She went to make the call. When she

returned, Doc was outside, walking slowly across the open meadow. David had fallen to his knees. As Doc drew near, David raised his fists toward the sun in silent rage.

Doc was wading toward him through the grass when David got to his feet and turned toward the house. Doc called out, but David ignored him. His features contorted, he moved in a daze. Doc reached out a hand. David brushed past and began to sprint, running around the house and out to the front. Doc ran after him, hampered by the heavy grass. Before he rounded the corner, he heard a car door slam.

When he reached the front of the house, his Chevy was already backing out of the driveway. As he watched help-lessly, David peeled onto the pavement, the car fishtailing under the acceleration, and was gone. Soon it was little more than a cloud of dust far down the road toward town. Doc shook his head and turned to the house as Maggie came out on the porch.

"That boy's gonna kill himself, if he don't kill somebody else first."

"I don't know, Maggie. Maybe we should just let him alone. He's too level-headed to do anything stupid."

"And he's too damned mad not to . . ."

"Why don't we go after him ourselves, then?"

"How? We don't know where the hell he's going. And he's got one hell of a head start."

"You must have some idea."

"Maybe I do."

David could barely see as he drove at speeds approach-ing ninety. Pat might be patrolling the highway, as was his habit, waiting to pounce on unsuspecting speeders. That would suit him just fine. He wanted to talk to Pat, but there was something he had to do first. At the intersection of Bay Road and Route 281, he turned into the latter, slowing just enough to make it. The car skidded into the corner, straightened, and David floored it. He smiled grimly at the clouds of burning rubber billowing up behind as the tires fought for traction on the sandy asphalt.

A mile ahead, he could see the Diem house, and he topped ninety as it drew nearer. A quarter of a mile before the driveway, he began to brake, and the tires squealed again. He was doing thirty as he reached it, slid recklessly into the drive, and slammed on the brakes. He was out and running before the car stopped rocking.

He didn't bother to knock; instead, he opened the door so violently it swung back and hit him in the shoulder as he went through.

"Mama, Mama, are you here?" he called. "Mama, it's David."

There was no answer, and he ran into the kitchen. There was a low flame under a pot on the stove, so she had to be here. He ran back to the living room and crossed to one of the bedrooms, sticking his head through the door and calling, then withdrawing before she could have answered. He ran back to the kitchen, and out the back door.

She was sitting on the lawn near a bed of recently planted flowers. By her side was a small galvanized watering can covered with dew, and a small pile of weeds, the soil clotted in their roots still dark with dampness. Ignoring the steps, he jumped from the porch and landed with a thud on the lawn, but she didn't turn her head. Walking now, he crossed the lawn and knelt beside her.

"Mama, I'm sorry. I came as soon as I heard. I . . ."

"Why? What can you do here?"

He didn't know how to respond.

"I don't know. I guess I just wanted to . . ."

264

"Wanted to what, David? To share my grief? I am sorry for your brother, but that is nothing compared to my loss. A son and a daughter. I am sorry, but there is nothing you can do here. Go home. Shed your own tears. I will grieve for my family alone."

And there it was, in a nutshell. Alone. Everything was gone now. His brother, Kate, Nancy, everyone and everything. For the first time since coming home, he wanted to be anything *but* alone. He couldn't handle this by himself. And if there was one person with whom he would have thought it possible, it was the woman before him. But she turned him away, shutting him out with impregnable finality.

"Mama, I . . ."

"David, please." She interrupted him so sharply it felt as if she had slapped him. His cheeks stung. "Do you remember the first time I met you?"

He did. He had brought news of another death in her family. Her husband had been falsely arrested by a corrupt ARVN colonel, using his influence to advantage in a small-time black-market operation. Diem had reported the colonel to the Americans, and the colonel, in turn, had brought charges of complicity with the Viet Cong against Diem. He used his influence to turn the tables before an investigation could get started. He knew his own actions would be nothing compared to the alleged crime of his accuser. Under "interrogation," Diem had died. That was the ARVN position. In fact, he had been thrown from a helicopter. On a temporary desk assignment in Saigon, David had been sent to inform the family.

"Yes," David whispered. "I do."

"That, too, was at a time of death. This time, your own family is involved, and that is difficult for you, I know. But a family should be left to itself at such a time. I want to be left alone."

"But . . ."

"David, there is nothing you can do. I don't want you here. It was your people who did this, not mine. Please, leave me alone."

David reluctantly got to his feet. He wanted to tell her that she was his family, that he and Nancy were going to be married, that she was to be Mama in more than banter. But he couldn't. He wasn't even certain it was so. Everything he touched turned to dust. Maybe he *was* responsible, in a way she understood more clearly than he. What was the point of telling her anything, now?

He turned and crossed the lawn toward the corner of the house. His chest felt constricted; his breathing was labored. It was a familiar sensation, one he hadn't felt for a long time. The nerves tickled at the back of his neck, as they had so many times, sometimes for days on end, in the jungle. It was fear, naked fear of the unknown, and of the known. He'd never been able to decide which was worse, but now he knew. He knew what had happened as surely as if he'd been there. And he knew that knowing was the worst.

Pat Riley was involved, somehow. Mrs. Diem told him that without saying it. He didn't know how, and he didn't know why, but it had come farther than he feared. He'd told Peter a long time ago it could be bad. But it hadn't been this bad even in his worst nightmares.

As he reached the corner of the house, Mrs. Diem called to him, "David?" He stopped and turned to face her. She looked at him for the first time since his arrival. Her features were impassive, but the look in her eyes was more than enough. The look of limitless forbearance, the stoic passivity that had always struck him as her most remarkable feature, was gone. In its place was a grief so deep and so unendurable that her eyes were blank, completely stripped of feeling. They were the eyes of a catatonic, totally detached from human emotion. Her circuits had overloaded and the fuse had blown. She could feel no more. And David envied her.

22

BACK in the car, David felt drained, as if the old woman's eyes had sucked all feeling out of him. The rage was gone, and nothing had replaced it. He was numb. With a momentary shock, he realized he had to arrange Peter's burial, and then that, too, passed away. There was nothing left now, nothing but a rigorous logic. There were things to be done, and he would have to do them. His face felt slack, as if molded of clay and set in expressionless vapidity. His determination was equally dispassionate, a certainty rather than an emotional commitment. He started the car and backed out onto the highway.

He drove straight to the sheriff's office, parking in the alley alongside. McHale's car was there, along with three others, including one from the Rangers. McHale obviously wasn't wasting time getting help. David walked out of the alley and up the broad steps to the office. The sheriff looked up as he entered and dismissed the two deputies with whom he had been talking.

"David," he said, "I'm sorry, son." He gestured to his private office and led him in. "I was worried about you. Doc called, too. He was afraid you was going to hurt yourself."

"Or somebody else, right?"

"That, too."

"It crossed my mind."

"Make sure it don't again, all right?"

"Where's Peter?" David asked, ignoring the implicit warning.

"Over to Madsen's. Luke's already over there."

"What happened?"

"I ain't sure, son. Doc told you all I know."

"You got some ideas, though, don't you?"

"Ideas don't mean nothing. I got to prove things before I can do anything about them. I want you to remember that."

"It was Pat; he was part of it, wasn't he?"

"Now I don't know that for sure."

"But you think he was, don't you?"

"What I think don't matter. What I can prove—that's what matters."

"What are you going to do?"

"Same thing I always do, David. Find out what happened and who done it."

"You better do it quick, Randy."

"David, now, I'm warning you. I know how you feel, but you let me handle it. I don't want any more trouble. You understand me, son?"

David nodded. "I'll leave Doc's car in the alley. Here's the keys." He tossed them onto McHale's desk.

"You ought to go over to Madsen's, David. I'll go with you, if you want."

"No, thanks, Randy. Luke will give me a hand."

"I'll let you know, I find anything you ought to know about."

David nodded again and left the office. He walked the block and a half to Madsen's in a light that seemed thick, syrupy. The sky's unnatural gold reflected from the windows of the shops and cars he passed.

At the funeral parlor, Luke was in the office, conferring with Leon Madsen. They looked up as David entered. Luke put down papers he was reading and walked out to meet David. When he said hello, his voice was nasal.

"David, I can't tell you how bad I feel, son."

"I know, Luke. You were good to him. He loved you."

"I know, and I loved him. You boys are like family to me."

"No more, Luke. It's just me, now. And I won't be here long."

Luke nodded that he understood. "I . . . uh . . . well, I think I took care of everything. You want to talk to Leon, or shall we go on home?"

"I'll talk to Leon a minute. Can you hang around and give me a lift? I don't have a car."

"Of course. I'll wait here."

David went inside to talk to the funeral director. Luke watched them through a glass partition. They talked for several minutes, and Luke wondered how things had come so far so quickly. He'd been wrong before, but never this wrong.

When David left the office, Luke asked, "You ready to go home, son?"

"May as well."

Luke led the way to his car. They got in without a word, and Luke drove slowly. David seemed too calm. Either what happened hadn't yet registered, or his thoughts were elsewhere, most likely on revenge. That possibility frightened Luke. There had been too much pain already, too many dead. If David was going to settle things on his own, there'd be more, David possibly among them. Reluctant to raise the issue, he decided a good night's sleep would be the best thing for everyone.

When they reached the Hodges home, Luke walked David to the porch. They said good night, but as David was about to climb the steps, Luke stopped him. "Wait a minute, son."

"Luke, you don't have to say anything. I know how you feel, but it's not your fault."

The older man embraced him. "You take care, son."

"Don't worry about me, Luke. I'm okay."

Luke nodded. David watched the lawyer drive off, then went to the side porch, where he sat down to look out at the darkness that surrounded him. He could see Peter sitting there, his face animated, smiling, joking. It had all happened so suddenly, they'd never had the chance to get to know one another again as well as they wanted. David cursed himself for being so cautious. Now it was too late. Someone had murdered his brother. That fact could not go unacknowledged.

David went to the kitchen and opened a beer. After downing it in three quick swallows, he tossed the bottle through the wreckage that had been the window. It landed with a crash in the broken glass and splintered frame outside. He knew what McHale and Luke were afraid of. He was afraid of it himself, but he couldn't ignore it. He had at least to talk to Pat, decide for himself. He wanted to look Pat in the face and dare him to deny that he had killed Peter. And Nancy . . .

He thought about walking into the Double Header and blowing Pat away. But as satisfying as that thought was, he couldn't see himself doing it. It was contrary to everything he'd learned about himself in the war. He couldn't, and wouldn't, allow himself to descend to that kind of brutality. He didn't want to leave Kate brotherless. He was leaving town, and that would be good enough. McHale would find out, in time, whether it had been Pat, and if it had been, he would be punished. But he had to confirm, now, for himself, what he already believed to be true.

He drove back to town in an icy calm, with none of the recklessness that had marked his last trip. That hasty passion had evaporated, and been replaced by glacial serenity. He couldn't imagine anything that would shatter it. When he parked the car, he stepped out and closed the door with a sense of finality. He would learn all he needed to in order to leave with no regrets. He wasn't even sure why he wanted to establish something he already knew, until he realized he was holding out to Pat this one last possibility. All he had to do was deny it, and David would believe him. Not because he wanted to, but because he had to.

The place was nearly empty. Rick was tending bar, and Louise was waiting tables. Pat was there, as David had known he would be, with a few of his cronies, sitting by the pool table. When David entered, everyone stopped talking, and Pat moved his chair away from the table a bit, as if he wanted freedom to maneuver. This subtle gesture evaporated whatever hope David had that Pat would fail to confirm his suspicions. Louise walked over to David and asked him if he wanted a drink. When he shook his head, she took him by the arm, tugging him back toward the door.

"David, he's been drinking all afternoon. Please, don't stay here. There's going to be trouble if you do."

"That's not why I'm here, Louise. I just want to talk to him."

"You can't, David. He's as ornery as I've ever seen him," she whispered. "I'm afraid. I'm afraid of him, and for him. I don't . . ."

Before she could finish, Pat interrupted her, hollering from his place by the pool table, "Louise honey, don't waste your time on Hodges, there. He don't like white pussy."

David pushed Louise aside as she turned to Pat with an expression of disbelief. It was as if she were seeing him for the first time. David walked toward the table where Pat and the others were seated.

"I think you owe Louise an apology, Pat," he said.

"For what? She's white. I ain't said anything about her. It was you I was talking about."

The others at the table laughed nervously. They seemed anxious, like pilot fish finding safety in the shadow of the shark. They stopped laughing as Pat continued. "I guess Katie'll feel better about things now, knowing that slant-eyed cunt ain't around anymore."

David leapt the remaining distance between them, sliding across the table to land feet first in Pat's lap. The deputy fell over backward in his chair and reached for his gun as he struggled to regain his feet. David kicked him in the jaw, and Pat groaned as he fell again. The gun flew across the floor to land against the base of the jukebox.

"Leave it," David snapped, as one of the others went to retrieve it. "Get up, Pat. I'm going to beat your face in. Get up, get the fuck up, you fat fucking slob."

Louise ran to the phone and dialed McHale while she kept an eye on the combatants. Again Pat tried to rise, and again David knocked him down. Pat's mouth was bleeding heavily, and his nose was split and smeared to one side, probably broken. Again Pat fought to regain his feet, and again David slugged him, this time with one fist clenched in the other.

Rick came out from behind the bar carrying a gun, and no one moved except for David and Pat. The others seemed disinclined to help Pat, and Rick seemed reluctant to stop the fight as long as no one tried to join in. Pat tossed his chair at David's legs, finally regaining his feet as David sidestepped. Pat looked helplessly at the others, who remained frozen, then saw his gun by the still blaring jukebox. The hope he might reach it vanished when he saw the pistol in Rick's fist. Instead, he moved in on David, bent low with his hands outstretched. David stepped aside, avoiding the deputy as easily as he had the chair. Pat, sluggish at the best of times, was dulled still further by heavy drinking.

As he passed, Pat reached out for David, who readily broke his grip and shoved Pat into the bar headfirst. The deputy's head struck the base of the bar with a loud, wet crack, and he collapsed on the floor. David was breathing heavily, his anger still hot, unsatisfied by the abrupt end of the fight. He hadn't wanted it to happen, but once it started, he knew he wouldn't be satisfied until it was finished, really finished. The motionless hulk on the floor marked the end of a battle, but not the war. It wouldn't end, now, until one of them was dead.

David turned and walked toward the door, and no one tried to stop him. He knew they wouldn't, and he knew, too, that Pat's influence over his friends, whatever its source, was now shaky at best, perhaps altogether broken.

As David got into his car, he saw McHale and a deputy pull up. He ignored the sheriff's signal to wait, driving off as serenely as if he were going out for the Sunday paper. There was no reason to stop. McHale knew where he lived. If he wanted to talk to him, tomorrow would be soon enough.

23

FOR two days, David refused to believe he was going to bury his brother. It seemed too unreal, but as soon as he convinced himself he couldn't be waiting for so unthinkable an event, something shattered his calm. A phone call of condolence, one of Peter's sneakers in the living room, Peter's books—all reminders of his brother, proving there was no mistake. Peter was dead.

The night before the funeral, he sat on the porch waiting for the sun, hoping its light would dispel more than the darkness. He wanted a reason to accept what he couldn't change, but there was none. Given enough time, perhaps the events would wither, their effect on him erode. But that would take time he didn't have. Something final had happened, something more final than Peter's death . . . and Nancy's death.

Events, memories, hopes, and fears all crowded him,

each slipping away before he could grasp it. At first he drank, but dullness eluded him. Soon the beer was gone, and the pain lingered, sliding in and out of focus but never absent. At three o'clock, he dialed Kate's number. The phone rang three times before he hung up. It seemed the thing to do, until he had done it. He had nothing to say to her that would matter, that would change things.

He hadn't heard from her since Peter's death, and it surprised him, though not as much as he would have thought. He had imagined every conceivable script for such a phone call, Kate expressing everything from sorrow as deep as his own to exultation that they were finally, irrevocably even. But he knew she was too distant now to share his pain, and incapable of rejoicing in it.

Once, he left the porch to walk out under the stars, ignoring the mosquitoes that droned in his ears and bit his neck and arms. They seemed to be the only things alive. Even the other insects were silent. The stars seemed to retreat from him, dimming slowly, then winking out one by one as an overcast moved in off the Gulf. He thought it might rain, and hoped it would. The coolness, the purity the rain would bring would be welcome, but even as he thought so, it began to clear. It seemed fitting that even so simple a comfort would be denied him.

He couldn't understand how things had come to such an end. He had been, and was still, a simple man. He had tried to do what seemed right, and now the foolishness, the presumptuousness of that notion seemed monumental. He didn't know what was right. No one did. No one could. Nothing was more elusive than knowing what one ought to do. And he didn't know now. It hadn't been pride, he was certain. He'd been proud of nothing, except perhaps his lack of pride. And now he was humbled beyond his comprehension. He would go to the funeral a baffled man, unsure why he was alive when so many he had known and loved were dead. Feeling, even as he grappled with the reasons, that it must somehow have been his fault.

And that was itself a kind of pride. Perhaps assuming such significance caused it all. How could he be responsible for so much? Who was he to have that effect on things? On the world? How could even isolated events, little more than dropped stitches in so large a tapestry, have anything to do with him? Who was he? And why should the answer matter so much now, when it was too late to make a difference? The questions hovered in the darkness, pressing in on him from every side. He wanted to understand, had to understand. But would he even know the answers if he found them? And if so, what would be different? What that mattered would be changed? His life was now beyond change, as immutable as the soil that would soon cover his brother's casket.

At dawn, the sky was full of red fire. The sun loomed on the edge of the earth, expanding as he watched and then, suddenly, collapsing as if it had all been a joke, an intimidating display. He thought it might be testing him, to see what he would do as it squeezed toward him, threatening to scorch and flatten everything between them. When he hadn't flinched, hadn't known what to do except stare, it backed off, satisfied that he was as helpless as he seemed.

He went indoors and showered, then dressed in his only dark suit and a wrinkled tie. Examining himself in the mirror, he realized he looked as exhausted as he felt. There were dark circles under his eyes, and his cheeks were a pasty, pale yellow. His eyes drooped, and his hair rebelled against the comb. His heart was racing, his breath shallow and rapid. The moment he had been dreading for two days bore down upon him like a runaway freight. It was time to go.

277

Out in the car, he paused, tilting the rear-view mirror to try once more to slick down his unruly hair, as if it mattered whether he were presentable. He started the car and backed out of the driveway, stopping to look at the house for a moment. It wasn't the same. It seemed empty in a new way. A final emptiness, as if the place were abandoned, seemed to hang over it. He fancied he could see the weeds moving in, the paint peeling as he watched.

The drive into town was interminable. All motion seemed to have slowed, with birds drifting imperceptibly, the grass taking forever to bend and spring back under the breeze. Time was conspiring to prolong the agony of the morning. But, dilatory as it was, the trip came to an end. David parked alongside the funeral home and sat for a long time before leaving the car.

Inside, there were a few friends, Luke and Doc among them, as well as Randy McHale and Father Rodriguez. David stood in the doorway taking in their faces, hoping to see Kate. He saw Maggie, but she was alone. Curiously, there were no Vietnamese, and he was angry, rather than surprised, that they had chosen not to attend. It seemed odd that they wouldn't pay last respects to a man who had given his life on their behalf. They had troubles as well as a funeral of their own to worry about, but that realization did nothing to relieve his anger.

As he entered, the muffled conversations died. Maggie crossed the floor toward him, extending both hands to grasp his, then letting one go to pat the back of the other with her free hand. She seemed about to speak, but just patted his hand again and let it go. David lowered the hand to his side, feeling its dead weight, wondering what to do with it. He looked around the room, quietly undistinguished in its labored solemnity, and walked into the chapel where Peter's casket lay. There were a few sprays of flowers, and a pair of wreaths, a small card affixed to each.

The floral fragrance was stifling. He thought flowers ought to be less aggressively present at such occasions. He examined the cards idly, noting the senders and their formulaic sympathy. A small spray of gladiolus bore a card in Kate's neatly ornate script. "I'm sorry for everything, Kate Riley." That was all it said. He smiled bitterly at the Riley, as if she had had to remind him of her last name.

David felt a hand on his shoulder and turned to see who it was. Luke had followed him in. The two men looked silently at one another. Luke shook his head slowly from side to side, as if trying to rid himself of something. David nodded that he understood, and squeezed the old man's shoulder in silent reassurance.

Al Rodriguez appeared in the doorway and beckoned to David, who followed him out. Rodriguez stepped into Madsen's inner office, David right behind. The priest reached around him to close the door.

"David, I'm so terribly sorry," he began, then stopped, as if he didn't know what to say next.

"It's okay, Padre."

"I feel as if this were all somehow my fault."

"I don't blame you, and Peter wouldn't, either. We do what we can. Sometimes it doesn't work out, that's all."

The priest nodded, gritted his teeth, and turned away. He seemed to be wrestling with something, whether it was something he wanted to say, or with some personal demon, David didn't know, and didn't want to guess. Rodriguez pounded his fist on the desk and wheeled back to face David.

"Damn it, David, it wasn't supposed to turn out like this. People are supposed to be better than this."

"These people? Not a chance."

"Hell, yes, these people. These are your people, too,

you know. And they're better than this. I know they are."

"That's where you're wrong," David said softly. "They're not *my* people. They're not even yours. They are what they are and they belong to themselves. That's why I'm getting the hell out of here as soon as I can."

"But you can't leave, David. You mustn't."

"Should I hang around until I get killed, too?"

"I guess I asked for that. But . . ." He stopped helplessly, his eyes fixed on David's impassive features. "These people, the Vietnamese, they're helpless here. I guess that's my fault, but . . . I mean, I should have listened to Luke."

"Look, Padre, you did what you thought you had to. If you didn't expect this, nobody can blame you. You're not in the business of expecting things like this. And you shouldn't be." David reached out to grip the priest by both shoulders. "Thanks for being here. I appreciate it." He turned and opened the door, then paused. "You know, just because I'm not willing to help you doesn't mean you're wrong. Maybe it just means you're a better man than I am." He walked through the door and left the priest in the office.

David walked over to a long leather sofa and sat down, hoping the remaining minutes before the ceremony would move more swiftly than the morning had so far. One by one, the others present drifted over to whisper their condolences, then drift back into the small group across the room. They seemed to be huddling together to protect themselves from something.

After a few moments, Rodriguez reappeared, and they filed into the chapel. For the occasion, the priest had chosen to wear civilian attire. He looked vaguely uncomfortable, as if he felt vulnerable without his collar. When they had taken their seats, he spoke briefly about Peter and what he had been like as a man, skirting carefully around the circumstances that had brought them together that morning.

David tried to listen, but his attention kept slipping away. He counted the flowers in each wreath and spray, then, doubting his accuracy, counted them again, trying to remember his first total. When he tired of the flowers, he turned to the weave of his suit, counting threads and stitches, looking for flaws in the cloth. But he found none. There was symmetry all around him. The weave of the coat was flawless, the numbers of flowers even, and neatly balanced by color and placement. Perfection, it seemed, order, were things denied only to him.

All that mattered had been taken away, or he had thrown it away. Either way, it didn't matter. It was all gone. The thing that had mattered to him above all else in his life was reason, and that too was gone. He had no reason to do anything, and there was none in anything that had happened.

The worst was being alone. That struck him as ironic. As much as he had wanted to be alone before, he now wanted companionship, company, love, something. Someone to share what was left of him, of his life. It wasn't much to offer, but it was all he had. He doubted there would be any takers for so uneven a bargain. He thought of Kate, and how unfair this had all been to her. She was blameless, a victim, asked to live with more pain, and more painful knowledge, than anyone could reasonably be expected to bear. That had been his fault. And Donald's, and Pat's. Maybe even Peter's. But certainly his.

He felt a hand on his arm and looked up to see Rodriguez peering at him expectantly from the front of the chapel. Luke was leaning into the pew. Did he want to say anything? No. What could he say, and to whom would he say it? Was there anyone in the room who would understand what he wanted to tell them all? He shook his head, and Luke sat down beside him while Rodriguez drew the service to a close. Then it was time.

David stood to take his place at the head of the casket. Luke and Doc Roth joined him, along with Halsey, McIlhenny, and McHale. Together they carried the casket to the hearse waiting in the alley, so ordinary it wouldn't have drawn a second glance from him before this. He supposed it was the same with everyone, but he would probably never know. This image, too, would leave him in time. In time. How hopeful that sounded, and how unlikely it seemed. He stepped back as the casket slid into the back of the hearse. When Madsen stepped forward to close the door, he reached in and placed his fingertips on the cold metal box for an instant, stepped back again, and flinched as the door slammed shut.

David rode in the front of the hearse on the way to the cemetery. Luke had wanted him to ride in his car with Doc, but he preferred the uncomfortable silence of the hearse to the company of his friends. There was nothing anyone could say, and nothing he felt like saying. He could only hope it would be over soon.

It struck him as cruel, somehow, wanting to hurry things. It wasn't as if he had anything to do later. There was no place to go, except away, and that was no place, and was noplace. He would get there soon enough. He couldn't understand his desire for speed. But as if for once wishing made it so, they reached the wrought-iron fence that surrounded Witman's small, overcrowded cemetery. In the distance, past aisles of weather-whitened stones gleaming in the sun, he could see a green awning. Beneath it, he knew, would be a few chairs. A mound of damp earth would be off to one side, discreetly distant, but near enough to do the job.

The hearse pulled up, and the driver quickly left his seat to open the rear door. David could hear other cars pulling up behind them, doors closing, more softly than usual, but no less tightly, no less finally. He sat staring straight ahead, his hands in his lap, until Doc stuck his head in through the driver's window.

"You ready, David?"

He nodded, and Doc patted the door once and walked back the way he had come. David saw him in the passenger-door mirror, talking about him, he knew, with Luke and Maggie. Maggie looked toward the hearse while they spoke. Her hair had never been a more brilliant white. She was wearing a dress for the first time David could remember; probably, he guessed, for the first time since Donald's funeral. And there was symmetry in that, too, he thought. The circle closing, as it was bound to do.

The ceremony at the graveside was mercifully brief, and he could hear the thud of the first shovelfuls of earth striking hollowly on the casket even before he slipped into the back of Luke's car. Doc and Luke sat in the front. David could hear their voices, but not their words, as they murmured softly on the way back. When they reached town, David asked to be let out. Luke looked nervously at Doc, who nodded his approval. When Luke pulled over, David opened the door of the car and slid out. Closing the door firmly, he leaned in through the open rear window.

"I feel like being by myself."

Luke nodded, and said, "You stop by the office later, hear? You and me got to talk some."

"I will. Later. See you, and thanks."

He started walking, not sure where he was going, but knowing he had to go somewhere, do something, anything, to get his mind off the morning. Luke was about to pull away from the curb, when Doc stopped him.

"Wait a minute, Luke. We better keep an eye on him for a bit."

"You're right, Doc. He don't seem himself. Not that he should."

The two men sat in the car, watching David's befuddled progress down the street. He was walking like a man not quite certain where he was, moving only to keep from standing still.

After two blocks, Luke said, "He seems okay, just a little dazed, is all. I reckon he'll be okay."

"I think I'll tag along anyway. Why don't you go on? I'll get out here."

"We're probably worrying about nothing, Doc. But then, my record ain't been so hot lately."

Doc didn't answer. He got out of the car, leaned in to say good-bye, then followed David. At the first corner, he stopped to let a car pass, and when he reached the opposite side of the street, David was no longer in sight. Doc realized that the Double Header was two blocks farther up the street, and was most likely where David had gone.

In the saloon, David paused to let his eyes adjust to the gloom. When he could see, he walked to the bar and pulled up a stool. Rick came to wait on him, mopping the bar self-consciously as he did so.

"David, what'll you have?" he asked.

"A beer, I guess."

"I wanted to go this morning, but, well, you know how it is, with the business and all."

"Sure, don't worry about it. We buried him anyhow."

Taken aback by the gruesome joke, Rick walked off to get the beer, wondering how long David was going to stay. There was something unsettling about his manner, the tone of his voice. Rick returned with the beer and pulled his own stool up to sit across the bar from David, who was the only patron at the moment.

"You going back to Maggie's boat?"

"Nope."

"What are you going to do?"

"Whatever it is, it won't be around here."

After a while, Rick moved off to find something else to do. Talking to David was a strain, their exchanges largely limited to labored questions on his part and cursory answers from David. Light burst into the darkened bar, and David turned as Doc came through the door. Doc looked around uncertainly, spotted his quarry, and walked to the bar to take the stool next to David. Thankful for the company, Rick walked down to see what the newcomer wanted.

"A club soda, I guess, Rick, thanks."

"Why don't you have a beer, Doc?" David asked.

"Too early, David." He smiled. "The only time in my life I drank this early in the day was right after my wife died. It didn't help me as much as I wanted it to, so I gave it up."

"I don't particularly want a temperance lecture, Doc."

"I wasn't giving one, son. Why don't we move over to a table? These stools are uncomfortable."

"Whatever you want, Doc." David got to his feet and grabbed his beer by its neck to lead the way to a table back near the jukebox. "You like shit-kicker music, Doc?"

"Not too much, no."

"You got to, to make it down here, Doc. Didn't anybody ever tell you that?"

Before he could respond, the door opened again. From their vantage point, the new arrival was little more than a broad shadow, framed against the bright light from the street. He ambled casually to the bar and ordered a beer, then walked in their direction. The exaggerated care with which he placed each foot suggested that the man was drunker than he wanted to appear. As he got closer, they could see his face in the dim light from the jukebox, and it confirmed Doc's guess. Pat Riley was just about the last person he wanted to see at the moment, but there was no way to avoid it.

"Well, if it ain't the sawbones. Still Jewish, Doc?"

"I guess I'll be Jewish as long as you drink on duty, Pat," Doc said. "They both appear to be permanent conditions."

"I ain't on duty. Fact is, I ain't gonna *be* on duty for a while. I been suspended. You don't seem to keep any better company than you used to, neither."

David kept silent during the exchange, whether because he was oblivious to the visitor or because he was keeping himself absolutely under control, Doc couldn't guess. Pat pulled a chair out and twirled it with an exaggerated motion, then sat down with its back against the table edge.

"Bring that beer over here, Rick," he yelled over his shoulder to the bartender. Turning to his reluctant hosts, he said, "You got a dead brother, Doc? This here seems to be the table for people who got dead brothers."

Doc, anxious to defuse the situation before it got out of hand, answered quickly. "That's in bad taste, Pat. Maybe you should go on home and get some sleep. You seem to need it."

"Shit, Doc. I got lots of time to sleep, now. Davey, boy, how you hangin'?"

When David ignored him, Pat shrugged and picked up his beer, draining nearly half of it in a single gulp. "How come this shit tastes so bad today?"

"Maybe it's the company, Pat," David said.

"Lookit here, Davey. You ain't got no call to be talking like that to me. We got a lot in common, now, me and you. Neither one of us is workin', we both like to drink, and we both got a dead brother. Why don't we just relax, and have a good time? What do you say?"

"Pat, I'd rather burn in hell than have a good time with you."

"Now that ain't exactly the kind of talk two out-of-work buddies ought to be sharing, is it? Listen here, I got an idea. How's about you get me my job back with Randy, and I'll talk to my old lady about taking you back? What about it?"

"Pat, you got more balls than sense. You know that?"

"Don't believe everything Louise tells you."

"Pat, Doc and I don't feel like company right now. Why don't you sit at the bar or something?"

"Fuck you, Hodges. You think you're too good for me, don't you? You always did. Shit, my own mother thinks more of you than she does of me. But you're no better'n I am," he said, slamming his fist on the table.

Rick looked up from behind the bar and shook his head in resignation. He had expected trouble from the time Pat walked in. He had been hoping it wouldn't get out of hand, but there was no way around it.

"Pat," David said, "I don't think about you at all, if I can help it. You're getting to be more of a pain in the ass all the time. But I don't expect it'll be a problem much longer. I'm leaving here, soon. The last thing I see will be your big, ugly face. But when I'm gone, I'm gone, and that last look'll be the first time I was glad to see you."

"Shit."

"You're more articulate than usual, this morning." David smiled almost angelically. It seemed to Doc he was deliberately trying to provoke Pat, and doing better than Doc would have liked.

"Maybe we should all cool off, just a bit," Doc said.

"Maybe you should mind your own fucking business," Pat snapped.

"You got no call to talk to Doc that way, Pat," David said quietly.

"I'll talk to anybody anyway I want to, Hodges," Pat said, getting to his feet.

David smiled more broadly, and Pat leaned across the table to grab his shirt. David broke the grip, getting to his feet at the same time. "You touch me again, it'll be the last thing you do, you fat fuck."

Pat reached for him again. As he did so, David swept his beer bottle from the table and brought it down across the bridge of Pat's nose. The deputy fell to the floor, stunned by the blow. He shook his head twice and tried to get up. David reached down to pull the larger man up, then, before Pat had regained his balance, drove his fist into Pat's midsection, knocking the air from his lungs. Pat collapsed, struggling to breathe, and David reached down to remove the deputy's side arm. He examined it briefly, and placed it softly, almost reverentially, on the table in front of Doc.

Rick placed his own gun on the bar, reached for the phone, and dialed the sheriff's office. David grabbed Pat's arms and dragged him unceremoniously across the barroom floor, leaving him in a heap at the base of the bar.

"I guess Randy'll know what to do with this garbage," he said, laughing. Rick nodded as he hung up the phone. David returned to the table, righting Pat's chair and taking it for his own.

"I'm not sure that was the smartest thing you could have done, son," Doc said with some concern.

"Oh, hell, Doc. Being smart was never my long suit. Whenever I tried, it just got me into trouble, anyhow. You see why I have to get out of Witman. It's a fucking zoo."

288

Doc sat silent, as if considering his next words carefully. "You think he killed Peter, don't you?"

"Yes, I do. I know he did, but I guess that just makes us even."

"What do you mean? What are you talking about?"

"Ask Katie sometime. She can explain it all to you." David drained his beer and stood up. "Look, I got a few things I got to do before I leave. I'll see you later, okay?"

"You leaving soon?"

"Yup, I am."

He walked toward the door, waving to Rick as he passed. Doc picked up his club soda and watched the bubbles bounce from place to place as they left the fluid, and it seemed their movements were more predictable than any human behavior he had encountered since moving to Texas.

His reflections were shattered by a shout. He looked up to see Pat leave the bar, Rick's gun clenched in one fist.

"Hodges," Pat yelled, raising the gun at the same moment.

For a second Doc sat immobilized. Galvanized by another shout, he recognized it was his own voice warning David to run. David was turning as Pat fired. The bullet caught him in the chest, under the right arm. There was another shot, and Pat fell forward, blood already staining his shirt below the left shoulder. Doc sat at the table in silent astonishment, shaking his head from side to side, staring mutely down at the revolver in his own trembling hand.

Doc had only wanted to help, to change what had been fixed long before. He wanted to help David forget an unforgettable war, to help Peter expunge an indelible scar, to help Kate redeem her sacrifice, to help displaced people find a home where the earth wouldn't tremble beneath their uncertain feet. In that arrogant self-assurance that so often passes as an antidote for impotence, he had tried, too little and too late, to staunch a flood he'd been too careless to oppose when it was a trickle. He'd tried to bridge the gulf between hope and happenstance, but, as they will, time and circumstance conspired against his best intentions. Now, withered into insignificance, the fruit of his own good will lay mute and meaningless as the palsied hand before him.

And as he stared at it, the hand receded, as if he were looking down on it from a great distance. His senses seemed simultaneously sharpened and disoriented. He could see himself, a small speck on the coast of Texas, now smaller still as Witman itself shrank and kept on getting smaller. Soon, his vision swallowed by the immensity of the silent Gulf, he lost sight of Witman altogether.